Buckshot

Buckshot

Also by Monty R. Garner

Card Jordan Series

Buckshot

Monty R. Garner

WOLFPACK
PUBLISHING
— EST 2013 —

Buckshot
Paperback Edition
Copyright © 2025 (As Revised) by Monty R. Garner

Wolfpack Publishing
1707 E. Diana Street
Tampa, FL 33610

www.wolfpackpublishing.com

Paperback ISBN 979-8-89567-111-5
Ebook ISBN 979-8-89567-110-8

Buckshot

Chapter 1

THE SUN GLOWED BRIGHT RED AS IT ASCENDED FROM the western horizon of the Lone Star State sky. It was late summer, and heat waves mixed with dust created a hazy mirage simmering off the dirt street that ran through the middle of the Texas town. Thirty-three-year-old Buck Reed stood on the boardwalk outside the bank, his shirt wet with sweat, and used the bandanna from around his neck to remove the droplets of perspiration seeping through the skin of his forehead and face.

With one more look at the deserted street, the gunfighter stepped off the boardwalk and put the handkerchief away in his left rear pocket. Moving like a man in a trance, he walked in a sluggish motion to the center of the street, the dust rising around his boots with each step he took.

He walked away from the sun, and its heat rays made his shirt so wet with sweat that it dripped onto his britches and the dusty ground. He raised his right hand to his mouth and blew on his thumb and fingers before lowering his arm so his hand rested beside the Colt holstered on his right hip.

As he made his way down the street, crowds of townspeople gathered on each side of the street watching him. But why? He had no reason for them being here. Buck looked to his left and examined the faces of the people, and all he saw were blank stares in their eyes; no one waved or said anything. To the right, the boardwalk was lined with stiff, unmoving forms, and no one smiled, cheered, or cried out to him. Why were they all here? Where had they come from? No one was there when he stepped into the street moments ago.

Half a block in front of Buck, two large, identical two-story buildings stood on opposite sides of the road. Each bore a sign that read *Saloon*.

The batwing doors on the tavern to his left swung open, and out came a young, blond-haired man wearing a black vest over a gray shirt. A two-gun, tied-down rig was holstered around his hips, and he crept along with a lumbering pace, stirring up dust with each step until he stopped thirty feet directly in front of Buck.

The young man didn't say one word, and his eyes were so black and motionless that they looked like coal. He slowly positioned both arms so his hands were even with his holstered guns.

Buck knew what was about to happen and wanted to leave the street and go into the saloon for a drink of whiskey, but his legs wouldn't move. The young opponent facing him smiled and reached for his guns and was still pulling them out of their holsters when he was hit with a bullet to the chest and then another.

It was difficult for Buck to see through the heat waves and gunpowder smoke, but he could make out the young man hitting the ground with his eyes wide open, staring up at the heavens.

A noise to Buck's right caused him to shift his eyes in that direction and notice a young blond man wearing a black vest over a gray shirt come down the steps and walk to the center of the street like the other man did. He, too, lowered his hands beside his guns and started to pull them out when Buck fired his gun and put three slugs in the young man's chest.

Buck watched the wannabe gunfighter hit the ground and stare up at him with blank, hollow eyes.

Another man came out on the street, and he, too, tried his luck but died. Then another and another and another. The gunfighter shook and took in deep gulps of air. He was scared that it could be him lying on the ground in a pool of his own blood. He wanted the killing to stop and the nightmares to go away.

An explosion filled the atmosphere, so violent that trees exploded and buildings shook off their foundations. Buck could see himself flying through gray clouds streaked with fingers of lightning. He tried to grab hold of the clouds as he flew by, but there was nothing there to hold on to.

What in the world was happening? Was he having an out-of-body experience?

The vision from the clouds placed him on a battlefield, lying on his stomach, shooting at advancing Confederate troops who came at the lone soldier at a dizzying pace. One after another the young men went down from the accuracy of Bucks shooting. But seconds later, they sprung back to their feet and kept coming toward him, bloodied and mangled. Why wouldn't they die? Buck became scared and confused. All of a sudden, the mutilated soldiers surrounded the gunfighter, holding their guns cocked and ready to kill him.

A light so bright that he had to cover his eyes shone down on him and swept him away. He heard gospel singing and opened his eyes to see a freshly dug hole in the graveyard. Cautiously moving to the edge of the grave, he saw a coffin and that was all he could take.

"No more! No more!" screamed Buck Reed as he abruptly came awake and sat up in his bed with his hands clenched into fists. His clothes and bedding were soaked in sweat, and he was tangled in the bedsheets. Deep breaths of air cleared his mind of the dream that had kept recurring for years. Each time it came, it never got easier. Why did his past come back to haunt him at two in the morning? The dreams drained him of energy, and they were disturbing to his state of mind.

He held on to the bedpost and stood up on weak legs before walking four feet to the washstand, where a pitcher of water sat beside a basin and a towel hung from a peg on the wall. With shaking hands, he poured enough water to wash his face and try to get the images of the corpses out of his mind one more time. The cool water refreshed him, and he lifted his head to look at himself in the mirror. The wrinkled face, gray hair, and faded eyes looked back at him with the hardness of the passing years.

What must I do to end these dreams? Will they ever end? He shook his head, returned to the bed, and lay back down. The time happened to be a quarter after two in the morning and time to rest. Age had caught up with him, but the dreams seemed new each time he had them. Over the years, too many towns and heartaches had taken their toll on him. Why did these dreams still come to the sixty-two-year-old man? This was August of 1885, and not some battlefield where he fought in the Civil War or some gunfight in one of the many towns of his past.

Too much of his time appeared to be used reminiscing over the past, and there wasn't one thing he could do to change it. Somehow, he needed to look toward the future and try to transform to who he wanted to be from this day forward. His new home happened to be a half-day ride away, and hopefully, the nightmares would finally stop once he settled there.

Chapter 2

Dodd City, Texas, came into Buck's line of sight through the heat waves that danced off the parched, dry ground. The heat still lingered on for late August as the lone gunfighter walked his horse toward town. Every once in a while, Buck closed his eyes, thinking that might help him focus on what was ahead. His eyes weren't as keen as they once were, and that wasn't good for a man who had lived by the gun for the last twenty years.

Buck pulled his handkerchief out from the pocket of his lightweight duster and removed beads of sweat from his forehead, face, and neck. The creases on his forehead and the crow's feet around his eyes were indications he had seen more sun and wind than most men. His once-bright blue eyes now showed shades of gray, along with his hair and whiskers. He decided a month ago that traveling around Texas, New Mexico, and Colorado, hiring his gun out for money must stop. The time had come for Buck to settle down and enjoy old age.

He wore a gray cowboy hat with the front pulled down to help shade his eyes from the sun. Buck dressed in his best clothing when he traveled on business. He wore a white shirt with a black string tie and gray tweed britches with the pant legs tucked into the tops of polished black boots.

Today, he wore his lightweight duster over his attire to keep the dirt off his clothing. Once in town, he would remove the garment and leave it across the saddle, then take a rag from his saddlebag and use it to remove the dust from his boots. Buck liked to look good, and he was particular how his boots looked when he was conducting business or essential tasks.

Buckled around his waist and attached to the wide belt was a custom-made holster holding a Colt .45 modified to his specifications. The barrel had been cut off by two inches, leaving it five-and-one-half inches long without a front sight. A Colt Lightning, .38 caliber, tucked under his left arm in a shoulder holster provided him a backup weapon when needed. A Henry repeating rifle inside the saddle scabbard, with the rifle stock pointing toward the front for easy reach, supported him for hunting. Other than the rifle and two pistols, he'd only brought a coiled-up rope and his travel bag, which hung off the horn of his Mexican saddle. He brought no bedroll along for this trip, but had saddlebags tied behind the cantle stuffed with books.

The gunfighter previously visited Dodd City more than a half dozen times over the past ten years to deposit money in the bank. The banker, a man by the name of O.W. Wisdom, was the only person the old pistolero knew in the Texas town.

The town seemed to have more businesses on Main Street than it did on his last trip here, seven months earlier. He counted seven grocery stores, two large dry goods stores, two drug stores, one saloon, and one bank.

Buck's four-year-old chestnut stud, Red, eyed the water troughs on both sides of the dirt street. Buck had won the red horse in a poker game two years earlier and had been training him ever since. He gave a slight tug on the reins to the left, and Red stopped at one of the water troughs and started sucking in water.

The sign on the building door in front of them read *Bank of Dodd City*, which happened to be his first stop. Three thousand, four hundred dollars lay in the bottom of his travel bag, and the time had come to deposit the last money he would ever earn as a hired gunhand. He had already decided he would not do any more gun work and no more killing. That was what he'd told himself over the past two years, and it was hard to live up to when he had a reputation as a top gunhand and fast draw.

Dismounting took more effort than it used to. His butt was sore from riding in the saddle. His knees didn't work so well anymore, and he had to stand beside his horse and hold on to the stirrup to give his legs, hips, and back time to straighten out before he walked into the bank.

O.W. met Buck as he came through the door.

"Hello, Buck. Did you bring another deposit?"

"I did. Here it is, and I'd like to know how much money I have in the bank," said Buck.

"Of course," said the banker. "Follow me into my office."

The bald banker put on his wire-rimmed glasses and looked at a ledger book. "Would you rather I write it down in case anyone wants to listen to what I tell you?" O.W. glanced toward the open door.

Buck looked around the bank and said, "Yeah, write it down for me."

The banker handed him a slip of paper with the total

of $32,456 written on it. "You're a wealthy man, Buck. Will you be staying long, or are you off again?"

"I'm calling it quits and going to my place to sit in my easy chair and not work anymore. I'll be on my way now," said Buck.

"I wish you the best in retirement, and you stop in to see me when you're in town," said O.W.

"Thanks, my friend," said Buck and walked out.

He stood at the hitching post and untied Red so they could go across the street to the saloon. A man who had made his living with a gun could never be too careful in any town, so he looked up and down both sides of the dirt street and glanced at the tops of the false fronts of the businesses, but nothing gave him any reason to be alarmed. Red followed him across the street to the saloon with the bridle reins laying across his neck. A cool beer would be nice to wash away the trail dust before he rode the five miles to his property.

With the duster readjusted across the saddle so it wouldn't fall off, the careful gunman made sure that the weapon holstered under his left arm would come out of its holster quickly, just in case he needed it. Once inside the saloon, he stepped to the side of the door, giving his eyes time to adjust so he could check out the establishment and see who was there.

Two cowboys stood at the south end of the bar, and four men sat at one of the tables. Three men at another table got his attention. They looked like other individuals he had encountered multiple times in his life—well-dressed, with flashy shirts and britches. One in particular stood out thanks to his hand-crafted holster sporting a Colt with fancy white pistol grips.

Young wannabe gunfighters always sported fancy guns and holsters, with the idea it made them look important or tough. The sad thing was, Buck couldn't remember any of the dead ones' names; just the cold stare of their eyes as they lay deceased on the floor in a pool of blood.

Buck removed the safety strap off the gun hammer on the weapon at his hip. He pulled the hammer back into the firing position and brought his right hand up to his mouth to blow on his right index finger and thumb. That was something the gunman always did when trouble came his way—he wanted to make sure there was no moisture on his shooting finger.

Deciding it would be best if the three men sitting at the table didn't know he was watching them, he went to the bar and found a place where he could see their reflection in the mirror on the wall behind the barkeep.

The bartender came over with a filthy rag hanging over his shoulder. He wiped a hand on his half apron. "What'll it be, stranger?"

Buck never diverted his eyes from the image of the three men in the mirror as he said, "I'll have a beer."

"Coming right up. That'll be a nickel."

Buck reached into his left pants pocket and pulled out some coins. He laid four bits on the bar top just as one of the men stood up, finished his whiskey, and placed the empty glass upside-down on the tabletop. That was when he gave away his intentions: he removed the safety from his gun, lifted it by its grips, and let it fall back into the holster.

Buck paused with the beer halfway to his mouth and thought briefly about what to do. He should leave, so he put the mug to his lips and drained the liquid from the glass. He put the empty mug on the bar top and started for the door.

"You hold up right there, Reed. I know who you are, and it's time you came against someone faster than you," said the young man, standing five feet behind Buck with his feet shoulder-width apart and his hand close to his gun.

Buck stopped, raised his right hand to his mouth to blow on his forefinger and thumb. He held his arms shoulder high and turned around before he lowered them and looked eye to eye with the young man.

"I don't know you, and I don't intend to know who you are. I came here for that beer to wash down the trail dust, and now I'm leaving town."

"I know you, Buck Reed, and I aim to take you down here and now."

"What's your name, kid?" asked Buck as he stepped toward the man.

The young man raised his voice so everyone in the saloon could hear him. "I'm Rex Reynolds, and I'm about to kill a gunfighter."

Buck smiled at the loudmouth Reynolds boy. "Rex, I've squared off against young gunfighters like you for more years than I can remember, and I'm still alive. You ain't no different than the rest of them, except you're still breathing. I'm not going to kill you today. Instead, I'm turning my back on you and leaving. I don't think you want to shoot me in the back and get the reputation of being a back-shooting coward."

Rex stood ready to draw, and Buck's last words caused him to turn red in the face out of either rage or embarrassment, Buck didn't care which. He turned his back to the man and walked out the door. He had already thrown the bridle reins over his horse's neck and was getting ready to mount when Rex and his two friends came out of the bar and onto the boardwalk.

"I'm not finished with you, old man," shouted Rex.

Buck looked sideways at the young man. "You and

your friends should go back inside and have a drink on me. I left enough money to pay for a shot of whiskey for each of you."

"I don't want your whiskey," said Rex as he took one step forward.

Buck took one step away from his horse and drew his gun before the young man knew what was happening. The draw startled Rex and he tried to take a step backward, but he tripped and fell on his butt. The other two men were so scared that they froze and didn't help their friend get back up. All three men had started sweating from being afraid.

"Today is your lucky day," said Buck. "I made a promise to myself when I woke up this morning that I wouldn't kill anyone today. You fellers shuck those guns and lay them on the porch. Go on! Do it before I get mad."

The three did as they were told. Rex rose off his hind end, stepped to the edge of the porch, and pointed a finger at Buck. "Old man, your days are numbered. The next time I see you, it'll be different."

"I'm sure it will be. Are you kin to Wilbur Reynolds?" asked Buck.

"He's my pa." said Rex.

"I suggest you go home and tell him you saw me in town. I'm riding out of here, so it's time for all of you to hightail it back inside. And Rex, if you come gunning for me ever again, I won't be so friendly," said Buck.

The young men hesitantly went back inside the saloon. Buck mounted up but kept his eyes on the door until he was out of pistol range. That had been a close call, and Buck sure didn't want to cause any harm to the Reynolds boy.

Chapter 3

BUCK DIDN'T TIP HIS HAT, SMILE, OR ACKNOWLEDGE anyone on the dirt street or boardwalk as he left Dodd City. Staying to himself and not causing people to wonder about him was a habit that had saved his life more than once. Over the years, Buck had seen more than his fair share of trouble because of his reputation. Men like Rex, who wanted to be famous, were the ones to avoid if possible, and then there were the lawmen who wanted him to leave town and not come back, even though he hadn't broken any laws.

Eight years ago, Buck had asked O.W. to purchase him a section of land three miles east and two north of Dodd City. The property consisted of two fenced portions of grazing land and one portion of farming land along a creek. Before the war started, the previous owners had employed a ramrod who lived in a two-bedroom house west of the barn, and behind that house stood another plain house where the five slaves had stayed.

The main house had three bedrooms and was home for the owner and his family. It had been built east of the stables, so the barn could be between the two residences, and accessible to both the owner and the hired hand. The corral took up a half-acre beside the barn and the chicken coop, which happened to be sixty feet behind the main house.

Bois d'Arc Creek flowed through part of the property, and at the homesite, fresh water was available from three hand-dug wells.

He had a plan to make it his forever home during his retirement. The years had finally caught up with him, and it was now time to settle down and do something besides hire his guns out. Killing had been a thorn in the side, and he thought that was the reason he had the bad dreams. The dreams reminded him of all the lives he had taken, and it was time to quit.

Riding to his land gave him time to think about what had transpired in town. This hadn't been the first time some young buck called him out, but he hoped it would be the last. He knew he had lost some of his reflexes and agility. It was only a matter of time before he faced off against a much younger and quicker man. It seemed like being fast was a curse, and it followed him wherever he went.

This was the first place in years that he could call home. The way of life he'd led had taken him to various places, businesses, ranches, and towns. Sometimes his stay was short, and sometimes he had stayed somewhere for over a year. None of the towns or ranches where he had worked were home. They were where he earned his money, and then he'd go on to the next job. Being a top gunhand required the people needing his services to pay him well.

He reflected on his past and realized many friends had either left the trade, or they were dead or so crippled they could hardly walk anymore. Being a hired gun left a man open to all kinds of trouble. He had been shot three times over the years, and as he aged, it became harder to get over the wounds.

Range wars were the worst kind of fights he had ever been in. They were typically rancher against rancher or rancher against ill-equipped sodbusters. At times range wars were simply murder, and he never wanted to be part of killing innocent women and children. But while on the job, he had no problem killing a man in a fair gunfight.

He had only seen his property and houses once in the ten years he had owned it. A month after he purchased the land, he went there and spent the night, leaving the following day to track down a murderer for the bounty. Back then, the houses and buildings had been solid and in condition for use. If his memory served him right, the corral consisted of split cedar logs nailed to upright posts. It should still be sturdy enough to hold his horse, at least for a few days.

The list of things he needed at the house, like kitchen utensils, food, bedding, towels, and furniture, was getting so long in his head that he knew he would have to write it down once he got there.

Home. That word had an exciting ring to his ears. He was going home and living off the land for a while. Who knew, he might even find him a woman to live out there with him. *Stop it, Buck.* He didn't need to think about a woman right now. He had to arrive at his home and put in some time cleaning before he had company come calling.

When he turned north off the main road to Bonham, Texas, he noticed that the homesteads began to thin out along the road. He'd have to explore the area soon in case enemies came gunning for him. Knowing his environment meant a lot when there was trouble. A man needed to have multiple escape routes as well as areas that he could defend if needed.

His land couldn't be more than twenty miles south of the Red River and Indian Territory. If the local or state authorities were ever after him, that would be the direction to go since he was more than familiar with parts of the Territory.

He laughed. He and Wilbur Reynolds, Rex's pa, had spent two months in Indian Territory, at Gilbert and Doaksville. But those days had passed and didn't need to be discussed. He did hope young Rex would tell Wilbur that they had met. Maybe his pa would talk some smarts into the young man's head.

A hot bath to soothe his aching joints sounded like a fine idea, and he sure hoped there was a washtub at the house. Taking regular baths had been one thing he'd liked about his job and the places he'd worked since the Civil War. A hot bath in the morning also helped to loosen his muscles and joints.

He also liked to wear clean clothes, shined boots, and look his finest out in public. Washing and ironing his clothes happened to be a trade he never acquired a skill for, so he would need to find someone who could wash and iron his clothes.

His mind had wandered, and he once again tried to focus on the items he needed for his property. A wagon was first on the list, so he could haul his groceries and other things from town. He couldn't remember if there was a wagon in the barn or not.

Speaking of wagons, he thought about the job he had one summer riding shotgun on a freight wagon hauling goods out of Austin, Texas. That had been the worst place he had ever worked, and the memory of it was still in his mind. He'd arrived in the middle of May 1871, and left in

October of the same year. It was hot and dry on arrival and stayed that way the entire summer. Some old-timers said it had been the hottest summer they could remember. By September he had had enough of eating dust off horse hooves, and packed up for a better climate. He did go back once in his later years, for a gunhand job that didn't pan out, and left within a week.

His houses and barn came into view, but something didn't seem right. It looked like smoke came from the backyard of the main house, and a few figures milled around a fire. Maybe he'd ridden to the wrong property. When he could take a closer look at the barn, he would know for sure because the previous owner had used his branding iron to write his initials on the wood door.

Chapter 4

A CAREFUL MAN NEVER WALKED INTO A SITUATION mindlessly, and this occasion was no exception. Buck stopped his horse after he rode past the first house where the previous foreman had lived and observed the main house and barn. The smoke came from the backyard and not a stovepipe for the kitchen stove or a fireplace. What were these people doing out back with a fire going? Maybe heating water under a big pot to wash clothes in, or they could be burning trash in a burn pit, or getting ready to scald and clean a hog. Whatever their reason was, they weren't supposed to be on his property.

Riding past the house would give Buck a better view of the front of his residence, so he nudged Red with his boot heels and the horse walked on. Cedar-shake shingles were missing in random places across the roof, and the outside walls needed painting. A few warped, twisted, weatherbeaten boards would need to be replaced thanks to the harsh Texas sun and wind.

A hundred yards past the house, Buck maneuvered his horse so he possessed a clear view of the backyard. Two men and what looked to be a woman were washing clothes in a large cast-iron pot over a fire. They hung the wet, clean clothes on a wire between two trees to dry in the sun.

Buck turned Red around and returned to the lane that took him to the front porch. He removed the safety strap off the gun on his right hip and pulled the hammer back. Out of habit, he brought his right hand to his mouth and blew on his index finger and thumb.

The element of surprise was always the best offense in a fight, and today was no different. Buck left Red in front of the house while he eased his way down the south wall until he could see the figures in the backyard.

The men were unarmed, and he was almost certain the woman didn't have a weapon. The woman held a wooden board that reminded him of a canoe paddle. She used it to move the clothing around in the large cast-iron pot filled with hot, soapy water. One of the men kneeled on his haunches, drinking a cup of something hot, most likely coffee. The other man held a basket that looked like it still had some dirty clothes in it. Buck figured he was waiting for the woman to make room in the pot for the garments.

"Hello," said Buck as he stepped around the corner of the house. "I'm Buck Reed, and this happens to be my property that y'all are on."

The man drinking coffee dropped his cup and started to stand. Buck said, "You make darn sure those hands stay in plain sight, or I'm liable to think you're going for a gun, and then I'll have to start shooting."

"Mr. Reed, I ain't armed. We're just out here washing our clothes."

"Who are you, and why are you squatting on my property?" asked Buck.

"I'm Alabaster Boswell, and my wife is Sally. This feller is a friend that goes by Runt."

"You didn't answer my question," Buck said. "Why are you living on my property?"

"Well, you see," said Alabaster, stopping to spit. "It was vacant, and we needed a place to live. So we moved in almost a year ago. Ain't no one said it belonged to you."

"So you saw a vacant house and moved in?" asked Buck.

All three people nodded.

"Why didn't you move into that other house over there?" Buck asked, referring to the foreman's house.

"This one was bigger and much nicer," said Sally, standing with the paddle still in the pot.

Buck assessed the situation, ready to draw, when he asked, "Do any of you have jobs or any way to make money?"

"Nah, we don't have regular work. We just take on odd jobs, and sometimes we sell vegetables from the garden over there," said Alabaster, pointing to the back of the barn.

"That's what I figured," said Buck. "I hate to give you bad news, but I want you to load up your stuff and get off my land. Since you have wet clothes in that wash pot, I'll give you until tomorrow morning to head out, and then if you're not gone, I'll come back, and we'll have a come-to-Jesus meeting."

"Now, you just hold on to your underdrawers a minute, mister," said Sally as she removed the paddle from the pot and started toward Buck. Runt dropped the basket and reached for a shotgun on the woodpile. Buck hadn't noticed it before but saw the stock when the man went for it.

Buck's hand moved and in a split second, his gun was

pointed at the woman, ready to fire. Sally stopped in her tracks, shocked that he was about ready to shoot her. Runt quit reaching for the gun, stood still, and wet his pants in fear.

"Ma'am, you put down that paddle and listen to me," said Buck. "This is my property, and I intend to live out the rest of my life here, and that doesn't include sharing it with you and your man. Your friend has soiled his pants, so you have more to wash. Finish your laundry, hang it out to dry, and pack up your belongings. Leave anything that was here when you moved in, and get off my land. Is that clear?" he asked.

Alabaster stepped forward and took Sally by the arm. "Mister, we have a wagon and two horses in the barn. We'll start loading up and be gone by noon tomorrow."

"Good. I'm riding back into town for the night, and I'll be back in the morning," said Buck. He put two fingers to his mouth and whistled. Red came trotting around the house and stopped beside his owner. It would be for the best if he didn't stay on the property yet, but left so the Boswells could start packing. A nice meal and bed at the Bonham Hotel would suffice for the night. It might also be a good opportunity to buy some furniture for his house.

The old man wasn't in a hurry and took his time riding to the county seat of Fannin County. He arrived around two and went shopping for some of the supplies he would need at his residence.

An hour before dark, Buck purchased a wagon and two horses to haul the new beds he'd bought at the furniture store to the house the next day. Two men from the store loaded the furnishings he purchased. He also bought some other items, like chairs, nightstands, and a washbasin for the bedroom. The store would deliver them for him tomorrow. Even though he planned to live alone, a second bed would come in handy when he did have company.

"Mister, there's only a little room left in the wagon for provisions and such," said one of the men when they had the load tied down.

Buck thought about what food he should buy. All he was used to cooking was coffee, bacon, eggs, and fried bread; he hadn't cooked a complete meal in years. Either he ate in a café, or he worked someplace that employed a cook for the hands.

The same went for sleeping, and he had to buy a new bed, mattress, and bedding. He hadn't slept under the stars on the cold, hard ground in a very long time. His old joints had spent too many years bouncing around the country on the back of a horse for him to sleep on the ground.

Buck took the loaded wagon back to where he'd bought it and made a deal with the owner to put it and the horses up for the night, saying he would pick them up at nine the next day. Red was housed at the livery stable for the night so he could be fed grain.

The mercantile was on the other side of the street, down the block a few buildings. Buck went in and walked around the store, looking at cooking utensils.

A young woman approached him. "May I help you find something, sir?" she asked.

"Yes, you may," he replied. "I need cookware and don't know what to buy."

"I see. Let's start with a coffeepot. Do you live alone, or are there others in your house?" she asked.

"I live alone and haven't cooked in years," said Buck.

She picked up a medium-sized coffeepot and a cast-iron skillet. "These are two of the essential things you'll need," she said as she carried them to the counter. "I think adding a stew pot and maybe a pan to cook vegetables in should do you for now, unless you want something else."

"What about things to eat with? I need forks, spoons, and knives," said Buck.

"Oh, so you need everything for a kitchen?" she asked.

"Yeah, I don't have anything. I may not even have a table," said Buck. "I haven't been inside my house in a long time."

"Are you in a big hurry, or can I take some time to gather everything that I think you'll need?" she asked.

"I plan on leaving town tomorrow, about nine in the morning. If you want to gather everything up, I'd appreciate it. Maybe you could also put together necessities in the way of food items," said Buck. He pointed at shelves of canned goods. "A variety of those readymade vegetables would be nice and quick to prepare."

"I can certainly do that, and I'll do my best to have it all ready by nine tomorrow. My name is Sammy, by the way. Me and my husband own the store, and we appreciate your business."

Buck stuck out his hand. "I'm Buck Reed, and it's nice to meet you, Sammy. I'll check back with you in the morning."

"I'll have your order ready, sir, and it's nice meeting you."

Buck smiled, tipped his hat, and left the store, heading to a café he had seen earlier.

After a delicious supper, the gunman walked to the hotel and rented a room for the night. He gave the hotel clerk instructions to have a hot bath ready at eight the following morning.

Buck woke up in his room the next morning, fully rested. But when he slowly scooted to the edge of the bed and put his feet on the floor, it seemed like every bone and joint in his body hurt. It took a few minutes of gentle movement before he could stand up and dress to go downstairs to have his morning soak.

The hot water did wonders for his joints; when he got out, he managed to shave, dress, walk to breakfast, and enjoy the lovely morning without grimacing in pain with every step.

Red was happy to see his owner when Buck entered his stall. He gave Red a piece of hard candy that he carried for that purpose. While the horse chomped on the sweet treat, Buck rubbed Red's neck and talked to him.

The hostler came into the barn. "Mister, do you want me to saddle your horse?" he asked.

"I certainly do, young man," said Buck, handing the boy four bits.

Buck rode down the street to pick up his wagon. It was already harnessed with the two horses, and the bedroom furniture was tied to the sides of the wagon bed.

A middle-aged man in bib overalls came over when Buck arrived.

"Everything's just like you asked, Mr. Reed."

"Thank you. I'll tie my horse to the back and be on my way," said Buck. "By the way, I need hay and oats delivered to my place, so I have plenty for my horses. Do you do that?"

"Yes, sir, I can deliver you a couple of wagonloads of hay and four towsacks of oats tomorrow."

Buck told the man how to get to his land and paid him for the feed. He took off, and when he was even with the Bonham Furniture and Supply business, he stopped the horses, set the brakes on the wagon and went inside.

"Morning, Mr. Reed. I'll have the rest of your furniture delivered first thing tomorrow morning."

"That's fine. I want to add a bathtub if you have one," said Buck.

"Yes, sir, I have one, and we can get it on the second wagonload."

Buck pulled out some money and paid the man for the tub.

Sammy had all his food and cookware in sacks and boxes at the mercantile. Her husband helped Buck load it in the wagon, which was so packed they had to put wooden containers filled with groceries on the seat with him.

Buck left for home with his horse trailing behind his new rig. He felt good about his future living in his own house. The incident at the property with the Bosworths could have been worse, and he felt a calm inside of himself for not having to use more force than he had. He wanted to live in harmony with his fellow man and not have to ever kill again.

Chapter 5

WHEN BUCK ARRIVED AT HIS HOUSE WITH THE WAGON loaded with his new bed, the Boswells and Runt were already gone. He parked the wagon by the front door of the main residence before checking out its condition after being used by the squatters.

The inside of the house was almost barren except for a few things. There was still a wooden table with two benches in the kitchen area. The kitchen and living room were separated by a wide, doorless opening. Two old wooden chairs remained in the sitting area, but they looked terrible and needed to be taken outside and burned. He gave Sally credit—she had kept the wooden floors swept and mopped.

One bedroom didn't have any furniture, although there was a pile of old clothes and other items, and he figured it was Runt's room by the size of some torn britches. In the second bedroom, a filthy feather mattress sat on the floor, and he assumed Sally and Alabaster had slept there. The third bedroom was empty and dusty, and he surmised that the squatters never used it for anything.

Buck went outside and took Red to the barn, where he unsaddled the horse and turned him into the corral. He put the saddle over a horizontal board between two posts on the corral and carried his saddlebags full of books to the house.

After leaving the wagon by the front porch with easy access to the front door to unload everything, he unhitched the horses and put them in the corral with Red. With his hat off and the sleeves of his shirt rolled up, he went to work cleaning the residence.

The kitchen table would have to stay for the time being, but he started hauling everything else in the house to the backyard to set on fire.

Eventually only the two old, rickety chairs remained. He took the two steps down from the back porch to the yard with one of the chairs in his hands, and after walking two feet away from the steps, the familiar sound of a rattlesnake shaking its buttons filled his ears. Before Buck could move out of the way, something hit his boot top around the ankle area. With speed he didn't know he still had, Buck dropped the chair, drew his gun, and pointed it at the snake that was ready to strike again. He let off three quick shots, and the snake's head exploded on impact from one of the slugs.

He bent down and turned the chair upright, sitting down to examine his leg. The snake had hit the boot on his right leg, so he pulled the boot off and looked for fang marks. It turned out to be a good thing that he wore his pant legs inside his boots—the two fangs had gone into the leather but hadn't touched his skin. The pants had been a buffer between his leg and the boot top.

He looked at the dead snake and thought about skinning it, but why bother? He could throw it out by the chicken pen and let the yard birds eat it, but he didn't know if he had any chickens. Buck decided to pick the serpent up by the tail and drag it away from the house. The predators could feast on it overnight.

By the time he unloaded the wagon and set up his new bed for the night, it was late, and time for supper. Not wanting to build a fire in the cook stove, he ate a can of cold beans along with a can of peaches. He had forgotten to buy lamps for the house, and it was almost dark, so he went to bed.

Buck hobbled around the following morning because of his rheumatism. His old joints hurt and seemed swollen, and he shuffled his feet as he made his way into the kitchen. He went to the outhouse once he got a fire blazing and a pot of water on to boil for coffee.

Later, with a hot cup of coffee in hand, he sat on the front porch and hoped his other furniture would be delivered soon so he'd have a nice comfortable chair to relax in.

The beautiful morning relaxed him, and a stroll around the house might allow him to look at everything that needed to be repaired. The missing cedar shingles on the roof would be a job for someone younger than him. He decided to make a list of all the materials he needed, and on the next trip into town, he'd hire a couple of carpenters to do the repairs.

Next, the corral and barn were up for inspection. When he'd written out the list of materials, two wagons loaded with Buck's new furniture pulled up in front of his house.

The men driving the wagons unloaded his things and carried them inside. Buck directed the workers where to place each item, and when they were finished, he said, "I need a carpenter to do some repair work on my house, barn, and corral. Do you know anyone in Bonham that I might hire?"

"I do. I'm Morell Farr, and my two sons and I do handyman work around town. I only make deliveries part-time for the furniture store. The owner is my uncle, and he hires me from time to time."

"When can you get started?" asked Buck.

"If I know what all you want done, we can start gathering the material tomorrow and get right on it," said Morell.

"Come with me, and I'll show you what I want to do. Did I hear that you would buy the supplies?" Buck asked.

"That's right. You can go to the lumberyard and the hardware store and make arrangements for payment, and me and the boys will load and haul it out here."

The other feller spoke up and said, "I don't have a dog in this fight, so I'm heading back to Bonham."

"I'll be along directly," said Morell. "Show me what you want done," he said to Buck.

Buck walked the man around the house, pointing out things he wanted repaired, including the roof. The barn and corral needed fixing also, but Buck said he wanted them to finish the house first and then work on the barn.

After Morell left, two wagons loaded with the feed he had purchased came toward the barn. The men were still stacking hay when Buck saddled up his horse and left to ride into Bonham, where he planned to do what Morell had suggested. He set up accounts at the hardware store and the lumber yard, then ate an early supper before riding back home.

Chapter 6

Buck closed the gate on the corral while Red ate the scoop of oats in his feed pan. There was plenty of water in the horse trough, enough to last till morning, so Buck headed back to the house. That was when he saw visitors turn off the main road and start up the lane to his home.

Five armed riders came his way, and he didn't trust their intentions at five-twenty in the afternoon. He removed the safety off his gun and cocked back the hammer so it was ready to fire. The shoulder gun was prepared also. He blew on his index finger and thumb while walking to the house.

Buck arrived on his front porch and waited until the riders stopped their horses. One of the men had on a badge, and one of the other four looked like the crew's boss or ringleader. He wore a large Texas-style hat and fancy clothes that didn't resemble the range wear the other riders were dressed in.

"Evening, gentlemen. Are you the hospitality

committee coming by to welcome me to the area?" asked Buck.

The man he thought was in charge spoke up. "I'm Bernard Sena. I own the ranch down the road a short distance, and I want to know what your intentions are on this property."

Buck didn't change his facial expression or make any movements. He said, "Well now, being that I own this land, I have the right to do anything I want as long as it's moral and legal."

Bernard urged his horse forward another step and pointed his right index finger. "I'm warning you right now, gunslinger, I won't put up with your kind coming around here scaring law-abiding citizens. Is that clear?"

"That's right neighborly of you, Bernard," said Buck. "Sheriff, did you hear what he just said to me?"

"I heard, and I agree with him," said the sheriff. "We don't want your kind around here. You would be wise to sell out and go somewhere else."

"Now, fellers, I can't believe that an upstanding rancher and the elected county sheriff are on my property threatening me," said Buck. "All of you get off my land. I don't appreciate getting threatened by loudmouth trespassers. I have the right to gun all of you down right here and now." Buck spread his feet shoulder-width apart, squared his shoulders, and dropped his hands by his side, ready to draw. He knew his actions would either cause them to turn and retreat, or result in one or more of them dying.

"Now you hold on, mister," said Bernard. "We don't want any trouble."

"You're a liar," said Buck. "You came onto my land to run roughshod over me and threaten me with violence. I don't run, and I'm sure not scared of you or your bought-and-paid-for sheriff."

The sheriff moved his horse two steps closer to Buck. "You listen to me."

"No! You listen to me," said Buck. "All of you get off my land right now and stay off. Sheriff, you better hope someone doesn't run against you in the next election. I'm liable to back them with money and put you out of office."

Bernard sat on his horse, seeming to contemplate his next move. Buck knew that he had the rancher stumped, so he took it to the next level. "Rancher, go ahead if you're considering pulling that hog leg. I'll even give you time to clear leather before I kill you."

"Whoa now!" said the sheriff. "There's no need for gunplay. Come on Bernard, we'll get off the man's property."

Bernard pointed his finger at Buck. "I'm leaving, but you heed my words. We won't put up with gunfighting and killing around here." With that said, he turned his horse around, and the five men left.

Buck stood on his porch smiling as the men rode away. The bluff had worked, and they would think twice about coming back.

After the carpenters started their work the next day, he would ride to Dodd City and withdraw enough money from the bank to pay for the repairs.

Back inside the house, he got a glass of water and sat in his new padded chair. The books he'd carried in his saddlebags were stacked on the floor. The one on top was a copy of the Holy Bible, the next was *Moby Dick*, then *The Adventures of Huckleberry Finn*. He picked up *Moby Dick*, found where he had placed a marker, and started to read. When it was too dark to see the words, he fried some eggs for supper by the light of a candle he found. After he ate, he sat outside watching the stars and listening to the sound of bugs and coyotes until sleep overcame him.

Around four in the morning, Buck sat up in bed with his gun in his hand. A noise had woken him up, and his first reaction had been to get his gun from under his pillow. There it was again. It sounded like horses running, and lots of them.

He swung his legs to the floor and stood up, then shuffled to the back door to see what was happening outside. Could it be Bernard and his men coming back to scare him away or burn him out?

When he made it to the back door and had it open, whatever made the noise was long gone. He would investigate in the morning. Herds of wild horses ran on the vast ranges of Texas and New Mexico, but he had never seen any in this part of Texas.

It was so close to daylight that he decided to get up for the day and make coffee and cook his breakfast. At first light, he was outside walking across his property, hoping to find what had woken him up.

Buck was about to give up on his search and return to the house when he saw a large patch of grass with broken stems. It looked like the area was nearly thirty feet wide. Unshod horses had ridden through his land. Hooves with no shoes meant they were either wild horses or they belonged to Indians. It was unlikely that it had been a herd of wild mustangs, so the question was, why would Indians ride across his land at that time of the morning? They had to be running from someone, or they had committed some crime and were trying to escape.

If he had time, he might follow the tracks later, but right now, he wanted to go back to the house and wait on the carpenters' arrival to start his repairs.

Chapter 7

On the way back to the house after finding the horse tracks, Buck saw a pile of logs about thirty feet from the cord of stacked-up firewood and assumed the Boswells had cut it and left it there. The wood looked to be the correct length for his stove, so after he washed the breakfast dishes, he put on his gloves and went to find an axe.

His goal was to split a wheelbarrow full of logs, take them to the house, and then come back and work up another load. After an hour of hard work, the old man sat on one of the upturned logs, catching his breath, and heard Morell coming along with a wagonload of material before he saw the wagon. This was the perfect excuse to stop working with the axe, double jack, and iron wedge for the day. As he put up his tools, Morell and his two boys unloaded their wagon.

"Good morning, fellers," said Buck. "I see you're ready to get started. How much do you figure I'll owe you for all the repairs?"

"I figure for me, the boys, and using my wagon to haul everything, the total will be about eight dollars a day. I estimate it'll take us two days on the house, and two days on the barn and corral," said Morell.

"So around forty dollars for everything?" asked Buck.

"Yep, that sounds right."

"I'll tell you what I'll do," said Buck. "If you also split that wood pile over there, I'll make it fifty dollars for all the work."

Morell looked at the wood and smiled. "It's a deal. My boys will go through that woodpile in a jiffy."

Buck walked over to the boys, who were still unloading lumber from the wagon.

"My name is Buck. What are your names?" he asked.

The taller boy, who appeared to be in his late teens, said, "I'm Jubal. It's a pleasure meeting you, Mr. Reed."

The other boy looked younger but had more facial hair, and stuck out his hand. "I'm Lester, Mr. Reed, and it's nice to meet you."

"You boys are now my friends, so you can drop Mr. Reed. Just call me Buck."

The young men smiled at each other, and Buck knew they had heard about who he was.

He went back to Morell. "I'm riding into Dodd City to do some business. Is there anything you need from town? I can take my wagon if there is."

"No, I don't reckon we need anything. You go on, and we'll get started," said Morell. "You be careful in town. There's some rumbling going on about you living out here."

"I'll be careful," said Buck. He started walking off but stopped. "I heard horses come through behind the house before daylight this morning. I'm pretty sure it was Indians on the run. Have you heard anything about a band of renegades riding through?"

"Yeah, there's an Army patrol after them. Most likely,

they're on the run from the reservation west of Fort Sill," said Morell.

Buck nodded and walked to the barn, where he saddled up his horse. Red followed his owner to the house and waited until Buck came back out with his gun belt strapped around his hips. The two young men stopped working and watched as the gunfighter mounted and rode off.

His horse started south trotting down the road, but that hurt Buck's back and butt too much, so he let Red walk. That gave the newcomer time to pay close attention to the other farms and ranches that he passed by. Bernard Sena's ranch must have been north of his place, since he didn't see anything that would make him think otherwise.

The countryside was primarily flat land used for grazing or planting cotton. Along the creek stood large cottonwoods, oaks, ash, and other species of native trees. The pastures had cedars, a few mesquites, and brush scattered throughout them.

Once on the main road that ran between Bonham and Dodd City, Buck urged Red to lope. Red liked to go faster, and it took only a short time for them to go the remaining three miles to town.

Buck had already decided to stay out of the saloons. He would do his business and return home. The last thing he wanted was trouble that got him run off by the law.

O.W. greeted him when he came into the bank lobby. "To what do I owe the pleasure of seeing you again so soon, Buck?"

"I want to withdraw five hundred from my account. I need to pay some men for repairs to my house and barn."

"Coming right up," the banker said. He walked to the teller window and collected the money.

"I heard you had squatters in the house when you arrived," said O.W.

"Yeah, but they left peacefully, and the house was clean when I took over," said Buck. "I have a couple of errands, and then I'm going home. I'll see you in a few days, O.W."

Buck gathered up Red's reins and walked across the road to the mercantile, where he bought three kerosene lamps and had the clerk wrap them in paper so the globes wouldn't break. He had forgotten to get the extra lamps in Bonham yesterday and wanted one in the kitchen, one in the living room, and one on the bedside table so he could lie in bed and read.

With his package tied onto his saddle, it was time to start back home. As he rode down the street, four men walked out of the saloon and stood on the boardwalk, watching him go by.

One of the men hollered out, "Hey, Buckshot! Come over and have a drink."

Buck guided his horse toward the man, and when he was five feet in front of him, Buck said, "Hello, you old windbag. You're a sight for sore eyes." He dismounted and let the reins hang to the ground. Buck approached the man and grabbed him around the shoulders for a bear hug.

"My boy told me you were in town," said the man. "It's really good to see you again, old friend."

"It's good to see you, Wilbur. I didn't know you were still alive until I met your son the other day." Buck looked over at Rex, who stood silently next to his father. "I bought myself a little spread northwest of here a few years ago, and now I'm going to finish my years on it. Where's your place located?"

"We're south of town and back east a mile or so. Come on in, and I'll buy you a drink," said Wilbur.

"I'll have one beer, and then I have to be going. There're some men making repairs on my house and barn who need to be paid before they finish today," said Buck.

He tried to slow down on the beer, but it was hard to do when meeting up with an old friend. He had a second beer while they talked and laughed until Buck put down his empty mug and said, "I need to get going. It takes me a mile or two before I can take the jar from letting my horse go fast. I'll be seeing you around, old friend."

As Buck turned to leave, Rex said, "You'll be seeing me. At some point, we have unsettled business in the street."

Wilbur backhanded his son across the face and knocked him out of his chair. "I've done told you once, you hard-headed fool. This man will kill you before you pull iron."

Rex wiped blood off his split lip and got up, looking embarrassed.

Buck walked out and mounted up. That had been a family matter in the saloon, and he didn't want anything to do with it. Rex would die if his father didn't beat some smarts into that boy's head soon.

Chapter 8

IT WAS LATE AFTERNOON WHEN THE GUNSLINGER arrived home and took the lamps into the house. The workers were replacing boards on the back wall and the back porch floor. There was a can of kerosene in the kitchen, so he filled the lamps and placed one in each room.

The wood box in the kitchen was almost empty, and with nothing to do, Buck hauled in enough wood to fill it to the top, then put enough in the stove to cook his supper.

Morell hollered from the back porch, "Mr. Reed, we're finished for the day. Me and the boys will be back tomorrow to start painting the house."

"Okay. Thanks fellers, for your hard work. Hold up, and I'll pay you."

When he had counted out the money and handed it to Morell, he said, "I'll see you tomorrow."

"Yes sir, and thanks for paying up front." Morell nodded and went to his wagon.

Buck waved as they left; then he went about gathering up what he would eat for supper.

When finished with supper and the kitchen clean, he went to the front porch to sit and enjoy the evening breeze. Sitting there in the early evening, the heat from the day cooling with the setting sun, reminded him of when he was a teen living with his parents outside the Antioch Community in Delta County, Texas.

In the hot summer months, the family sat outside in the evening after working in the cotton fields all day. Those days in the cotton fields were some of the hardest work he had ever done, but he'd been much younger than and more robust. As a young man, he'd aspired to become an apprentice lawyer and study the laws of Texas, but life had a way of changing dreams.

The year 1850 had changed his life forever. The strapping twenty-two-year-old man fell in love with Mary Jean Evers, and they courted over the summer. After the cotton harvest, he asked Mary to be his wife that fall, and she said yes. The wedding took place at her folks' farm in March 1851.

Buck went to work at the local cotton gin and seed company in Cooper, Texas, which was about six miles west of a little two-bedroom house they rented. His first duty had been to work on the cleaning floor, where they separated the cotton from the seed. It was hard, dirty work, and the dust off the trashing floor caused him to have breathing problems, so the boss assigned him to the loading docks instead.

In January 1853, he and Mary grew tired of paying rent and had saved up enough to make a down payment on something, so they bought a lovely tiny home in the settlement where the gin was located.

That first year in the house, Mary got a job doing housework for Mr. Goldberg, who owned the cotton gin and gristmill. It took everything they made to pay their bills. Buck then took a job driving freight wagons around the area, hauling seed, cotton, and other products. It paid more money, but he had to be away from home a few days a month.

The two lovebirds made ends meet and had even started to save again when, after three years of marriage, Mary became pregnant. She continued to work even after the baby girl was born in November 1854. Her name was Belinda, but they called her Linda most of the time.

The family prospered, and the child grew. Buck worked long hours and even took on extra work, and they paid off the house early in 1857. A year later, they were in the process of building on when Buck's world was turned upside down.

Smallpox had been running rampant, and sure enough, Mary and Belinda became infected. Belinda died first, in 1858, at the age of four. Two days later, Mary passed during the night with Buck at her side. He was devastated by the loss of his loving wife and little girl. At the funeral, his folks, who were getting up in age, had to hold on to him as they walked to the graveyard that miserable day so he wouldn't collapse.

Buck was mad at God for letting this happen, and he felt so guilty that it was them who had died and not him. Grief ate at his every thought so much that he couldn't think straight and didn't know where to turn or who to talk to about it. After a week of mourning, the distraught widower and father saddled his horse and headed to the next town over, where whiskey could be purchased. The only thing he could think of to make him forget his loss was to drink.

Sorrow and whiskey became his friends each night as he consumed the fiery liquor. His daily routine for the next two months was to get up and work all day, go to the café to eat, and then drink himself to sleep every night. With each passing day, his health began to suffer. He didn't care for his work anymore, and he got fired for showing up drunk.

The money he and Mary had saved to expand the house was running out, so he sold their home and moved into a one-room shack in Pecan Gap, Texas. It took him five months to become flat broke, and he had no means of making more money.

One morning when he woke up lying on the dirt floor in his shack, he realized he had no more money for whiskey. He felt sick inside because his body was dependent on the alcohol. Empty bottles were scattered on the floor, and his pockets were empty. How would he survive without whiskey to get him through the day? He would have to find a job or start stealing. Never one to go against his upbringing and break the law, he had to get clean and find a job.

All his clothes were filthy and smelled of sweat mixed with stale whiskey and puke. He'd need to scrub himself with lye soap and hot water to remove the months of dirt from his body. The saddest thing was, he didn't even know if he had a tub to bathe in. Standing on weak legs, he managed to gather up what few items of clothing he had. Next, he searched for something to wash them in and found a tin washtub in the outbuilding behind the house.

It took him all day to wash clothes and take a bath. He needed two baths because the water was so dirty after the first one.

Bathed and wearing clean clothes, he walked into town to search for work. As he walked along the dirt road, a thought hit him, and he stopped. Where was his horse? What had he done with his horse?

That first afternoon after getting cleaned up was not

good for Buck Reed. He got sick to his stomach and broke out into a cold sweat. It wasn't long until he stood bent over, puking in an alleyway between two businesses. The sickness was so intense that his hands shook, and it was hard to breathe. The withdrawal from the whiskey was having its way with his body, and his mind told him he needed to get a bottle. Standing up was not an option, so he sat back down with his back to a building and went to sleep.

Chapter 9

SHAKING, SWEATING, AND SICK, BUCK WOKE UP LYING in the dirt between the two businesses in Pecan Gap. When he finally got to his feet, he leaned against a building to catch his breath. Step by step, he made it to the end of the alley between Jefferson and Duke streets. All he could think about was a drink of whiskey.

A door slammed up the alley, and a man came toward Buck. His eyes were on the ground, not watching where he was going. Buck wanted a drink so bad that he changed that day. The withdrawal pain took over his mind and body so much that he frantically looked for a weapon to rob the man. He found a length of lumber about four feet long and picked it up. Hidden at the corner of the building, he waited until the man was three feet past him.

Buck rushed the man and clubbed him on the back of his head with a blow so hard the man fell forward onto his face, unconscious. Buck hurried to the man with a newfound determination and rolled him over. The man wasn't anyone he recognized from around town. Buck quickly searched the man's pockets and found one dollar and seventy-two cents.

The man began to move and mumble, so Buck took off back the way he had come and immediately went to the saloon. Standing at the bar, he motioned for the barkeep to bring him two rounds.

"Evening, Buck," said the bartender. "Do you have money to pay for your drinks?"

Buck laid four bits on the bar top. "Darn tootin' I got money. Now pour my whiskey."

He picked up the glass with a shaking hand and downed the first shot. The fiery liquor hit his empty stomach and fed his discomfort. He recovered enough to drink the second one in two swallows.

"Do you want another?" asked the bartender, holding the bottle.

"Not yet. I'm going to the café for my supper and then coming back for one or two more," Buck said, and he left.

The whiskey helped him feel better, but he was starving. He couldn't remember the last time he'd eaten, and since he had a little money, he could eat and buy a bottle of liquor to take home with him.

The shaking had all but stopped when he arrived back at the saloon. He stood at the bar drinking when someone came in talking about the man from the freight office getting hit on the head and robbed of two hundred dollars.

The liquor affected Buck, and he almost said out loud that the man who got robbed was a liar—the man Buck robbed had had less than two dollars on him. But Buck stopped himself from weighing in and had another drink instead. By nine o'clock, he was drunk and broke again, without enough money to buy another shot, let alone a bottle.

"Hey, bartender, can I get a bottle on credit and pay you tomorrow?" Buck asked in a slurred voice.

The bartender reached under the counter and came out with a hardwood stick about two feet long and round as a beer mug. "I ain't giving you any credit. If you don't have money, get out or I'll throw you out. Is that clear?"

"You don't have to be mean about it. I'm leaving, and I ain't coming back," said Buck, and he staggered to the back door. He often left that way since it was closer to his shack.

When he got to the door, he turned the knob, but instead of going out, he opened the door to the supply closet and went in. After moving a couple of crates of empty bottles, he sat on the floor with his back to the wall and went to sleep.

When the drunk woke up, the room was pitch black. At first, he was a little frightened, not knowing where he was, but when he opened the door and saw the empty saloon, a smile formed on his face.

There was just enough light coming through the big window at the front of the building for him to find his way to where the whiskey was stored behind the bar. He took a bottle in each hand, went to a table, and sat down. There was no need for a glass; he put a bottle to his mouth and gulped the burning liquid down. He could hardly stay seated in the chair when he'd emptied the first bottle. His mind and body had been taken over by the alcohol one more time.

Buck had just enough wits about him to realize he had to leave the saloon. He stood up and took one step before passing out and landing on a table, shattering it into pieces.

Chapter 10

THE FOLLOWING MORNING, HE WOKE UP AND FELT severe pain in his side. There it was again, and it hurt even more now. He opened his eyes and saw the bartender standing over him, kicking him with his booted foot.

Buck tried to get up, but a fist to his chin knocked him back out.

Something cold and wet hit him in the face, and he came awake to find he couldn't move his hands. He could hear talking in the room, and all of a sudden, two men lifted him off the floor. His bloodshot, swollen eyes finally focused, and he recognized the men as the town's marshal and his deputy.

"Buck, can you walk, or do we have to drag you to jail?" asked the lawman.

"I don't know, just leave me alone," said Buck through bloodied lips.

"Let's take him on to jail," said the marshal. He and the deputy each grabbed an arm, lifted him off the floor, and escorted the drunk out of the bar.

Buck spent the remainder of the day and that night

sleeping in a jail cell. In the morning, the deputy woke him up and offered him a cup of coffee and a biscuit for his breakfast. The ribs on his left side hurt when he moved, and he felt discomfort when he took deep breaths. His swollen, cut lips, along with the rest of his battered and bruised face, hurt when he ate and he grimaced as he chewed.

"Who beat me up?" asked Buck.

"Miles, the barkeep, found you in the saloon passed out and took his boots to you. I reckon you broke in and stole whiskey and then destroyed one of his tables," said the deputy.

"What's going to happen to me now?" asked Buck.

"I don't know, but I suspect you'll go before the circuit judge when he comes to town for court. In the meantime, you get to stay in our little hotel rent-free," the deputy said with a laugh.

That afternoon, the marshal came in and hollered for Buck to get up.

"I've been over at the saloon, and if you pay the owner twenty-five dollars for damages, he'll drop the charges against you."

"I don't have twenty-five dollars, and that barkeep can kiss the south end of a northbound horse," said Buck. "He had no right to take his boots to me and break my ribs."

"You're lucky he didn't shoot you," said the marshal. "You make yourself at home, and the judge will be by in a few days to assign your fate. In the meantime, I'll have my deputy bring you breakfast and supper daily."

"I appreciate that, Marshal," said Buck. "By the way, what is your name?"

"It's Olen Wayne Long, and the deputy is Jerry."

By that night, Buck was shivering and sick to his stomach. The deputy put a piss bucket in his cell for him to vomit in. Every time he started throwing up, his ribs hurt so badly that he couldn't breathe.

By the fifth day in jail, he felt better and had begun to eat the food that the deputy brought him, which consisted primarily of beans and cornbread. On the twenty-sixth day of captivity, things changed.

The marshal came into the jail and said, "Your trial before Judge Marriott will be at two this afternoon in the saloon. I suggest you be on your best behavior, or he'll throw the book at you."

Sure enough, the judge set up court in the saloon, and when the marshal brought Buck before the elderly Judge Marriott, the man hit his gavel against the tabletop to start proceedings.

"Mr. Reed," said the judge. "You have been charged with breaking and entering, theft, and destruction of property. I find you guilty of all charges."

"That's not fair. I didn't break into the saloon," said Buck.

"You shut your mouth," said the judge. "You, sir, are a drunk and a menace to society. I find you guilty, and you will either go to the territorial prison for three years or go into the Army. What will you choose?"

Buck stood in shock at what the judge proposed. "I reckon I'll join the Army," said Buck, defeated.

The judge hit the table with his gavel again. "So be it. I'll notify the Army immediately, and they'll come after you. Court dismissed."

Buck was escorted back to his cell to wait until a detachment came from the Army to pick him up.

Chapter 11

THE DAY AFTER THE TRIAL, THE TOWN MARSHAL dragged a straight-back chair in front of the cell where Buck lay on his cot. Buck was still sick from detoxing from the alcohol and not eating much, but he was doing much better. The nights and days of withdrawal torment had finally eased to the point that he didn't shake anymore.

"If you promise to stay put and not run away, I'll unlock this cell, and you can go to the outhouse, sweep the floors, and make coffee," said the marshal. "It may be months before the Army comes to collect you."

Buck worked inside the little office and jail area for four months. In February 1858, five soldiers and a sergeant came riding in from Fort Gibson, Indian Territory. They had a spare horse in tow with a bag hanging off its crude Army saddle. Buck's uniform and papers were in the bag. Upon arrival, the sergeant read the oath to defend the Constitution of the United States to Buck, who swore allegiance with his hand on a Bible.

Buck put on his Army uniform, which was two sizes too big for him, and a secondhand coat. After getting dressed, he rode off with the patrol and they headed back to Fort Gibson. The long trip made him miserable—he had to sleep on the cold ground without a bedroll. He used the saddle blanket as best he could for warmth and stayed close to the fire at night. The meals the first couple of days consisted of jerky and hardtack. On the third day of the trip, one of the soldiers killed a deer, and they ate well that night and the next day.

Buck's first military assignment was to the Garrison Regiment, and he was confined to the fort for the first six months. The commanding officer didn't think it would be in the Army's best interest for the ex-prisoner to leave the confines of the fort for quite some time.

After two years, he had the opportunity to join the cavalry regiment. Being a cavalry soldier required extra training since they were on duty most of the time, protecting the Five Civilized Tribes from hostile Indians and Whites. Buck saw no real action until his term of duty, which happened to be three years, was almost over. His unit had the assignment to guard west of the Three Forks region, where the Arkansas, Verdigris, and Grand Rivers came together. Rifle fire surprised the Army patrol, and after locating where the shots had come from, the soldiers split up and converged on a camp of outlaws. A short skirmish occurred. Three outlaws were killed, and two escaped.

Buck killed his first man that day, and when the battle was over, he confiscated the gun and holster from the bandit he'd shot. The weapon was one of the new Colt Walkers made for the Army. Buck was fascinated with it and kept it hidden once they made it back to the fort.

In February 1861, he was discharged from the Army with the clothes on his back, his Colt rolled up in the coat that he carried in his hand, and thirty-six dollars that he had saved over the three years. As soon as he cleared the fort, he unrolled his coat and put on his pistol. The ex-soldier started walking to Texas with the holster buckled around his waist. He stopped to rest and practiced drawing the gun when tired of walking.

On the third day of drifting south, a Cherokee Indian family also traveling south in a wagon gave him a ride to a town on the banks of the Arkansas River. There, he bought a couple of blankets and a hot meal before going out on the road again.

It took him ten days to reach the confluence of the North and South Canadian rivers, where the Methodist Church had established the Asbury Manual Training School.

After dark, he snuck into the stable behind the school and waited until everyone was asleep. The stable had three horses penned in stalls, and after some consideration about getting caught as a horse thief, the need outweighed the punishment and he took one so the weary traveler wouldn't have to walk anymore.

Chapter 12

Buck stood up on the porch and wiped the tears from his eyes. Losing his wife and daughter had been hard enough, but losing everything they had worked for and the embarrassment of being the town drunk were enough to make even the toughest man cry. He cleared the tears off his face—he'd reminisced enough for today. But it was good to reflect on the memories of his wife and daughter every so often so they wouldn't fade away.

It was late and time for him to turn in and rest. He went to his room and blew out the lamp, crawled into bed with his gun under the pillow, and drifted off to sleep.

That same dream that he'd had many times over the last five years saw him standing in the middle of a dusty street, waiting as young men lined up to face him. He drew against them all, but his bullets didn't kill them. They kept coming at him over and over until he woke up covered in sweat.

He got out of bed, washed off, crawled under the sheets, and finally fell back to sleep. Just like always.

He didn't wake until the sun was rising in the eastern sky. After getting dressed, the image he saw in the mirror while he combed his hair got his attention. The gray hair was longer than usual, and even though the stubble of his gray whiskers was longer too, it still didn't hide the wrinkles covering the leathery face. Those eyes that were once a pale blue stared back at him, gray now. They seemed shadowed, recessed in the sockets and looking empty of gentleness or caring.

The eyes didn't lie. It had been a very long time since anyone or anything had been important to him except retiring. At least the dreams about the men who had died by his gun didn't come as often as they used to. This was now his home, and it was time to change his ways. Hopefully, the dream he'd had the night before would be the last time he had to endure its horrors.

The rattle of trace chains on a wagon brought him out of his thoughts. Morell and his boys had returned to work on his house.

"Good morning, Morell," said Buck. "What are you planning on doing today?"

"We brought the paint with us, and I hope to finish the house today," said Morell.

"You go ahead and get started. I have work down at the barn, and then I may ride over to the creek and try to kill a deer or turkey," said Buck.

"Okay, we'll talk to you later," said Morell.

The old barn could use a good cleaning, and most things inside needed to be discarded or burned. By noon, Buck had created a big pile of junk a hundred feet from the barn which couldn't be set on fire today. The wind was out of the south, and he would wait until another morning when it was still before starting the fire.

Plenty of daylight was left to hunt for a deer or turkey. Buck saddled Red and led him to the house, then grabbed his rifle and a couple of flour sacks to put the meat in.

It didn't take long until the creek appeared in front of him. Trees lined both sides of its banks. Not being familiar with where the deer drank or where they fed, Buck rode alongside the banks looking for tracks. A narrow trail filled with deer tracks led toward the water, and he decided that would be an excellent location from which to watch. Red was left to graze a hundred yards away from the trail, and Buck found a good hiding place behind some brush. He was comfortable lying on the ground on his stomach, waiting for that night's meal.

Position behind the clump of saplings and sage grass with a rifle caused him to think back to a similar time when he'd waited on the enemy. After his discharge from the Army, he met Elmer Greenwood, who let him share his campfire on the way back to Texas.

When Buck first rode up to Elmer's camp south of Doaksville, Indian Territory, on the Kiamichi River, he stayed hidden behind the large trees and brush. "Hello in the camp," he said. "Can I come in and have a cup of coffee?"

"Ride on in, but make sure those hands are clear," called out someone to his left.

No one was sitting by the fire, and he couldn't see anyone in the direction where he heard the voice. Buck dismounted with his back to the small campfire and tied his horse to a tree limb. When he turned around to go to the fire, he came face-to-face with a gun pointed right at him from less than five feet away. "What's your name? State your business," said the man.

"I'm Buck Reed, and I just got discharged from the

Army. I'm heading back to Texas. I mean you no harm. I'm tired and need a hot cup of coffee."

"I'm Elmer, and I hunt outlaws for the bounty. So rest assured if you try anything, I won't think twice about killing you."

"I don't have a cup. Would you happen to have an extra one?" Buck asked. "I don't have anything to drink out of or anything to eat with."

"Yeah, I got a cup and an extra plate. I don't always kill the men I go after, so I carry extra utensils with me."

Elmer had a rabbit roasting about two feet above the fire with a stick through its body. Two other sticks stuck in the ground held the rabbit up. Buck eyed the meat while pouring himself a cup.

"When was the last time you had anything to eat?" asked Elmer.

"Last night," said Buck, blowing on the steaming black liquid.

"I reckon I can spare some of that swamp rabbit with you tonight."

"I would surely appreciate it."

Elmer divided the meat, and the two men ate until nothing was left but bones. Elmer leaned back on his elbows with his legs out straight and asked, "You any good with that gun you're wearing?"

"I think so. I'm fairly quick at drawing it, and I normally hit what I shoot at," said Buck.

"Have you ever killed anyone?"

"Yeah, the unit I was in had a run-in with some outlaws a while back, and I killed the man that owned this gun I'm wearing."

Elemer sat upright. "What outlaws?"

"I don't rightly know all of them, but I heard later that

the main man that got away was named Joe. Heck, I can't recall his last name," said Buck.

"Does Joe Wilcock sound familiar?"

"Yep, that's it. Do you know Joe?"

"I have a wanted poster on him with a fifty-dollar reward. Where did you find him?" Elmer asked.

"We were west of the Three Forks region where the Arkansas, Verdigris, and Grand Rivers come together over by Fort Gibson," said Buck.

"Do you think you could take me there?"

"I have no reason to go back there unless you want to hire me to help you," said Buck.

Elmer got up off the ground, walked over to a tree, and pried loose a chunk of bark with his knife. He came back to the fire and pointed at the tree trunk. "You see that bare place on that tree? I want you to stand ready, and when I say shoot, you pull leather and fire."

Buck stood up, blew on his thumb and forefinger, and exhaled. When Elmer shouted, "Shoot!" Buck drew and fired one shot that splintered the wood where the bark had been removed.

"You're a good shot, and with a little more practice, you could be very fast with the draw. If you want to join me in tracking down outlaws, I'll give you half of the bounty."

Buck sat back down and took another drink of coffee before deciding. "I reckon you have a new partner. I have nothing else to do, so count me in."

"Good. Now we better sleep because tomorrow we go after Joe and his gang."

"They most likely won't be where we found them," said Buck.

"No, but I've observed that outlaws tend to find a

place they like and use it as their home base. Joe likes to
rob in the Cherokee and the Creek Nations. He's still
close to the location where the Army found him."

"I'll be ready to ride when you are. I'm turning in for
the night," said Buck, lying down on his saddle blanket
with his head on the saddle for a pillow.

Chapter 13

Buck and Elmer headed north toward the Kiamichi mountains, and it took the two men eight days to finally make it to the Three Forks region not far from Fort Gibson.

After three grueling days of climbing over rocks, riding through brush, up and down ravines, and maneuvering through thick forest, they located Joe and two other men from information a man gave Elmer for five dollars. The man told them that they were holed up in a shack behind the store that bartered with the locals between Fort Gibson and Muskogee.

Elmer and Buck found the store and stayed hidden where they could watch the place. Buck snooped around where he could see horses tied in a makeshift corral. After he told Elmer what he saw, his mentor wanted him to go inside the store to spy on what the men were doing. His instructions were for Buck to see if Joe was there and find out how many men were with him.

Buck was apprehensive about going inside and told

Elmer, "I don't like doing this. Why can't you go in with me?"

"Look, man, if you're going to be my partner, you have to get brave and mean. You watch yourself, and if there is any indication that Joe or one of the men with him suspects you're a bounty hunter, just pull your weapon and start shooting. Remember the wanted poster says dead or alive."

Buck took his time pondering what his partner told him. He looked Elmer in the eyes and said, "Okay, I'll go in, but I'm not giving them a chance to shoot me." He pulled his gun from its holster, held it behind his back, and entered the store.

Buck recognized Joe sitting at a table with two other men. He would have to pass by their table on his way to the counter to buy a mug of beer, which was stacked with goods for sale.

Joe looked up at Buck when he was about to pass their table. The outlaw paused, his hand holding a pint jar of whiskey on the way to his lips. That pause was the last thing he ever did. Buck brought the gun from behind his back and fired one lead ball, which hit Joe in the forehead. Instinct took over, and Buck then shot the other two men. When his gun fell on an empty chamber, the new bounty hunter realized what he'd just done.

Elmer rushed through the door with his gun ready to fire but stopped when he saw the carnage in the room. "Store man, you keep those hands where I can see them," said Elmer. "These men are outlaws and wanted dead or alive."

Buck still stood in disbelief with the gun at his side.

"Buck, reload your gun," said Elmer. "You want to make it a habit to reload as soon as you finish shooting. You never know when you'll need your weapon again."

Buck responded by doing what his partner told him. Elmer went through the dead men's pockets and removed anything of value. "Buck, go get their horses and bring them close to the door," said Elmer.

It took both men about thirty minutes to get all three men loaded on their mounts and tied so they wouldn't come off during transit.

"Let's get going. We can haul the outlaws to the Indian agent outside the fort and get paid. I have all their valuables, and we can sell those to one of the stores in Muskogee that I've done business with before," said Elmer.

After they collected the rewards, sold the dead outlaws' guns, saddles, and horses, and took what money was in their pockets, the two partners had over four hundred each, which was more money than Buck had seen in a long while.

The first thing he did with his money was buy new clothes and boots, as well as a hat. His old Army-issued clothing went into the trash. Then he purchased a good bedroll and slicker for the rainy days. When he'd stolen the horse from the school, the only saddle he could get his hands on had no saddlebags, so he bought a shiny new set plus a cup, a tin plate, and eating utensils.

He worked with Elmer for the next year and saved up most of his share of the bounties. Elmer wasn't fast drawing his gun but was a good teacher. Buck had to practice his quick draw every day, and the exercises involved shooting at targets once a week.

Elmer didn't want to bring in any of the outlaws they went after alive, and Buck grew tired of killing men. Even though they were outlaws and had broken the law, they were still humans and should be given the right to surrender.

Buck saddled his horse one winter day, dissolved his partnership with Elmer, and rode away.

Tracking down outlaws paid more than any job he had ever had. Buck made his way into Texas from Indian Territory so he could get closer to home. The first job he picked up came from a sheriff's office in Paris, Texas. There he found reward posters on three individuals, and he was back in business. It took five months on his own to finally make any money tracking down the lawbreakers. Texas was a big state, and most folks preferred to avoid bounty hunters coming around asking questions.

By the end of his first year of working alone, Buck had made a name for himself for bringing in hardened criminals. Then rumbles of war came into Texas through the newspapers and people riding through from the south. Men from Texas were joining up with the Confederacy and in doing so, a lot of locals thought that Texas would be a battle state.

One sunny day in Fort Worth changed the young bounty hunter more than anything had up till then. Curt Right was the man on the latest wanted poster Buck had picked up, and he was standing in the middle of the street when Buck came out of the mercantile where he had just purchased a new shirt.

"Bounty hunter, I've heard of you, and you'll have to kill me if you plan on taking me in. Either come out into the street and draw or walk away—your choice."

"It doesn't have to be this way, Curt. You can give up and face a jury of your peers."

"Nope, we settle it right now, facing each other."

Buck had never been in a gun battle like this where he faced a man before, but knew he was fast. Standing on the boardwalk, thinking about what to do next, one belief kept coming to mind. If he walked away, every outlaw he went after would call him out. The only choice was to face Curt and shoot it out.

"Curt, you had your chance to live. I'll oblige you, and we'll see who the faster man is."

Buck put his package down and started out to face Curt. He brought his hand up to his mouth and blew on his forefinger and thumb, and when he was in the street, he realized Curt had set him up. The sun was in his eyes, and it was difficult to see, so he turned to his left slightly, and that was when Curt made his move.

Buck didn't think about what to do; it just happened in reaction to his opponent's movement. Curt brought his gun up into firing position but was struck in the chest. He staggered backward.

Again Curt brought up the gun and Buck could tell that it started to feel very heavy to the dying man, because he had difficulty getting it into the firing position. When he pulled the trigger, the gun fired into the ground. He slumped to the dirt in the street and fell forward onto his face, dead.

Buck's first face-to-face gunfight, where someone had called him out, turned out well in his favor. He reloaded his weapon and waited until the sheriff came running up with his gun drawn.

"Sheriff, that's Curt Right, and I have a wanted poster on him for a forty-dollar reward."

"You can come by my office in an hour and collect your money."

That was a turning point in his ability to bring in the men. He wasn't afraid to face them and give them the choice to draw or give up. His bounty hunting provided him with money and some gratification knowing the bad guys he went after were in jail or dead. All that changed one day when he went to arrest a young man for stealing a horse. The boy's folks swore that the boy had been home at the time of the theft and it wasn't him. Buck took him to the sheriff and they held his trial a week later. The judge ordered the boy to hang from the gallows for horse theft.

Two weeks after the boy died, the county sheriff arrested the real horse thief, and Buck was devastated when he heard the bad news. Thanks to the fact that he hadn't listened to the boy's folks and he hadn't taken a little longer to investigate, an innocent young man died.

Killing the outlaw Curt Right in a gunfight and three months later being responsible for the death of the innocent boy caused Buck to question if bounty hunting was still something he wanted to do for a living.

Two months after the boy got hanged, each sheriff in the Texas towns Buck visited gave him the same bad news. If a wanted man was brought in, no reward money was available to be paid out. That fact, along with rumors about a war coming, made him start looking for other work.

The bounty hunter returned to Lamar County and acquired his first wanted posters there. He wanted to listen to the lawmen and see if the federal courts were still paying rewards for the men arrested in the Indian Nation. Paris, in Lamar County, saw a lot of turmoil like the rest of Texas. Men left their families to join the war, and working the farms was left to the wives and kids. Most of the Texas men joined the Confederate army and were shipped by trains out to the front lines of the fighting.

Buck met a woman named Ginny Meadows outside Paris, Texas. After a brief courtship of only four weeks, he moved in with her to help her on the farm she owned. The work was hard, and after three weeks of working behind a plow, he packed his things and saddled his horse. Walking behind two mules all day plowing was not in his cards, and left while Ginny was in town buying groceries.

Stories of the fight in the South followed him everywhere he went, and things in Texas were getting worse every day with the men going off to fight. There were no jobs available because no one had any money to hire workers. Buck had to do something to earn a living, so he rode back to Fort Gibson and joined the Union army again.

Chapter 14

THE SOUND OF A TURKEY GOBBLING IN THE BRUSH IN front of him brought the hunter out of his reflections. Three large birds were coming his way, and when they came into range, he took aim and pulled the trigger. The shot missed, and all three birds ran off a few yards and then took flight. Well, the hunting was over now. There was no way a deer or turkey would come close after hearing the gunshot.

On the ride home from the spoiled hunting trip, thoughts of his life kept coming back to him. Things could have been different if he had stayed in Lamar County with Ginny; he wouldn't have fought in the war. But leaving someone he didn't love or want to spend the rest of his life with and working behind mules all day made the decision for him. Maybe he should've gone to Colorado or Arizona where jobs in the mines could be had, but he didn't.

Buck had a little over four hundred dollars in reward money when he left Paris, Texas, in 1863 and headed to Fort Gibson. Being familiar with the area, he didn't bring a lot of provisions since most of his meals could be purchased in towns along the route. It took a total of eight days to arrive at the fort.

When he entered the post headquarters, the officer in charge remembered Corporal Reed and placed him back in the Army with the same rank as before, assigning him to an infantry platoon under the command of Captain John Oliver and Sergeant Bates. Buck had never met the captain before, but he did know First Sergeant Bates, who was over the squad he was assigned to. He had met the first sergeant during his first duty at the fort.

Buck was almost back to the barn when his newly painted house came into view. Pulling back on the horse's reins, he admired the color and beauty of his residence. It looked like the workers had already left for the day, and that they had completed the painting. Hopefully they'd start on the barn the following morning.

Buck stopped Red at the barn and sighed heavily. After all those years of being a traveling gunhand, this was now to be his home for the rest of his life. Remembering the past gave him a sense of deprivation for all the bad things that had transpired over the years. So much of the past was hard to remember, but the events became new again once he started down a particular path.

Dismounting, he led the horse inside the barn, removed the saddle, and combed the horse's hair. He'd planned to put Red in a stall, but Morell had stored the materials for fixing the barn in front of the stalls, making it challenging to use them. Instead, he took Red to the corral. After filling the water trough and putting oats in a feed bucket, Buck entered his residence through the back door.

He stood just inside the doorway. The sound of silence filled the living room. It would be nice to have someone to share the house with. Maybe if he played his cards right, he might entice a lady in Bonham or Dodd City to be interested in him. Perhaps a couple of day trips into Bonham could provide him an opportunity to meet some single ladies. Tomorrow, when Morell was here working, Buck could ask him if there were some unattached ladies around town.

Once he finished his evening meal and the dishes were washed, dried, and put back on the shelf, he wanted to go outside and sit on the porch and enjoy the evening breeze.

After ten minutes of looking at the neighbor's cattle on the other side of the road, Buck's thoughts returned to the day Sergeant Bates ordered the squad to start marching toward Arkansas. Each man was issued a Springfield .58 caliber rifle and a belt set with a cartridge box, sling, cap box, and bayonet scabbard. The only other items the soldiers had were a haversack, a pocketknife, and a canteen. The sergeant told his men not to bring ground sheets, blankets, or tents because they could take them from the dead along the march.

Sergeant Bates commanded thirty soldiers, and Buck, as a corporal, was next in command. Most of the infantry soldiers were young troops still in their teens or early twenties, except for Buck and three other men.

For the first three days, the soldiers only traveled a total of approximately twenty-one miles through the rough terrain. By the sixth day, they had traveled sixty miles total. The hills and rugged forest were taking their toll on the men. On the sixth night, while resting beside a fire, Sergeant Bates said, "Tomorrow I hope to arrive at Fayetteville and meet up with the rest of Captain Oliver's platoon. Corporal Buck, I want you to send a scout out in advance of our men to make sure we don't get bushwacked on the trail. Tell him to keep his eyes peeled for Johnny

Rebs hiding along the path. They've been digging in around our Fayetteville encampment for the past month. Captain Oliver is anticipating gray coats will attack the smaller forces so groups like ours can't reinforce the main regiment, and that's the reason we were assigned to relocate. I sure don't want to engage them out here where we're outnumbered."

It surprised Corporal Reed that the sergeant had given him the responsibility of picking a scout. It was the first real task he had received. "Yes, sir, I'll get right on it."

He left the campfire and walked about twenty feet north, where six men were lounging around another fire. Buck sat on the ground beside an older man by the name of Butch. Buck decided to pick Butch because he was a hunter and constantly told stories about tracking down deer.

"I've been ordered by Sergeant Bates to send out a scout in the morning, and I chose you," said Buck. "As soon as you have breakfast, get going and be on the lookout for Rebels who could be waiting for us. Don't confront them or get shot. All of our lives are in your hands."

"I don't rightly know where we're supposed to go. Do you have a map that I can use?" asked Butch.

"Yeah, come with me and the sergeant will instruct you on where to go," said Buck.

The two men walked back to Sergeant Bates. "Sarge, can you give Private Butch directions on where to go in the morning? He'll leave early but doesn't know the direction he needs to scout," said Buck.

"Sit down and I'll show you," said the sergeant. He pulled a leather binder from the inside of his shirt, took a paper from it, and unfolded it on the ground with the top edge pointed north. The sergeant began to explain the route they would take.

Butch sat in deep thought for a few seconds before he asked, "If I take that road you showed me, won't I be a sitting duck to any Johnny Rebs hiding along the path?"

"Yeah, I guess you could be," said the sergeant. "Walk off the road about fifty feet and if you see some gray coats, you turn tail and come find us."

"Sergeant, maybe we should send two scouts and have one on each side of the road checking for the enemy," said Buck.

"Yeah, let's do that. Corporal, you go ahead and take care of that detail. I have other things to do," said Bates.

Buck and Butch left Sergeant Bates and went to find a man in his twenties named Jerry, who would be the second scout. Buck informed him of the route to take and gave him instructions on what to do on the trail if he saw the enemy.

The two scouts left right after daylight the following morning, and the rest of the squad followed about an hour later. The terrain was rugged, going up and downhill, with trees, brush, rocks, and boulders. The sun was floating toward the west when the troops had to cross the Muddy Fork River. Everyone had to carry everything they had that couldn't get wet above their heads while they crossed the stream. It was miserable walking with wet boots and clothing. The men's feet were hurting, and some were getting blisters. By the time the squad made it to the shoreline of the Illinois River, they were dead tired.

"You men take a break. Corporal, I want you to send someone upstream and someone downstream to look for a place to cross. Tell them to see if anyone has any boats we can commandeer," barked Sergeant Bates.

Buck did as he was told, randomly picking out two men to do as the sergeant had ordered, and then found a patch of tall grass to lie down in to rest. In less than an hour, he heard a commotion on the river, and a soldier paddled toward the group in a canoe, with two more canoes behind him. Buck went to the edge of the water, and the soldier told him that they had found a Cherokee Indian village and borrowed the boats from them. They had even offered to help take the soldiers across to the other side.

When Sergeant Bates saw the Indians paddling the canoes, he barked out orders. "Get your weapons ready to fire. Those Cherokees fight for the Confederates."

The soldiers took up their arms and got down on one knee, ready to fire. But Buck and the soldier in the boat called out, "Hold your fire. These men ain't fighting. They are farmers and fishermen."

Bates assigned several soldiers to keep the Indians in their sights until all the men were on the far side of the river. There was only an hour of daylight left, so the men took off to find a campsite for the night. After thirty minutes, the troops came to a small clearing to rest for the night.

Buck went to Sergeant Bates and said, "How about I send a couple of sentries out to secure our camp so the rest of the troops can cook some of their salt pork for supper?"

"You do that. I'll assign a few privates to rustle up some wood for a few fires."

The area was cleared and the men cooked their supper, which consisted of salt pork and canned beans, and ate it with hardtack. The two men who had left that morning to scout in front of the squad never made it back to camp that night.

Chapter 15

BUCK ROSE FROM HIS PORCH CHAIR AND STOOD looking at the evening sky. He'd had enough of recalling the horrors of war and how he'd managed to survive. It was a miracle that any of them lived through the fighting. He, along with a lot of other men, made many mistakes that could have gotten them killed. War was bad enough, and making mistakes only magnified the danger.

It was getting late, and after he stood for a few more seconds, the old soldier made his way back into his house and fired up the lamp in the front room. It gave him enough light to walk into the kitchen to fill a glass of water to take to his bedroom.

Dreams flooded his mind during the night, and he kept waking up to clear out the images he had seen hundreds of times before. Young men lying dead in the street or on the battlefield. The nightmares always made him wake up sweating and thirsty. The water on the bedside table helped quench his thirst and soothe his dry lips and mouth, but it didn't relieve the picture of lifeless eyes he kept seeing.

More dreams came sometime around dawn, but this time, they were of a child playing in a yard, carrying around a rag doll. She laughed, danced, and ran in circles. She was so happy in her little dress, bare feet, and pretty brown hair done up in pigtails.

"Papa, come play with me?" she asked.

Buck came awake with a smile on his face and tears in his eyes. He still missed his little girl and was always happy to dream sweet memories of her. Not wanting the dream to end, the old dad closed his eyes in hopes the images would return, but they didn't. He often wondered if there was something he could have done differently to save his wife and daughter. His few years with them were the best times of his life.

It was morning, and time to stop reflecting on the past and start embracing the day by going into the kitchen. With the fire stoked in the cookstove and water on for coffee, he sliced some bacon and placed it in a skillet. Then he heard horses behind his house.

A man who lived by the gun always strapped it on while getting dressed. Buck pulled the Colt and opened the back door to see seven soldiers at his well, filling their canteens with water from a bucket.

"Morning. Can I help you fellers with something?" Buck asked, standing with the pistol in his hand, pointed at the ground.

A young officer left the others and took a few steps toward the house before he stopped. "I'm Lieutenant Randy Webb. Me and my men are needing fresh water. We're hunting a band of Comanches that have left the reservation. We tracked them through these parts but lost the trail. Have you seen them or any sign that they may have been by?"

"I'm First Sergeant Buck Reed, and they came

through my place about four in the morning a few days ago. I didn't see them, but I heard them, and it sounded like they were in a hurry," said Buck, putting the gun back in its holster. "I can show you the direction they were headed, if you want. The trail is over there a couple of hundred yards." Buck pointed at the grass where he had seen the trail.

"We can most likely find it," said the lieutenant. "You say that you were a First Sergeant?"

"That's right, I served in the Army twice. Once before the war and then during the war."

"Are you the same Buck Reed that hires out your gun?"

"I was, but I'm retired now and taking it easy."

"We'll be on our way. It was nice meeting you, sergeant. Maybe we'll meet again sometime," said the lieutenant. He returned to his horse and mounted up.

Buck watched them ride in the direction he had pointed and then turn south to follow the Indians.

The breakfast dishes were washed and the kitchen floor swept when Morell and his boys returned to work on the barn. Not wanting to disturb their work or slow them down, he sat in one of the new living room chairs and read a few pages of *Moby Dick*. After three pages, he closed the book and contemplated the meaning of what he had read, but nothing came to mind about the story because other things had taken over his thoughts. His fellow soldiers heading to Arkansas was back on his mind, and the only way to get rid of those thoughts was to recall the events and put them behind him.

Sergeant Bates mustered the squad at the break of daylight the morning after the soldiers had crossed the Illinois River. They were instructed to spread out in the forest and divide into two columns once they found the road. Two more scouts were sent ahead of the troops as lookouts. Buck was concerned that the two scouts he'd sent out the day before were dead, since they didn't return to camp the prior night.

Two hours into the march, they came upon the road that led to Fayetteville. Buck stopped the troops before they ascended into the roadway and found themselves in the open.

Sergeant Bates came to him and spewed out, "What do you think you're doing, holding up the soldiers? I'm in charge here, not you."

"I have a bad feeling about marching on the road. The two scouts we sent out yesterday haven't come back, and the two we sent this morning are still within hollering distance. I think we're walking into a trap," said Buck. "If the Rebels have snipers out here, they can pick us off like ducks on water."

"They didn't come back 'cause they had no reason to. Now get the unit headed out and stop your nonsense," shouted the sergeant as he turned and walked away.

Ten minutes later, the men were in single file on both sides of the road when shots sounded out behind them, and three soldiers near the rear were killed. The rest of the squad took to the woods on each side of the path but held their fire, not knowing where the shooters were. They could only see a dissipating cloud of spent gunpowder smoke in the air, but the shooter could be hiding anywhere since the breeze moved the smoke.

Buck didn't like the squad's situation, so he took it upon himself to find the shooters and try to eliminate the threat. The thick underbrush made it challenging to crawl on his stomach, but he managed by taking his time and getting close to the spot where the powder smoke had been in the air. The shooters had to be hidden somewhere with a clear view of the road. What if the shooters were higher up, like in one of the trees? Changing positions while still lying on his stomach made it difficult to see into the trees because of the leaves on low-hanging branches. It was quiet with no wind to speak of when Buck saw a small flock of birds flying toward the trees he had been watching. At the last second, the birds turned and flew to different foliage. The shooter must have been hidden behind the branches that the birds turned away from.

Rolling to his left a few feet gave him a better view, and sure enough, two rifle barrels stuck out of a fork where a limb connected to the tree. On the opposite side of that branch was another rifle barrel, which moved slightly. Buck could see the right side of the shooter's body. Buck slowly moved his rifle into position, took careful aim, and squeezed the trigger. The shooter yelled out as he tumbled to the ground onto a fallen log, still holding his weapon.

Buck stayed where he was and kept watching the other two rifles, but neither one moved. Maybe it had only been the one ambusher with three guns. He took a deep breath, got up as quickly as possible, and ran to the large oak. Sure enough, there was no one else in the tree, and the man he'd shot lay dead.

Chapter 16

THAT NIGHT BUCK SAT OFF BY HIMSELF, THINKING about the events of the day. His instincts had been right that morning, but the sergeant had ordered the men into harm's way. From now on, he would trust his intuition to stay safe. Killing the enemy and protecting oneself was another thing the young, inexperienced troops would have to get used to. This was war, and each man had to get mean to survive.

Most of the squad, especially the younger ones who didn't know any better, slept bunched up close to the fire. Buck and a few other soldiers found places to sleep away from most of the greenhorns as the more experienced soldiers called them, so they wouldn't be disturbed by snoring and anyone talking in their sleep. Plus, if they were attacked during the night, the ones closest to the fire would be the first ones killed.

Buck lay on the ground trying to sleep, but the reality of war had become true to him that day when he killed the enemy without any regrets about it. The Rebel soldier wasn't the first man he had ever killed, but it was the first man who wasn't a criminal or someone who was about to shoot him. Pulling the trigger on his rifle that was pointed at the man in a tree had been like target practice. If any of the men in the squad wanted to survive this war, they had better not pause for one second in battle. Kill the enemy at all costs.

The old soldier put away his thoughts when he heard leather harnesses squeaking and horse hooves pounding on the ground outside. Morell and his boys got out of their wagon when Buck walked out on the front porch.

"Good morning, Morell. The house looks really good. I assume you'll start on the barn today?" asked Buck.

"Yes, sir, we sure will. I'm also thinking about painting it the same color as the house. Is that all right with you?"

"Yep, I like that," replied Buck.

"Do you want to do any repairs on the other two houses on your property?" asked Morell.

"I don't think so right now. I may in the future, or I may burn them down. I'm not sure just yet what I want to do with them," said Buck. "I was also wondering if you know anyone I might hire in Bonham who will wash and iron my clothes."

"I don't rightly know of anyone off the top of my head," said Morell.

"How about Miss Lucy?" asked Jubal.

Morell nodded. "Yep, I plumb forgot about her. Lucy is a widow and takes on work to make money. She lives in a little whitewashed house about two blocks behind the livery stable."

"I think I'll give Lucy a visit later. Do you need me to pick up anything while I'm in Bonham?" asked Buck.

"No, we have more than enough materials for today."

"I'm going to harness up the horses to the wagon. If

you think of anything, let me know before I leave," said Buck, walking to the barn.

The workers were replacing broken boards on the barn walls when Buck headed out to Bonham with his dirty laundry in a basket. He had only traveled about a mile south toward the main road when two men rode out of the timber on his right and demanded that the wagon come to a halt. Buck took the safety off his gun when he laid the reins on the wagon seat.

"You Buck Reed?" asked one of the men.

"Who wants to know?" replied Buck.

"Listen here, old man. We have a message for you. You sell out and leave Fannin County, or you will have to deal with the two of us."

"Well, since you put it that way..." Buck brought his right hand to his mouth and blew on his thumb and index finger. "There ain't no better time than today to deal with the two of you. Heck, I'll even give you the benefit of the doubt. You boys make your play anytime you feel lucky."

"We're just here to deliver the message. We ain't fighting you today."

Buck was mad and knew the one mouthing off was all talk and no action. "You listen to me. I have a message for the two of you to take back to the person that sent you out here. I don't scare easy, and if they want a piece of me, I live north of here two miles. And if you ever feel like squaring off against me, I'll kill the both of you and never look back."

The man who did the talking moved his horse's head using the bridle, and Buck drew his gun and cocked the hammer back before the two had time to react. "Now turn those nags around and hightail it out of here. The next time I see you, I may start shooting."

Both riders backed their horses up a few steps before turning and riding back into the trees.

Buck holstered his weapon, picked the reins up off the seat, and slapped them against the rumps of the horses. This wasn't the first time someone sent their stooges to try to run him off. It didn't work then, and it sure wouldn't now.

Bonham was a lively place of commerce, but Morell's directions were sound and Buck easily found the little white house. It had to be the correct place because there was a sign in the yard that read, *I wash, iron clothes, clean houses, and do odd jobs*.

As the old man stepped onto the porch, the door came open and he was taken aback by the beauty of the woman standing before him. The sun's reflection made her hair sparkle, and she had the prettiest hazel eyes he had seen in a long time.

"Howdy, ma'am. I'm Buck Reed. I was told you might wash and iron my clothes."

"I'm Lucy Smith. Do you plan on stripping out of those you have on?" she asked.

"Oh no, ma'am. I have a basket in the wagon."

"Don't just stand there, Buck Reed. Go get the basket. I ain't got all day to spend jawing with you."

"Yes, ma'am. I'll be right back," said Buck. He rushed to his wagon, collected his clothes from the bed, and went back to the house, where Lucy was still standing on the porch with her hands resting on her hips.

She took the clothes basket, saying, "I'll have your things ready to be picked up tomorrow after dinner."

"Thanks. It may be the day after tomorrow before I'm back in Bonham."

"Fine, I'll take care of them until you get back," she said and entered the house.

Buck began walking back to the wagon but stopped and looked back at the dwelling. A smile formed on his leathered face as he returned to the wagon. She was a looker all right, and someone he needed to know better.

The next stop was the mercantile, where he purchased three more changes of clothes, including under-drawers and socks. Still not comfortable cooking a wide variety of meals, he picked out jerky, red beans, potatoes, tins of green beans and fruit, and five pounds of salt pork. The smell of food filled the air outside the mercantile as he put the sacks in the wagon.

Two buildings south was the diner, where locals were having their noonday meal. Buck found a vacant chair at a table with a man, woman, and boy. "Howdy, folks. Would it be okay if I ate with you all today?"

"I reckon so," said the man. "I'm Steve Spears. That's my wife Dorothy and son Jeff."

"Nice to meet you."

Buck sat down, and he and the Spears talked about Bonham and some of the elected officials. Buck learned the folks lived south of the main road and farmed two hundred acres. When everyone was finished, Buck got up and motioned for the waitress to come to their table. "How much for everyone's meal?" he asked.

"That'll be two dollars, Mr. Reed."

Buck was surprised she knew his name. He handed the girl two dollars and fifty cents.

"Thank you, sir."

"You're welcome." He tipped his hat at Steve and Dorothy and said, "Thanks again for sharing your table."

"Thank you, Buck, for buying our food," said Steve.

Buck paused just outside the doorway to look up and down the street, a habit he'd had for years. He didn't see anyone who looked like they might be waiting on him.

Bonham didn't need Buck Reed lollygagging around town, so he headed home.

Chapter 17

THE INTERSECTION THAT HE USED TO TURN ONTO THE road that would take him home was coming up on the left, and as the horses turned onto the eastbound road, a medium-sized, long-haired, spotted dog came running at the team. He barked and growled, showing his teeth.

"Whoa, horses," said Buck, pulling back on the reins. "Dog, you hush up and go mind your own business." Buck turned on the seat and grabbed a couple of chunks of jerky out of one of the bags from the mercantile. He pitched one at the dog, who caught it before it touched the ground and swallowed in seconds.

"You want another one, boy?" asked Buck. The dog sat on his hind end and looked up at the man with sad eyes. Buck tossed another piece of the dry meat, and this time the dog leaped up and caught it with his teeth.

Buck slapped the reins on the backs of the team, and off they started down the road. A quarter of a mile north of the intersection, Buck looked back to see the dog following behind the wagon.

"Well, I'll be. I think he likes me." Buck stopped the

wagon, climbed to the ground, and walked to the rear. He lifted the tailgate off the wagon, patted the bed, and said, "Come boy, hop in here."

The dog ran forward, leaped into the wagon bed, and lay down. Buck climbed back into the seat and continued on home.

When the man and dog arrived at his house, Buck parked the wagon at the back door so he could unload his things. The dog hopped down and explored the yard, hiking his leg and marking his territory on anything he could find.

Once the wagon was unloaded, he took the rig back to the wagon shed and tied the horses outside the barn with the dog watching every move that Buck made. Buck racked his brain, trying to decide what to call his new friend.

As a child, a mutt named Blue had stayed at his house and was his best friend. They would play and run through the cotton fields.

When his daughter, Belinda, had turned four, he and Mary Jane gave her a puppy for her birthday, but now he couldn't remember what had happened to the dog after his wife and little girl died.

Morell and Lester came around the corner for more boards that were stacked inside the barn door. "Mr. Reed, did you get a dog?" asked Lester.

"I reckon so. I found him on the road, and he came home with me. I'm still trying to decide on what to call him," said Buck.

"Well, he looks like a biscuit eater to me, so I would call him Biscuit," said Lester.

Buck looked down at the dog and nodded his head. "I think that's a fitting name for my dog. Biscuit, come on, boy, let's work on these harnesses."

Of course the dog didn't help; he wandered off and did his own thing. After the team was back in the corral, Buck found the carpenters behind the barn replacing boards. "Morell, I'm thinking about buying some chickens. Would you mind taking a look at the chicken house and pen?"

"Of course. We'll do that after we're finished with the barn."

"What about something I can haul the chickens in when I buy them? Something like a coop that I can slide in the back of the wagon?" asked Buck.

"We can most likely make you something that will work," said Morell.

"Good, I would appreciate it. I need to go back to Bonham tomorrow, and if I had that cage, I could bring the chickens back with me."

"Do you want us to build you the pen today?" asked Morell.

"Yes, I think that would be great," said Buck. "While you're busy doing that, I'll look the chicken pen over."

"Come, boys, let's go to the barn and see if we can find anything to use," said Morell.

The chicken pen was in good condition, and there was even a feed tray and water can. Buck returned to the house and sat on the porch with Biscuit beside his chair.

Buck thought back to the war and remembered his squad had adopted a bluetick hound when they were away from their main camp for three weeks. This event took place five months after they had gone to Arkansas and were back at their camp, which had also moved closer to the Arkansas line. The hound was a hunting dog whose owners were most likely dead. The mutt was malnourished when he tried to sneak into their camp to steal bones and food. One of the soldiers felt sorry for the hound and started giving him scraps. It wasn't long until he stayed around. If he began barking in the woods, some soldiers would find him and shoot squirrels and rabbits.

Three weeks after the dog found them and the soldiers were back in the main camp, things got a little chaotic. Captain Oliver was in charge of a platoon of two hundred fifty men and an entire medical staff, which included a tent hospital with twenty cots. Adjoining the hospital was a tent that served as an operating room, where the post doctor cared for the injured. The post physician was Captain Charles Ward, and he had a staff of six who worked in the hospital with him.

The area outside the operating tent was a pigsty. There were parts of legs piled on the ground, and also arms, hands, and bloody rags. When soldiers were brought in wounded, the doctor and his team did what they could for each man. But the injured piled up, as well as destroyed body parts. When Captain Oliver could spare a few men, they were assigned the detail of burying the body parts.

The day Buck and his squad returned to camp, the hound smelled the decaying flesh and dried blood. He made a beeline to the operating tent, grabbed a foot and part of a leg in his mouth, and ran. A young private grabbed the dog as it came by him and held on until another soldier made the dog let go of the foot. Once the foot was out of the dog's mouth, the soldier turned him loose, picked up his rifle, and fired at the mutt as he ran into the brush. As far as Buck knew, they never saw the hound again.

Although Buck had enjoyed a large dinner in town, it happened to be almost seven p.m. He was getting hungry and knew the dog was probably starving. He got out of the porch chair, went into the kitchen, and built a fire in the cook stove. Leaving the kitchen with the water bucket in his hand, Buck had a thought, but he would go ahead and get water for coffee before he acted on it.

Once he had a steaming cup of coffee, the old man walked back to the barn where Morell and his two boys had put up their tools and were calling it a day.

"We put the chicken coop in the back of the wagon for you, Buck," said Morell.

"Thanks, I appreciate that," said Buck. "I also have another job I'd like to discuss with you. I want to put a hand pump in my kitchen and one in the corral to fill the trough with water for the horses. Is that something you know how to do?"

"It sure is. We can dig ditches, lay iron pipe, and install the pumps for you. I can check on the price of the materials when we get to Bonham," said Morell.

"I don't care about the price. You go ahead and get the materials, and I'll pay for it tomorrow while I'm in town."

"Yes, sir. The hardware store may not have everything, but they can order anything else we might need. We'll measure the distance now, and I'll know more tomorrow."

The Farrs wrote notes on a scrap of paper, and when Morell had everything he needed, he and the boys headed to town. Buck and Biscuit returned to the house where he cooked taters and sugar-cured ham for supper.

After supper, the dog lay on the front porch where he could be cooler, going in and out of sleep. Buck came outside with one last cup of coffee after he had cleaned the kitchen.

Chapter 18

THE SUN FADED TO THE WEST, AND THE MAJESTIC colors coming through the scattered clouds brought back a memory. It must have been the fall of '64 when his squad were on patrols north of Fayetteville. They had made a dry camp one night, and he remembered sitting on the ground with his back to a tree, eating jerky and hardtack. The sun with its fascinating colors slowly went down to the west. Then, all hell broke loose.

Cannonballs exploded in and around their camp, and men scurried for cover like squirrels hiding from a hawk. The forest where they had set up camp became chaos for a few minutes, with men crying out in pain and others running away. Buck stayed where he was because he knew the Rebel soldiers would advance on the camp and take potshots at the men in his squad while they tried to respond to the mayhem. Sergeant Bates was nowhere to be seen, so Buck took it upon himself to give orders.

He knew the cannons were at his back, which meant they were east of their location. "Everyone, find you a place to fire from on the west side of camp. They'll be here shortly with bayonets to finish us off. So get in position to defend yourselves."

Buck ran to the west edge of the clearing and took cover behind a fallen tree to lie in wait. What was left of the squad followed him, and soon, most of the soldiers were hidden and ready for a fight. Sergeant Bates and a man who had been wounded also showed up. A few minutes later Buck saw movement on the east side of the camp clearing. Buck whispered to the men on either side of him, "Hold your fire until I shoot. Pass it on."

Buck counted fourteen Rebel soldiers as they showed themselves leaving the timber and walking across the small clearing. He took a deep breath, eased the slack out of the trigger, and pulled it gently. The soldier who was in his sights hit the ground. The rest of the squad opened fire, and the battle ended in seconds. Seven Confederate troops lay dead on the ground.

Buck called out to the men, "Reload and get ready to march west. They'll be back with more men in a little bit."

Sergeant Bates approached Buck. "You did good here today, Corporal. You take the lead and get us out of harm's way."

The sun went down thirty minutes later, and darkness overtook the squad as they decamped. Buck assumed more Rebels would come after them, so he changed directions and headed south. Their original plans were to go north and then swing to the east and back south. The detachment traveled another hour until they stumbled upon a small creek and camped there for the night.

"You men can make enough small fires to heat food and water for coffee. Someone attend to the wounded. As soon as you finish cooking, extinguish the fires. We don't want any more company tonight," said Buck.

With their hunger pangs subdued, the men slept

without any more disturbances. The ambush had been a close call, and it would have been bloody if Buck hadn't taken charge and prepared the men. The next day, the squad continued south and made their way back to home camp. Why did he remember all this, and what significance did it have for him now? As he thought about that entire ordeal, a few things came to mind. He did look out for the men in his squad. He took command and saved lives in the face of fear. He never gave up. That second duty in the Army taught him to meet his fears head-on and to do what was right.

Buck was brought back to reality by Biscuit jumping up and growling. The dog started off the porch but stopped when Buck grabbed him by his neck. "You stay right here and keep quiet," said Buck.

Then he heard the pounding of horse hooves as riders came through his yard to the west of the house. In what little light was left, he counted nine Indians. They kept going past his barn and never paid him any attention.

It was odd that they came through for a second time... unless they had made camp on the creek at the back of his property where the Union soldiers couldn't find them. He went inside the house, lit a lamp, sat down, and picked up *Moby Dick*.

After two hours of reading, his eyes were tired, and he needed to go to sleep. Lying in his bed was a good time to consider what he would do the next day. He thought about going back to Bonham, but the dog had to stay home in case the Indians came around. The other day he'd seen a sign for someone selling laying hens. But first he'd go to town and pay for the material for the water lines and pump at the hardware store. Next, he needed to buy chicken feed and then pick up his clothes at Lucy's house.

It would be nice if he could take Lucy to the café for dinner. Yep, he might just do that.

Buck had already eaten breakfast and was on the porch when Morell and his boys came for work. He drained the last of the coffee from the cup and left it on the porch while he and Biscuit walked down to the barn.

"Hello, Morell. What did you find out about the water pipe?" asked Buck.

"I have some of it with me and was hoping you could bring the rest when you come back from town today."

"I'll do what I can. Where do I need to go?" asked Buck.

"Go to the hardware store. Albert will take care of you and have a bill figured up."

"That sounds good. I'll go ahead and get the horses hooked to the wagon and head on out. You boys be careful. It may be this afternoon before I get back," said Buck.

"Okay. We have a lot of work to do, so I better get the boys lined out," said Morell.

Thirty minutes later, Buck was on his way to Bonham. The wagon seat felt better on his old body than riding a horse. Maybe he should buy a buggy to take to town and quit riding Red so often. That was a good idea, but this trip might not be the time to check on prices. He already had a lot to do this trip.

He had just turned the wagon onto the main road when he spotted a buckboard sitting on the edge of the roadway with its right rear wheel off and the axle lying on the ground. A man and woman were trying to put the wheel back on but were having problems.

Buck stopped his wagon where they were working and got out to greet them. "Morning, folks. It looks like you could use some help."

"We sure could," said the woman.

"I got this pole to pry the wagon up, but I can't hold it up long enough for Ruth to put the wheel on," said the man.

Buck looked over the situation and said, "I have some experience with wagon wheels. Let's move that pole over here, and I'll find something we can use as a fulcrum. Then me and your wife can pry the frame up while you put the wheel on the spindle," said Buck.

With a log in place on the ground close to the axle and the pole as a lever, Buck and Ruth lifted the wagon while the man got the wheel back on and the spindle nut tightened.

Buck threw the pole to the side of the road and dusted off his hands. "I'm Buck Reed. My place is two miles north of here."

"I'm Roy Crawford, and this is my wife, Ruth. We're neighbors, I reckon. We live a mile east and a half north. The creek splits my land and yours."

"You may want to keep watch on that wheel. They tend to loosen up after the hub is worn, and that one's likely to come off again," said Buck.

"Yep, we'll probably get a new one," said Roy.

"Good idea," said Buck. "Well, I best be on my way. I have a lot to do in Bonham today."

"Thanks again, Buck. If you're ever close by, come see us," said Roy.

"I sure will." Buck tipped his hat to Ruth, returned to his wagon, and took off by going around the Crawfords. It felt nice helping someone in need, and a few years ago that was not something Buck the gunfighter would have done. The Good Book said we're supposed to love our neighbor as ourself, and that's what he did today.

Chapter 19

WHEN BUCK ARRIVED IN TOWN, THE HARDWARE store was busy with customers purchasing tools and other items. He took his time moseying up and down the aisles and taking inventory of the goods sold, providing adequate time for the owner and worker to finish helping other customers. Buck picked up a few items that he wanted to purchase as he walked around the store.

The store owner came to him and said, "I'm Albert Hammers, and I suspect you're Buck Reed, am I correct?"

"Yes, you are," said Buck, setting the items down on a table and sticking out his hand. "I reckon I owe you some money. And I've got my wagon with me to load more materials."

"Let me carry some of your items, and you can follow me to the counter," said Albert. "I have your bill figured up, but I'll add these to it."

Buck settled up and then asked, "Where are the materials that I need to load?"

"Follow me. They're out back."

A bundle of pipe and one hand pump sat on the back

loading dock. Buck looked at the items and turned to Albert. "I only see one pump. Did Morell already get one?"

"Yes. He couldn't haul everything, and this is what's left."

"I'll bring my wagon around and get loaded up," said Buck, and he started back through the store.

With the materials in the wagon bed, he went to Lucy's house to pick up his laundry.

"Hello, Miss Lucy. Are you home?" he called out as he knocked on the screen door.

When she didn't answer, he walked around to the back of the house and found the pretty lady in her wash shed, washing clothes from a large basket.

"Morning, Lucy. I'm here to pick up my clothes."

"Why hello, Buck. Wait here and I'll go fetch your things."

"Yes ma'am. I ain't going anywhere."

Lucy came back with his clothes folded and tied with some twine. "Here is your clothing, and that will be four bits."

Buck handed her a dollar and said, "I'm grateful to you for doing this. If it's okay with you, I'd like to bring my dirty clothing by once a week."

"That's fine, you do that. By the way, I can also mend anything that needs attention."

Buck couldn't get over her looks. She was around five foot six inches with a slender figure. Her brown hair was streaked with gray, and her hazel eyes lit up when she talked. He figured her age to be in her early fifties but wasn't sure, and before walking away, he conjured up enough nerve to ask, "Miss Lucy, would you have dinner with me at the café in an hour or so?"

"I certainly will, Buck, thanks for asking," she replied, smiling.

"That's great. I have another errand to run that will take about an hour, and then I'll be back to escort you to the café."

"That'll be fine. I'll be ready when you return," said Lucy.

Buck decided to go ahead and buy the chickens so that when dinner was finished, he could go directly home. As he drove his wagon to pick up the hens, he noticed a black single-bench seat buggy with a *for sale* sign on it. It wouldn't take long to look at the carriage and talk to the owner, so he stopped in front of the house and knocked on the door. An elderly woman opened the door. She wore a cream-colored dress, her gray-and-brown-streaked hair in a bun.

"May I help you?" she asked.

"Yes ma'am. I'm interested in your buggy for sale."

"It's my late husband's carriage, and I'm asking forty-two dollars for it and the gear for the horse."

Buck reached into his pocket, brought out his paper money, and handed her forty-two dollars. "I'd like a bill of sale. Could I leave it here until tomorrow?"

"Yes you can, and I have the document ready. We can fill in the blanks. You wait here, and I'll get it."

When she returned, Buck wrote down his information, and she signed it as Mrs. Rita Stewart. "Would you mind taking the sign off as you leave? You can come after the carriage when you're able," she said.

"Thanks, ma'am. I'll be back tomorrow."

It was turning out to be a great day. He had a dinner date with Lucy and had purchased a buggy. Next came the chickens to take home.

Buck bought a dozen laying hens, one rooster, and six

young pullets. The cage was big enough for them until he could get home. The man he purchased the chickens from put a pan with water in the makeshift coop so the birds could drink.

Buck parked the wagon under a shade tree by Lucy's house, and they walked to the café. The two blocks to the main street gave Buck time to make small talk and tell her about buying a buggy. They stepped onto the boardwalk, and at the first building they passed by, a man stood beside the structure urinating on the ground. He turned toward the couple, and Lucy put her hand to her mouth and turned her head.

Buck stopped and calmly said, "Mister, you put it away or lose it."

The man spun away from the couple but continued doing his business. Buck pulled his gun and fired one time into the ground between the man's feet. "I said put it away or lose it. I won't tell you again."

The man shook as he tried to button up, and while doing so, wet his pants. "You done made me wet my britches, mister."

"That's too bad. Don't ever show yourself to this lady again, is that clear?" asked Buck.

The fellow stood staring at them with a large wet spot on his clothes. "I apologize, ma'am. I've had a little too much to drink and didn't realize what I was doing."

The couple started off, and Lucy took Buck by the arm. "That was quite a show of chivalry you performed back there," said Lucy.

"Thanks. I have a thing about modesty and respect for a lady. Here's the café. Let's find a table and eat."

Buck pulled the chair out for Lucy, and she smiled as she sat down. They spent their time asking each other questions like, what they like to do for entertainment and what was their favorite color. The food came and both of them ate in silence. Buck didn't know how Lucy was raised, but at his house there was no talking at the table.

The couple finished the tasty food and had a cup of coffee to settle the meal. On the way back to Lucy's house, Buck asked, "Can I come calling on you again? Maybe we can have supper and go to the opera house for a show sometime."

"I would love that, Buck," she said and put her hand over his. "I've never been there, but I hear the traveling troupe is wonderful entertainment."

"Great. I'm coming back to town tomorrow to pick up my buggy, and I'll go by the opera theater and see when the next performance will be."

"Oh good, and you be sure to come by so we can talk some more. I have to get back to work, so I'll see you tomorrow," said Lucy, and she started into her house.

Buck was flying high on his way back home. What a wonderful time he'd had dining with the prettiest woman in town. Although he didn't know any other women in Bonham, he still thought she was the prettiest, and he was excited that she wanted to go with him to the theater.

Chapter 20

LESTER AND JUBAL HAD THE DITCH DUG FROM THE well to the house and were digging the trench from the well to the corral when Buck pulled the wagon up in front of the chicken pen. "Can you boys give me a hand with this coop?"

"Yes sir, we need a break from these shovels anyway," said Jubal, wiping droplets of sweat off his brow.

The two boys lifted the cage from the wagon and placed it so the birds could go right into the chicken pen. Then they unloaded the pipe Buck had brought and placed it beside the open ditch going to the corral. Biscuit never got up from his cool spot under one of the trees.

Buck took his clothes and the items he'd bought at the store into the house while the boys finished unloading the wagon. They were making significant progress on laying the water lines, and he couldn't wait to stop carrying buckets to fill the water troughs. A modern house would be so lovely. All he needed now was a woman's touch to decorate the inside.

Morell was installing the new hand pump in the

kitchen and was about to start assembling the pipe and making the joints with yarn and molten lead. Buck watched as the man went about packing the yarn into the bell end of the pipe, and then headed outside to get a pot of lead heating above a fire. Morell brought the pot inside and poured the lead into the bell to make a waterproof joint.

"That's something else. I never knew how that was done until now," said Buck.

"I worked for a plumber in Chicago years ago, and we did this a lot in the city," said Morell. "I hope to have this pump operating by the time we leave for the day."

"That'll be so nice to stop carrying water buckets. I'll get out of your way and sit on the porch."

He took a glass of water with him and sat overlooking the land across the road from his. The dog came to him and wanted to be petted, so Buck rubbed him behind his ears. A minute later, Biscuit finally sat down on his butt.

Buck remembered the day's events and was glad everything had turned out well. There had been long periods in his life when things hadn't been so good. His first time serving in the Army wasn't too bad, but that second time when he joined to fight in the war was a different ordeal, and in fact, his entire enlistment was awful.

That first year and a half in Arkansas held some of the worst, gut-wrenching experiences in his life. It wasn't just the killing that made for a horrible time. The food not only tasted dreadful but most days, there wasn't enough of it to feed all the men. Some nights, all they had was jerky and hardtack to quell the hunger pangs. Their water came from nasty streams, and the men suffered from diarrhea and stomach issues. Sleeping conditions were disgusting, having to sleep on leaves where bugs and spiders crawled on you, and they didn't have adequate covering to fight off the cold most nights. Fires couldn't be lit because the enemy might attack during the dark.

Those days were behind him, and he never wanted to live in circumstances like that again. The nights having to sleep on the cold, hard ground most likely contributed to some of the ailments that bothered him now.

Buck remembered one incident when he and six soldiers had gone on patrol to find the enemy's camp and figure out the best way to attack it. It was December, and on their second day away from camp, the sky became overcast and the temperature fell to somewhere in the mid-thirties. As they hiked to the place where the Rebel forces had last been spotted, it commenced to mist. It wasn't heavy, but enough to get everything wet and chill everyone to the bone. The temperature started dropping before dark, and tree branches froze and began to break off.

Buck knew they were in for a very cold, miserable time. "Men, start looking for shelter where we can get out of this weather. We may have to hole up for a few days, so watch for someplace dry."

"Corporal, won't we need food and water too?" asked one of the men.

Buck felt like shooting him for asking a stupid question. "Of course we'll need those things. Go over to that store and buy it for us."

The soldier looked around and asked, "What store? I don't see any buildings."

"Private, try to follow along. There ain't no stores out here," said Buck, and he walked off.

They finally found a rock protruding about twelve feet from the side of a two-hundred-foot-tall hill. The area under the rock ledge was large enough for the seven men to take cover and have a fire. "We need an abundance of firewood to last all night. I want everyone to gather limbs and stack them on each end of the ledge, just far enough in to stay dry."

As the wood piled up, Buck lit two fires against the back wall to heat the rocks so the men could start to dry out and get warm. The freezing rain started falling harder about the same time the troops had enough wood stacked for the night. The fires were a welcome sight since it was turning colder by the hour.

It rained almost all night, and the sound of tree limbs breaking off from the weight of the ice kept waking him up. Cold was not a good word for the weather; it was miserably cold, and the men huddled together by the fires to keep from freezing.

Shortly after daylight, the rain stopped, and hints of sunlight flickered through the hazy morning. The wood pile was almost gone. Any wood they collected that morning would be wet, but they would have to use it anyway. Walking over the ice-covered rocks was treacherous, as was stepping over fallen trees, but they gathered up what damp kindling they could find and stacked it up under the rock ledge.

The heat of the fires began to melt the ice from the branches the men had stacked up.

"Corporal, won't those Johnny Rebs see our fires and come to investigate?" asked a soldier.

"Billy, if you saw smoke a quarter of a mile south of here, would you go look to see who it was?"

"I don't know if I could make it over there with ice covering everything."

"Well, the same goes for our enemy. They ain't walking here on ice," said Buck.

By noon, the sun's rays were melting the ice off the

tree limbs and ground. The soldiers heard limbs breaking as sheets of ice fell from the sagging limbs, and the branches shot upward and snapped, which made it dangerous to walk under the trees. At midafternoon, Buck moved the patrol out and they started walking toward their original destination before the storm, which happened to be their platoon camp.

The patrol made camp that night on the banks of a creek that had once been someone else's campsite. There was still wood for fires and plenty of flowing water in the creek to fill the canteens.

The next day, they walked into their home camp to find their fellow soldiers hard at work repairing the tents that had collapsed under the weight of the ice. Buck and his men pitched in, and it took another full day before the site was back to normal.

Certain times in his life had been hard, but he managed to make it out of the war in one piece. A lot of good men didn't. Life could be hard on folks, and he should look back on his life and see the mistakes that he made and help others so they didn't have to struggle and have setbacks like he did.

Buck stopped reminiscing and stood from his chair when he heard someone call his name. He looked toward the barn. Morell and his boys approached the house in their wagon.

"Buck, we're done for the day. You have water in the house," said Morell.

"Thanks fellers. I'll see you tomorrow."

Chapter 21

THE HAND PUMP WORKED LIKE HE'D HOPED, AND IT would be wonderful if he could figure out how to have hot water without heating buckets on the cookstove. He walked to the corral with a two-gallon pail in each hand and dumped it in the horses' trough. This would hopefully be the last time he'd have to haul water to the livestock.

One important habit that a gunhand never did was get into a routine. Buck thought about that as he cleaned off the kitchen table after his and Biscuit's supper. After all these years, he had an evening routine: cook supper, clean the kitchen, and go out on the porch to sit and think.

He sat on the porch until it was almost dark, then went into the house and read until he got sleepy and went to bed. There were no dreams that night and he rested without incident.

The next morning, after he had bathed and put on clean clothes, he sat at the kitchen table thinking about using Red to pull the buggy. His riding horse didn't need to be demoted to a carriage horse. He decided to ride Red and lead one of the horses that pulled the wagon into town to get the buggy. What about the harness for the buggy? He didn't remember seeing it, but surely the woman had one inside the house or outbuilding. If not, he could buy a new one at the wagon yard or mercantile. Then he remembered she had said she had one that went with the buggy.

Lucy...now, she was a delightful thought. He must go by and see her after he finished with getting the buggy. He really liked her company and hoped they could build a firm relationship. Then he laughed and thought, *Buck Reed, this ain't the first woman you were ever sweet on, and it's probably not the last.*

He'd go by the opera house when he was in town and find out when it was open. If the date went well, he'd like to invite her to his house and get some ideas on fixing up the inside of a couple of room so they had a warmer touch.

The pocket watch showed that it was only six-thirty, too early to ride into town. Buck lit the lamp in the front room and sat down to read a few pages before sunup.

With *Moby Dick* opened to the last page he'd read, he thought back on how he first took an interest in reading. He was laid up on the IOA Ranch with a gunshot wound to his left side. He got shot in a skirmish with a few Comanche and recovered in the bunkhouse. A cowhand named George Boles loaned him *Uncle Tom's Cabin*. He enjoyed it so much that he read it twice. Reading became a pastime, and he bought books and carried them in his saddlebags.

Biscuit had two kinds of barks, the first one playful and the second one fearful. Buck came up out of his chair when he heard his dog barking and growling from the front porch.

Buck walked just enough to see out the front window. Twenty-five feet from the porch, sitting abreast of a horse, was the same lawman who had come to visit with Bernard Sena.

The last thing he wanted to do was startle the sheriff, so Buck stood beside the door and opened it. That way the lawman wouldn't get the notion that something was wrong.

"Howdy, Sheriff, I'm coming out on the porch," said Buck. He walked outside unarmed to see why the man was back at his house.

"Mister Reed, I came by to inform you that we're having a problem in the county with some Indians who deserted the reservation in Indian Territory. The Army has a patrol after them, but those imbeciles can't or won't find where the renegades are holed up. You be watchful, and if you happen to see Indians, just back off and let the authorities take care of it."

"I certainly will. I don't reckon they are around here, or my dog would have raised all kinds of cain."

"By the way, I hope there ain't no hard feelings about the other day. I thought I was doing the right thing by coming out here with Bernard, but I've changed my mind about you."

"Thanks, Sheriff. No hard feelings on my part, and thanks again for coming out with that information about the Indians."

"I'll be on my way now. I'm stopping in on as many farms as I can today. You be careful out here all by yourself." The sheriff tipped his hat and rode off.

Buck stood on the porch digesting what the lawman had said about him being out here all by himself. Had that been a warning that something was going to happen because of someone like Bernard Sena?

Buck returned to the house, buckled on his gun, and went back outside, chuckling to himself. The Indians had come by his house at least two times and hadn't bothered him, but he sure wasn't going to let the sheriff know about any of that. He didn't care what they had done, as long as they didn't steal from him or interfere with his land.

By the time he finished feeding the chickens and horses, Morell and his boys had arrived to start back to work.

Buck joined Morell as he lined out the two boys. "Good morning, men. The pump worked great in the kitchen this morning. I bought a one-seater buggy yesterday, and I'm riding into Bonham to fetch it in a few minutes. Is there anything I need to pick up or anyone I need to pay while I'm there?" he asked.

"No, we have everything to make it through the day. You go on whenever you want. We have plenty of work to keep us busy," said Morell.

Buck nodded and started back to the house with Biscuit following behind him.

He shaved and changed into his black clothing and shiny boots, since these were the nicest clothes he owned. When he visited Lucy later that day, he wanted to look good and impress her.

It didn't dawn on him until he was almost to Bonham that he hadn't brought a horse to pull the buggy home. He wasn't used to having a carriage, and he'd forgotten to bring an extra horse. He'd have to change his plans and go by the livery to see if they had a horse that was broken to a harness.

Bonham was alive with shoppers, merchants, and slackers leaning against porch posts or sitting on benches. He rode down the main street and around the square where the county courthouse sat. As he turned onto the street to the livery, a man sitting on a horse got his attention. Buck did a double-take and realized he knew the man. It was John Flemming in the flesh, and Buck hadn't seen the man since they'd robbed that mercantile in Dallas and parted ways with him and Sid Dill at Fort Worth. The last he had heard anything about John had been a couple of years earlier, and it seemed the ex-soldier had taken the outlaw trail of robbing stagecoaches, banks, and payroll shipments in Colorado.

Buck guided his horse to within six feet of John. "Hello, John, it's been a long time. How have you been?"

"Well well, if it ain't Buckshot Reed. I'm faring well, and it looks like you're doing okay for yourself," said John.

"I'm doing well. What brings you to our little city?"

"Me and a few fellers are just passing through. Are you living here now?" asked John.

"Not really. I have a place east of here a little ways. Who else is with you?"

He could tell that John didn't like being questioned by the way he looked around him like he didn't want to be seen talking to Buck, but that didn't deter Buck from asking again. "Who're you riding with these days, John?"

"Do I have your word that you'll keep this between us?"

Buck shifted in the saddle so he had easier access to his gun. "John, I don't care who you have with you, but I do care what your intentions are here in Bonham. I don't want anyone killed or hurt in the process of whatever it is you're aiming to do." Buck nudged his horse and started off.

John called out, "Hold up, Buck."

Buck backed his horse up until he was alongside his old acquaintance again. "What is it?"

"I'm with Sid Dill and a few more of his crew. I don't know what Sid is planning, but I do know it's not here at Bonham."

"Sid Dill, that's a name I haven't heard in a long time," said Buck. "Much obliged for the information. You watch your back with Sid."

Buck rode off with a queasy feeling in the pit of his stomach. Five years ago, he wouldn't have thought twice about John or Sid being in the same town as him, but now it bothered him that career outlaws were in Bonham where he did business and kind of called his home. He would stay quiet about seeing John and go about his dealings, although he would watch for any indication they were up to no good in Fannin County.

Chapter 22

THE HOSTLER WAS LEANED AGAINST THE BOARDS ON the front of the barn on the two back legs of a chair as he braided a lead rope when Buck rode up to the livery stables.

"Howdy, Mr. Reed, what can I do for you today?"

"I bought a one-seater buggy off a widow yesterday and need a good horse to pull it. Would you happen to have such an animal?" asked Buck.

"No, but I know who does. I think you bought the carriage from Mrs. Stewart over off 6th Street. She sold the horse that pulled it to Samual Curry a couple of weeks ago, and he has it for sale down the street. Three blocks south and two west," said the man, pointing south.

"Thanks. And you can call me Buck. What might your name be?"

"I'm Glen Mason, and it's my pleasure to meet you, Buck."

"The pleasure is all mine." Buck mounted back up and rode in the direction the man had told him to go.

Buck began to inspect the horse and engage in a bit of haggling over the price.

"How much do you want for him?" asked Buck as he picked up one of the front legs and examined its front foot.

"I reckon one-hundred-twenty-five is a fair price. He's only eight and still has a lot of strength in him."

"His shoes are worn out and needs his hooves trimmed. I'm thinking more like one hundred dollars," said Buck as he continued to walk around the horse.

The man stopped Buck as he rounded the horse's head. "I'll take one-hundred-fifteen and that's as low as I can go."

"I'm thinking one-hundred-ten is as much as I want to pay," said Buck. He reached into his pocket and brought out a roll of bills. The man looked at the money in his hand and said, "You drive a hard bargain. I'll take the cash."

With the horse trailing behind Red, Buck went straight to the blacksmith shop and left the animal there while he rode to the opera house to gather information on the next showing of the play.

As he looked at the flyer nailed to the side of the theater's double doors, a young, voluptuous woman came out of an office to his right. "Good morning, sir. Are you interested in attending one of the upcoming performances?"

"Why, yes, I am. I'm here to get a schedule so I can bring my lady friend to watch a presentation."

"Have you or your friend ever been to the opera?"

"I have once, but it was some years back," said Buck.

"So, your sweetheart has never been. Let me suggest our Saturday night act. I'm confident she will enjoy the music and comedy acts in the play. You can purchase tickets now so you can get seats up front with a perfect view of the stage and the actors."

"Thank you, I believe I will," said Buck. He followed the woman inside to her office and paid for his seats.

With the slips of paper tucked away in his shirt pocket, Buck rode to Lucy's house to find the front door open. Through the screen door, he watched her in the living room iron clothes. "Good morning, Lucy. May I come in?"

She set the iron on the wood stove where three more sit heating and came to the door. She opened the screen and hugged Buck as he entered the house. "Good morning, handsome. Did you dress up to come see me?" she asked.

Buck was in a good mood and said, "I certainly did. A homely man like myself has to dress up to see the prettiest woman in town."

"Oh, hush your mouth. You are not homely looking by any means, and I thank you for believing I'm pretty," Lucy said, blushing.

Buck pulled the opera tickets out of his pocket. "Lucy, would you be my date on Saturday night for dinner and the opera?"

"Of course I will. I'm so excited to finally see a stage act where professionals perform."

"We have great seats. The play starts at eight, so I was thinking I could pick you up at six-thirty, and that would give us sufficient time to enjoy a meal before the show," said Buck.

"I think that's a wonderful plan, and I can hardly wait until Saturday," she said. "I'm sorry, but I have to get back to work. I have a lot to do before Saturday gets here."

"I have things to do also, so I best be on my way. I'm

picking up my buggy today and heading back home," said Buck.

Lucy was full of surprises. She came to him and gave him another hug. He looked down at her at just the right moment, and she went up on her tiptoes and kissed him. He went weak in the knees, and when she broke the kiss, she said, "If you come to town before Saturday, come by. If not, I'll wait for dinner and the opera."

"With kisses like that, I'm sure I'll be back before Saturday," said Buck and went out the door.

"Hey, handsome," called out Lucy from the door. He turned as she blew him a kiss. He smiled and blew one back.

Buck left Lucy's house a changed man. He was beside himself with happiness and pride since the beautiful Miss Lucy had just kissed him on the lips. He wanted more but didn't want to make her uncomfortable. He laughed. *Here I am, an old man acting like a teenager getting his first kiss.*

The horse was ready at the blacksmith when he arrived. The smithy emerged from behind his forge, wiping oil off his hands on a soiled rag. "His hooves are in good shape and ready to go, Mr. Reed."

"Thanks for the quick service. What's your name?"

"It's Israel O'Brian."

"You can drop the mister and call me Buck."

"I can do that. If you ever need anything else, you come to see me."

"I sure will," said Buck as he untied his horse and led it away to get the buggy.

The buggy was in the exact location where it had been the day before, and Mrs. Stewart had hauled all the rigging out to the buggy as well. The reins, bridle, breast collar, girth, tugs, and associated parts sat on the bench seat.

He was hard at work putting the gear on the horse when the woman came outside. "Good morning, Mr. Reed. That horse looks mighty familiar."

"Good morning," said Buck. He stopped what he was doing. "Yes, ma'am, it should. I was told he was your husband's horse and used to pull the buggy."

"Well, I'll be. That is a nice coincidence, ain't it."

"Yes, it is. I'm almost finished here, and then I'll be on my way. It's been my pleasure meeting you, and I hope I see you around town in the future," said Buck. He finished with the horse and went to Mrs. Stewart to shake her hand.

"Thank you, Mr. Reed, and I'm sure you'll enjoy the smooth ride."

"Yes, ma'am, I'm sure I will. Thanks again. I best be heading home now."

Buck tied Red to the back of the carriage and climbed into the seat before slapping the reins on the horse's rump and taking off.

As he rounded the square, John, Sid, and another man Buck didn't know sat on a long bench under the awning of the courthouse. He gave them a small wave and kept going. He already had enough people talking about him without being seen talking to the likes of Sid Dill.

He had known Sid for about ten years and didn't like the man at all. Buck thought Sid was a cold-blooded killer who killed for the fun of it. The last time the two men were together, they almost drew on each other.

The ride home was delightful. His back and knees didn't hurt, and he had decided that the buggy would be his mode of transportation anytime he needed to go into Bonham or Dodd City.

Chapter 23

THAT EVENING AFTER SUPPER, BUCK AND BISCUIT
went out on the front porch to sit in the cool evening air.
He wondered what Sid Dill might be up to in this part of
Texas. Buck would call John a personable man, although
he was a thief and robber. As far as he knew, John had
never raped or murdered anyone.

He could still remember the first time he'd seen the
young, lanky Union soldier marching into camp northeast
of Fort Smith, Arkansas. It must have been March of 1863
or '64 when the unit Buck was a corporal in received rein-
forcements. There were thirty-three green troops with
their bedrolls hanging on their shoulders and bags
dangling off the sides of their shooting arms.

Sergeant Bates had assigned Buck the duty of finding
the new troops a place to bed down out of the cold. Buck
divided them into tents closest to the large hospital tent.
None of the seasoned troops wanted to be close to the
infirmary.

John introduced himself as the leader of his group, but

that didn't matter to Buck. He was just another greenhorn grunt and would have to earn the respect of the other men.

Shortly after he had all the new troops settled in, a runner came for Buck and told him that the captain needed to see him in his tent.

The Yankee corporal made his way around the crude tents and makeshift lean-tos that the soldiers had put together with pine branches to keep the rain and cold of the harsh March weather at bay. As he passed by campfire after campfire, he noticed the attitude of the troops around the fires was somber. The men sat with their heads down, their palms facing toward the blazing fire as they tried to stay warm.

Corporal Buck Reed had been summoned to the tent of Captain John Oliver, the commanding officer. "Corporal, I started with a hundred and fifty fighting men. How many soldiers do we have that can still fight?"

"Sir, I counted earlier today and we have thirty-five able-bodied men, plus the thirty-five new replacements," said Buck.

"I spoke with the camp doctor, and he said we have twenty-two injured in the hospital, and five of those are not expected to live. When I look out over the camp, all I see is disappointment and despair. I want you to order the men to move their tents away from the hospital. I'm hoping that will lift their spirits by getting the soldiers away from the sickness and screams they hear constantly," said Captain Oliver.

"Yes sir, I'll gladly have the men move the tents," said Buck and hurried out to spread the orders.

Buck despised having to look inside the operating tent. What he saw almost made him throw up. There might be arms or legs on the ground, and of course, blood was everywhere. Meat saws and bone saws hung from the center post holding the tent up. In Buck's opinion, sometimes men were better off dead than to live through getting their legs cut off. He could only imagine the pain they endured, and in most cases, the men eventually died from infection or bleeding out. Once, when he was helping to carry an injured soldier into the tent, the doctor was using a hot piece of metal to cauterize the end of a man's severed leg. The stench of the burning flesh was too much for the corporal, and he emptied his stomach on the ground.

Buck pitched in helping to move the tents, until the captain's aide came and said, "Captain Oliver wants to see you again."

He made his way to Captain Oliver's tent and announced himself before he went inside.

"Corporal Buck reporting, sir," said Buck as he saluted the commanding officer from the tent's doorway.

"Come in and sit down, corporal."

Sergeant Bates was also in the tent, drinking a scalding cup of coffee. The captain got up from the rickety makeshift table and picked up two tin coffee cups. "I'll get us a cup while Sergeant Bates explains your new orders." The captain left the tent while the sergeant blew on his coffee and took a sip.

"I hear that you're a dead shot with a rifle. Is that a fair statement?" he asked, then took another sip of coffee.

"Yes sir, I usually hit what I shoot at," said Buck.

Captain Oliver came back into the tent and handed Buck a cup of coffee.

"Corporal, your orders are to go east of the camp where that large meadow is and find you a good place to watch the other side. I want you to watch for Rebel troops coming this way to shoot up our camp. Our spies are saying that a detachment of Rebel troops is heading our way, and we need to turn them back or kill them. If you encounter any troop movement coming at us, fire off as many rounds as possible to slow them down and hightail it back here so we can be ready for the yellowbellies."

"Yes, sir, but don't you think it would be better if some other soldiers went with me? I don't know how much I can slow them down by myself," said the corporal.

"I don't want you to fight them all; I only want you to kill as many as you can until they take cover, and then you can head back here as fast as you can. Sergeant Bates will take thirty men and place them strategically in the path between you and the camp. When they follow you back here, they'll be caught in an ambush and eliminated," said Captain Oliver.

Sergeant Bates went outside again and came back in with a new Henry repeating rifle and a leather pouch full of bullets. "You find some strong cover and stay put until you see them coming. They'll be trying to return fire, but I doubt if lead from their muskets will even hit close to you. Kill as many as you can before they hunker down or retreat. Is that clear?"

"Yes, sir. I'll go get my canteen and bedroll so I can keep warm lying on the ground and then head on out."

Buck mulled over why they wanted him to do this by himself.

He found a large tree that had been blown over years earlier. It would provide him adequate cover. From his spot, it would be easy to escape unnoticed when he needed to leave.

The ground was cold and wet. The single blanket didn't do much to keep the cold away. He lay on part of it and threw the remaining cover over his legs. The sun was already past noon when he saw a slight movement, a blur of gray across the field. He pulled the hammer back and got ready to shoot.

Two Confederate soldiers emerged from the forest and stood looking right at where he was hiding. He didn't move or make any noise, and waited with his face against the rifle stock, the sights centered on one of the enemy.

Three more men joined the first two, and he watched them talk to each other and point to the trees to his right. That meant they didn't see him, and he had the advantage. The five men moved forward, and when they did, eight more Rebels came in behind them, and all thirteen started across the clearing, moving slowly and scanning the trees where Buck lay.

Buck took careful aim, exhaled, and squeezed the trigger. The barrel of the gun bucked in his grip, and in one swift motion, he ejected the spent shell and fired again. He continued to work the lever on the rifle and fired at will at the opposing troops, who had dropped to the ground and now began to return fire.

Buck reloaded his rifle and fired off three quick rounds before slithering away from the fallen log and run back to camp. He dashed through trees, around brush, rocks, and up and down gullies. He was coming up the side of a gully when he heard a blast and felt a sting followed by pain in his back and backside.

He had been hit but had to keep running since his life depended on it. He could see leaves and limbs being torn from a small tree by lead balls that missed him. With his legs moving as fast as they would go, he ran past Sergeant Bates and his men. In a few seconds, the sounds of multiple gunshots could be heard behind him.

By the time the corporal reached camp, the fighting had stopped. He sat on a log to catch his breath, and the private he had met earlier came to him. "Corporal, you're all bloody. Let me help you to the hospital tent."

"Yeah, I think I'm hit in the back. Here, take my rifle. What's your name, soldier?" asked Buck.

"It's John Flemming, sir."

"Let's go, John, I better see the sawbones."

John helped the corporal to the hospital tent, and when the doctor pulled Buck's shirt off, he said, "It looks like you took a blast from a scattergun. We'll have to pluck out the buckshot, and you'll be all right in a few days. Now, drop those pants and lay on that table so one of my assistants can go to work on you."

John came in, looked down at the corporal and said, "I guess you'll be called Corporal Buckshot now that you're carrying around some lead." He chuckled and left the tent.

By the time the medic ward had removed all the lead shots from his back and buttocks, Buck was in more pain now from the medic digging out the shots and was ready to get off the table. Around that time, the men who had bushwacked the enemy returned to camp with the wounded and dead. Sergeant Bates was one of the dead, and Buck watched as the four young privates laid him out for burial.

Buck only had a few bandages on his back because none of the pellets had gone in very deep and only had minimal bleeding. He walked to the supply tent for some new pants, a shirt, and a Union suit since his pants had lots of holes in them. When he was dressed and ready to eat, a runner came for him with orders that Captain Oliver wanted to see him.

Buck entered Captain Oliver's tent and saluted him. "Corporal Reed reporting, sir."

"Have a seat." The captain motioned to a straight-back

wooden chair. "Sergeant Bates has been killed, and that means you're now the first sergeant under my command." Captain Oliver placed some cloth sergeant stripes on his little desk in front of Buck. "Here's your new stripes. You can sew them on tonight after you move your things into the sergeant's tent and assume his duties. Are there any questions?"

"Yes sir, what about the ambush? Don't we need to keep a detachment out there in case the gray coats come back?" asked Buck.

"Yes! You assign a detail to watch our backside day and night. We don't need a lot of men out there. I think fifteen should do it, and you'll need to assign someone to lead."

"Yes, sir, I have just the man. He's new, but he wants to be a leader. His name is John something or other."

"That's fine. You take care of that and then come back here. I have a detail for you tomorrow," said the captain, waving the new sergeant off.

Sergeant Reed left Captain Oliver's tent with a new determination and a chest full of pride, as he was now the second-in-command. The tent Sergeant Bates had occupied was nothing to brag about, but he would be alone and not have to hear the other men cough and snore during the night.

Buck went through Bates's possessions and found a new shirt with sergeant stripes already on it, tucked away in a bag. He changed into the top and found a few more items he could use. He left the tent and walked to the spot where he had been sleeping, and as he passed by Sergeant Bates laid out on the ground, he noticed the pistol still around the dead man's waist. Buck kneeled beside the corpse and removed the gun and leather ammo bag slung across his chest and shoulder. Bates had been shot in the head, and as Buck removed the dead man's gun, he realized there wasn't any blood on Bates's coat. That would also come in handy, since it looked to be in better shape than the one he wore. Plus, it had stripes to let everyone know he was the sergeant now.

Chapter 24

SERGEANT BUCK REED WORE THE NEWLY ACQUIRED Colt .44 when he entered the tent of Private John Flemming and five other green soldiers where they sat on their bedrolls eating jerky.

"Well, look who has come to see us, boys," John smarted off after Buck came through the tent flap. "It's Sergeant Buckshot in the flesh."

"Private, you're now under my command, and I'm going to let your disrespect pass this one time," said Buck. He reached down, grabbed a handful of John's shirt, and jerked the young soldier to his feet. "From now on, you answer me as sir and salute me when you see me. Is that clear?"

"Yes, sir. My apologies, sergeant, sir."

"I have an assignment for you and these men. You're in charge of protecting our flank to the east where we had that skirmish yesterday. Come with me, and I'll find you nine more men to take with you."

After Sergeant Reed had assigned some men to go

with John, he went back to the captain's tent to get his next orders.

Sergeant Reed had on the shirt and jacket that had previously belonged to Bates when he received his orders from Captain Oliver. He wanted his commanding officer to see that he had taken the initiative to take on his new rank. The captain instructed Buck to take two wagons and ten men to meet up with a supply convoy that was on its way to Little Rock, Arkansas.

The supply wagons would be on the Arkansas River west of Ozark, Arkansas, which was a three-day journey for Buck and his men.

They left at daylight. Buck ordered two privates to serve as guides and lookouts ahead of the two wagons they'd brought to carry their supplies. One of the men he assigned to scout was Wilbur Reynolds, a young man who had seen his share of fighting and could be counted on in a scrape.

It was a hard three-day journey, but the small detachment made it on time and was able to successfully load their supplies. The small group was also given an extra wagon loaded with ammo, and one of the soldiers would have to drive it and not be on his horse in case of trouble.

They spent the night in the supply convoy's camp, and Buck overheard the men talking about a Confederate payroll convoy that was coming through the mountains and headed to central Arkansas, where a large contingency of troops was assembling.

The following morning, Sergeant Reed and his detachment headed back, and after traveling a few hours they stopped at a creek to let the horses take on water. Wilbur came riding up from his scouting position.

"Sergeant, I believe I've found that payroll shipment up ahead about five miles watering their horses in that creek we stopped at. I saw five men dressed in civilian clothes on horseback, but every one of them had on a military pistol and holster. The two men driving a wagon were also armed, and they had the bed tarped like they were hiding something. I suspect it's the payroll since the wagon looks like it's not heavy loaded—it's not making deep tracks. I suspect those men are protecting something mighty valuable, and it's there for the taking."

"So, why are you telling me this, private?" asked Buck.

"I came here by the route that I think they will take, and I found a place where we can ambush them. They'll be like sitting ducks on a frozen pond. We can take whatever they got hidden under that tarp and do well for ourselves when this war is over."

"We must get these supplies back to camp. There's a lot of men relying on medicine, provisions, and ammunition. I can't just change our orders and go after that payroll," said Buck.

"Look at it this way. If we stop that payroll from reaching its destinations, won't it help cripple the war efforts here in Arkansas? The men it's going to will get discouraged and not want to fight if they can't get paid," said Wilbur.

"We could all get court-martialed if this goes bad and we lose some of our men. How many of us do you think it will take?" asked Buck.

"Send the wagons on and use the men on horses. We can hit them hard, and they won't expect us. We take the money and skedaddle out of there as fast as we can," said Wilbur.

"Okay, I'll send the supplies on while you gather the men," said Buck, and he took off to give the drivers orders.

Two hours later, Sergeant Reed and six Union soldiers waited, hidden along both sides of the road. The payroll group came into view. Three riders were in front of the wagon and two at its rear. Buck fired the first shot, and the shooting started. The smell of burned gunpowder hovered strong in the air, and the smoke that came from the rifle barrels made it difficult to see. When the ambush ended, seven men lay dead, and three horses were also down hurt and in agony. Buck and Wilbur stripped the canvas off the wagon bed to find it empty.

Buck stood dumbfounded for a second and then hollered out, "Everyone mount up, and let's put some distance behind us. This was a decoy, and we need to get going quickly before the backup arrives."

They lit out like scalded cats and ran their horses until they were about ready to drop from exhaustion. After a short rest and water break an hour later, they let the animals walk for the next few miles. An hour before dark, the troops caught up with the three wagons and they made camp for the night.

That night, Sergeant Reed assigned sentries in case they were attacked. He called Private Reynolds off to the side and said, "I'm disappointed in what we found in that wagon today. They set us up like tinhorns and we took the bait hook, line, and sinker."

"I take all the blame, sarge. I was certain that was the payroll under that canvas. What are we going to do if word gets out about us leaving the supplies and killing those men?"

"We tell the captain what we did and make it sound like we were helping the war effort."

"Okay, I'll let you take care of that," said the private and they went back to camp.

The following morning, with the horses rested, they took off and watched their back for scouting parties since the Rebels most likely knew the decoys had been killed.

The supplies made it back to camp without any other confrontation with the enemy. Buck and Wilbur reported what they had done to Captain Oliver, and he was fine with their explanation.

Sergeant Reed had to calm his nerves when he left the captain's tent. He needed to get away from camp, so he went to check on the soldiers who were with John protecting the camp's flank. John had the troops positioned in a defensive location, and he rotated the men every four hours.

The night air brought a slight chill to the old man sitting in his rocker. Buck got up and held onto the porch post until he was ready to start inside. He had sat on the porch too long again, remembering another time in his life. "Biscuit, let's call it a night and get some shuteye."

Buck went inside, lit the lamp in the living room, and carried it to his bedroom.

As he lay in bed, he thought about Wilbur and his son, Rex. Rex would most likely die at the hand of some fast gun that the boy would call out. Buck hoped for Rex's and Wilbur's sake that it wouldn't be him the boy went after.

John Flemming had turned out to be a good soldier and even advanced to the rank of sergeant with another detachment before the war ended. Buck had concerns about John riding with Sid Dill. Sid had a mean streak in him and couldn't be trusted. He was a seasoned criminal wanted by the law in three or four states for a variety of crimes like robbery, murder, rape, and cattle stealing. Sid used people to do the things he didn't want to do or was too scared to do. He and Sid had a history, and he always figured that he would one day have to face him in a fight. But it wouldn't be tonight. Buck closed his eyes and went to sleep.

Chapter 25

Buck stayed home and piddled around his house and yard for the next two days. Morell and his boys finished up the work by Friday afternoon. Saturday morning after breakfast, Buck went down to the barn and pulled the buggy outside. He used his new pump to put water in a bucket, added some soap, and washed the dirt and grime off the carriage so it would be clean for his date with Lucy that night.

He snacked on jerky for dinner and then heated water for a hot bath. When he had finished his bath, he put on his Sunday go-to-meeting clothes, which consisted of a black shirt, black string tie, black-and-gray striped britches, and, of course, his shined black boots. He examined his rugged good looks in the mirror as he combed his hair and trimmed his eyebrows. He was pleased that he still had a full head of hair, even though it was primarily gray. The wrinkles around his eyes were from the miles he had traveled. He still had a nice smile and hoped Lucy would enjoy their date tonight.

Ever since he'd been discharged from the Army, he

liked to dress well and present himself cleanly and fashionably. Tonight, he would do what he had so many times before: wear his duster over his clothes until he arrived in Bonham to keep the dust off his clothing and then leave it in the buggy.

The last thing he did before he left was open his medicine cabinet and take down a little glass container that contained lavender water. He poured a little in his hand and applied it to his face and neck. He not only wanted to look good, but also wanted to smell good for his date.

Bonham was a busy city when he arrived on North Main Street and started around the square. He went around the west side of the courthouse and began to turn onto East 5th Street when he saw Sid Dill and another man come out of the barbershop. Buck didn't want Sid to know he'd seen him, and after he made the turn on East 5th, he pulled over and watched the two men walk across the street and continue past the courthouse until he couldn't see them anymore.

Buck knew that Sid and his crew were planning something, he just didn't know what it was. He thought about letting the county sheriff in on his thoughts, but since he didn't trust the man, it probably wasn't worth the effort.

If he saw John again, he would ask some more questions and try to get him to talk. They'd had a good relationship in the Army, and he didn't possess any ill feelings toward him at all. The only thing he hoped was that if he ever had to face Sid, John wouldn't get involved.

He stopped in front of Lucy's house and took off his duster before getting out of the buggy seat. He went up to the front door and was about to knock when she opened the door. "My my, Buck, you look very handsome today. Come on in, and let's sit a few minutes before we go eat."

"Thank you, Lucy. I must say you are always very

pretty, but tonight you are even more elegant in that gorgeous dress you have on."

She smiled. "This old thing? I haven't put it on in years."

"You would never know it by the way it fits you."

"I must tell you that there's an uproar in town about the performance at Russell's Opera House," said Lucy. "Some locals are unhappy that the traveling entertainer is putting on the play of *Uncle Tom's Cabin*. They say it's still too close to the war for those kinds of theater acts, even though the war has been over for fifteen years."

"I'm not worried about it," said Buck. "Some locals would be mighty upset if they knew I fought for the Union. I learned a long time ago that we can't please everyone."

"I agree with that. Come on, let's go have supper so our food can settle before we go to the opera," said Lucy.

Ever the gentleman, Buck helped Lucy get into the buggy. They had the town folks turning their heads toward them as they rode down the main street to the café. It took a few minutes to find a place to park the buggy because of all the construction in town.

Lucy spoke up when they finally parked two blocks from the café. "Ever since the railroad came through in 1873, it's been constant construction in town. I hear a new fancy hotel will be built right off the square."

"That's good news for the people around here; there are still many towns struggling to get past the hard times of the Reconstruction Act. Most Texas families were devastated because of the war and the carpetbaggers that came in after it was over and basically robbed the landowners of their property," replied Buck.

"You're correct about that. I had a hard time making a living during the fighting and the first four years after it was over. I'm so thankful for my neighbors and friends in town who came to my aid during the hard times."

The couple entered the café, which was almost full. Buck and Lucy were able to find a vacant table and enjoyed a delicious meal topped off with a bowl of cobbler. Lucy was so excited about going to the play that she kept Buck entertained by talking to him about everything from her job to what the town leaders were planning.

Buck finally laid money on the table, stood up, and extended his hand to Lucy. "I do believe it's time we started walking to the opera house."

She took his hand and rose from her chair. As she did, she intertwined her arm with his. He looked down at her and smiled. The couple walked arm in arm to Russell's Opera House, where a line was forming to get inside.

Seven people—three men and four women—were out in the street chanting something about slavery and war. Buck ignored them and focused on the beautiful lady by his side. They entered the theater, and a gentleman in a suit seated them and handed them each a program so they could follow along with the performance.

The auditorium was sold out, and there were no empty seats in the house when the piano started playing and the curtain opened. The performers came out onto the platform from both sides of the stage and began to sing and dance when pandemonium erupted. Three men rose from their seats and started firing their guns into the ceiling. Chairs were turned over as the patrons tried to get up and escape.

Buck took Lucy into his arms and whispered in her ear, "Stay seated. They don't mean you any harm. They're protesting the play."

When the men stopped shooting, the stage was empty,

and most of the people in the auditorium were either up and running to the exit or on the floor for protection.

Buck stood up and held his gun, ready for battle. "Gentlemen, I'm Buck Reed, and I came here tonight to see a theater performance. If you fellers are finished with your protest, then I suggest you holster your guns and leave peaceably. Otherwise, I'm going to start shooting. I'll be aiming at you and not at the ceiling, and I don't miss."

One of the men looked at Buck for a moment before he said, "Buck, I lost two boys in that war, and so did a lot of other folks in Bonham. We don't appreciate performances like this in town."

"I fought in that war myself and saw many good men die on both sides. The war has been over for fifteen years, and it's time for us all to heal and start being one country again. I paid good money to see the opera with my lady friend, so I suggest you leave now before there's more shooting," said Buck.

"We'll leave, but you better know that I ain't afraid of you. I'm leaving because I've had my say. Is that clear?"

Buck cocked back the hammer on his gun. "I'm clear. Now leave, and don't cause me any more trouble."

About that time, the town marshal and two of his deputies came running in with their weapons pointed at the three men. "Samual, you boys, drop your guns and come with me right now. You know better than to cause a ruckus in town."

It took close to thirty minutes until the auditorium was packed again and the first act started.

When Lucy and Buck were back at her house after the performance, she was still full of energy from the date. They stood on her porch and she turned to Buck and planted a long, tender kiss on his lips.

"Buck, that was the most fun I've had in years. I hope

you enjoyed it as much as I did." She kissed him again, then said, "It's getting late, and I have church in the morning. Are you coming into town to go with me?"

"I'm sorry, Lucy, but I'm not much on religion. In the future, I'll try to go with you. I had a wonderful time, and I hope we can continue to go out and have fun."

"I would like that very much. You come by the next time you're in town." Lucy kissed him again, opened her door, and went inside.

Buck walked back to the buggy but turned back to the house to see Lucy waving at the window. He waved back and left.

Chapter 26

BUCK SCANNED THE STREETS ON HIS WAY OUT OF Bonham after leaving Lucy's house. He looked for the horse that John had ridden when they'd talked the other day. His search didn't turn up the horse or any clue to make him think John was still in town. He urged his horse to go faster when he was clear of Bonham and on the open road.

The shooting at the opera and the fact that John and Sid had been in town bothered him so much that he tried to think of the different places they could rob. And the most likely place was the bank.

Once he was home, he took the buggy to the barn and unharnessed his horse. He then ensured the water trough was filled and his horses were fed before entering the house.

Buck couldn't get Sid and John out of his mind and wasn't ready to sleep, so he sat in the living room with the lamp trimmed down low and reflected back to his past experiences with them.

When the war was over and the troops were being

discharged, Buck, John, Wilbur, Sid, and two more men, Slim and Rawhide, rode together back to Texas, where they were all from.

Slim and Rawhide separated from the rest of the men after they forded the Red River and headed southeast, where their kin had farmland and jobs waiting on them, while the rest headed to Dallas.

Buck felt uneasy when the four ex-Union soldiers rode into town, still wearing Army clothing. Texas was known to be a Confederate state, and a lot of men had been killed or came home maimed for life.

The four ex-soldiers rode down the clay-brick street. They were too poor to house their horses in the livery or get rooms at one of the hotels. The men camped on the city's northeast side and began searching for jobs. No one would even talk to them about work for two reasons: there were no jobs available since times were hard because of the war, and they had fought for the enemy, and no one wanted anything to do with them.

After the third day of being shunned and rejected all over the city as they looked for employment, the men talked that evening and decided the first thing they had to do was get new clothing. Clothes cost money, and they would need what little money they had for food, so the new plan was to steal the clothing and then leave Dallas.

Wilbur said, "I heard that the silver mine in Clear Creek Canyon at Georgetown, Colorado, is hiring guards to protect the ore wagons leaving the mines. I vote that we break into the mercantile tonight and steal clothes and enough provisions to last us a couple of weeks, and head out of town."

"Do you know the way to Colorado?" asked John.

"No, I've never been there," said Wilbur.

"I've been to Denver before, and Georgetown is a

couple of days ride west of there. I figure it'll take us three weeks to make it, weather permitting," said Sid.

Buck remained quiet during the talk and knew they had to do something soon, or he would run out of money. His work options could have been better, and he agreed he needed new clothing to get a job. He didn't like the idea of stealing them, but that was the only option.

"I'm in on getting clothing and provisions, but I don't want any killing. Is that clear?" asked Buck.

"Listen to me, mister high and mighty. I've seen you kill more than your share of men, so why are you so adamant about not killing now?" asked Sid.

"I killed in battle, and that's different than murder," said Buck. "If anyone starts killing innocent people, then you and me are going to lock horns, and I guarantee you won't live to tell about it."

Sid stood up and pointed his left index finger at Buck while he removed the safety thong on the pistol. "Don't you ever threaten me, Buckshot! You ain't no sergeant in the Army that I have to take orders from anymore."

Buck changed position so he faced Sid. "Pull that hog leg on me if you have to. I'll even give you time to clear leather before I kill you," said Buck, straight-faced and not showing any other facial expression that might give his opponent the advantage.

Sid kept looking into Buck's eyes, and then he smiled. "No, we don't need to do this now. We need each other, and there is no sense in us fighting. Let's shake hands and be friends." Sid extended his hand. Buck looked at the hand and said, "I ain't shaking your hand. I don't think you'll let this conversation pass, so I'll make this easy for you."

"Hold on, you two," said Wilbur. He moved so he was almost between his two associates but stopped short in case they escalated their disagreement and shot at each other. "We need everyone's help to break into the store. But this could get us all in a jam if we get caught."

Sid nodded and said, "You're right, Wilbur, and I'll behave for now." He pointed a finger at Buck. "You need to walk wide of me, Buck, because me and you aren't so friendly."

Buck took several steps forward and stuck out his left hand. "Let's bury the hatchet and work together. We can always square off at a later date."

"Why the left hand? Don't you trust me, Buck?"

"Not really, and I'm not allowing you to try to hurt my gun hand," said Buck, smiling at Sid.

"Okay, you two, let's head on to the mercantile and get a good layout of the place before it closes," said Wilbur. "Sid, you try on a new pair of boots and get the worker's attention. I'll come in and mosey to the rear of the store to get a good look at the back door. John, you walk down the alley behind the mercantile and determine where we need to post a lookout and what tools you think we'll need to break in the door."

"I can do that. Do you want me to see if the back door is open now?" asked John.

"No, I don't want anyone to do anything to cause suspicion or alert the worker inside," said Wilbur. "Buck, you find us a good place to leave our horses so we can get to them fast and vamoose out of town. Sid, after I leave the store, you thank the proprietor for his time and leave. We'll meet back up behind the old rundown building about a block south."

Chapter 27

THE THREE SALOONS IN DALLAS CONTINUED TO DO business at one in the morning with drinking, piano music, and loud laughter as Buck and Wilbur walked their horses down Pearl Street and then turned down the alley at the rear of Pacific Street. Their plan to break into the mercantile had Buck and Wilbur meeting up with John and Sid behind the store at one-fifteen in the morning. John stole a crowbar earlier in the night from the livery stable to pop off the lock from the back door.

John and Sid's horses were already tied behind a vacant business that had a grassy area between the building and the alleyway. There was enough room to keep the horses hidden until the men stole what they needed from the store.

When Buck and Wilbur arrived, John and Sid were already behind the mercantile, working on prying off the lock. John positioned the crowbar into the padlock and heaved on the steel bar. The lock came open. Buck looked both ways, and John pushed open the door and went inside. The other three men followed, and Buck shut the door in case someone came down the alley.

Buck went to a shelf filled with stacks of britches and found a pair that he thought would fit. He removed his boots, the old Army-issue pants, and his shirt. He tried on three different sizes before he found the right pair. Finding a shirt was much easier, and when he was dressed, he tried on boots and then a new hat.

Fully dressed in his new clothing, Buck found a stack of bags under the counter, so they could carry their old clothing with them. After handing out the bags, each person packed their old clothing away, and the men began to gather provisions. With a bag of his old clothes in one hand and provisions in his other hand, Buck went out the back door and once more looked both ways to make sure the coast was clear for them to leave.

When the four robbers were back where they had left the horses and had the sacks secured to their saddles, Buck and Wilbur left the same way they had come, and John and Sid did likewise. They planned to meet back at their camp and go to Colorado from there.

When everyone returned to their camp, the campfire was still going. The four thieves rolled up their bedrolls and stowed away what few possessions they had.

Buck said, "We need to ride heavy with all our old clothing until we're far away from town. We don't want anyone to see our Army rags and figure out it was us that robbed the store."

"So what if they do?" replied Sid. "We'll be long gone, and they ain't going to send a posse after us over some clothes."

Buck didn't want to get into another disagreement with Sid, so he kept quiet and crammed his old clothes in a bag, not caring what Sid or the others did.

They were on the road again by three a.m. and continued riding until they were on the outskirts of Fort Worth.

Wilbur said, "I vote we bypass Fort Worth and head toward Colorado."

"I agree. If we're going to get work in the mountains, I'd much rather work while the weather is good," said Buck.

Sid spit on the ground. "You boys go ahead and ride on. Me and John have different plans here at Fort Worth."

"Come on, Buck, let's ride." Wilbur tipped his hat to the two men staying in Fort Worth and urged his horse forward. When they were out of hearing, he said, "Good riddance, you would have killed Sid sooner or later."

"That's water under the bridge now. Let's find a gully to get rid of these old clothes in and be on our way," said Buck.

Buck was still sitting in his chair in the living room when he woke up. Remembering back to the past had made him so tired that he had nodded off. On aching knees, the sleepy man got up out of the chair and had to stand a few seconds before his legs wanted to move. Walking slowly, he made his way to bed.

Chapter 28

WHAT JOHN HAD SAID TWO DAYS AGO MADE BUCK think more about what Sid might have planned for his gang. John said that Sid was planning something, but it wasn't in Bonham. Buck was cautious about what to do. Did he need to confront Sid, or should he let the local law know what his assumptions were? That might be the best plan: let the law know Sid and his gang were up to something and let them handle it. He wouldn't get involved. His strategy was to stay out of a gun battle and be a concerned citizen.

The next morning another matter was on Buck's mind. It was about his involvement with robbing the mercantile in Dallas. After thinking about what they had done all those years ago, he wanted to make it right with the store's owner, even if it caused him problems with the law. Making amends for his actions was the right thing to do.

Buck finished his breakfast and cleaned his kitchen before he went to the barn. Instead of riding his saddle horse, he hitched up the buggy. It would be much better on his old bones than Red's jarring gait. He parked the buggy in front of the house while he left enough feed and water for his livestock and dog to last them until the next day. Then he packed an overnight bag and took off for Bonham.

He wanted to see Lucy and be honest with her about what he was up to. He also wanted to ask her opinion on the two situations he was about to take care of.

With the buggy parked in front of her house, he walked up the dirt sidewalk to the porch. Instead of knocking on the front door, he walked to the back of the house, figuring she was in the washhouse working.

"Hello beautiful," said Buck from the doorway. Lucy was putting soapy clothes through the wringer with one hand and turning the crank handle with her other, making the rollers rotate in opposite directions. The movement pushed the garments into a tub of rinse water.

"Good morning, Buck. What brings you to town so early?"

"Let me do the cranking while we talk," said Buck, taking over the task. "I saw an old acquaintance in town yesterday. He rides with an outlaw, and I'm concerned they're planning a robbery here in town. I think I should notify the local town marshal so the law can be on the lookout for them in case they try to rob something here in Bonham. Do you think I should tell the law, or wait and see what Sid and John do?"

"You should definitely tell Marshal Coggins what you think might happen."

"Okay, I'll go there in a bit. The other thing is embarrassing, but it bothers me. Me and some men broke into a mercantile in Dallas right after the war and stole clothes so we could find work. I want to take the train to Dallas and pay the store for what we took."

"That was a long time ago, and the people who owned the store back then may not be the owners now," said Lucy. "I would let it drop and not worry about it."

Buck kept turning the crank handle, and when the last garment was through the double rollers, he said, "I'm trying to change who I was back then, and it bothers me that I stole those things from that store. I want to make amends for the bad deeds that I've done, starting with this."

"Then by all means, you should do it," said Lucy.

She approached him and put her arms around his midsection. "You be careful in the big city, and don't get into any trouble." She kissed him, and he smiled down at her before he planted a long kiss on her lips.

"I'll talk to the marshal and catch the train to Dallas. If it's all right with you, I'll come by on my way back home and let you know how it went."

"I'd like that. Now, get going before you miss the train."

Buck saw the town marshal walking down the boardwalk as he took the buggy down North Main Street toward the livery stable. He pulled over to the edge of the street and called out, "Marshal, can I have a word with you?"

"What can I do for you?" asked the marshal.

"I'm Buck Reed," said Buck, holding out his hand.

"I'm Marshal Coggins. Now, what do you need me for?"

"I saw a man named John Flemming in town three days ago. He's an outlaw that rides with Sid Dill, and I suspect they're planning on a robbery here in town since both of them are here. I wanted to let you know about them."

"I've heard of Sid, and I have a wanted poster on him

and his gang. I appreciate you letting me know they're in town. I'll notify the Fannin County Sheriff so he can also be on the lookout."

"I best be going now. I have a train to catch. It was nice meeting you, Marshal Coggins," said Buck. He pulled away and continued to the livery to stow his horse and buggy.

The next train to Sherman, Texas, was scheduled to stop in Bonham within the hour. Buck would ride the Texas and Pacific Railroad to Sherman and then swap over to the MK&T Railroad to get into Dallas, since the T&P went to Fort Worth.

Buck was impressed with the Pullman car the ticket agent assigned him to travel in. This happened to be the first time he had traveled by train in ten years, and the new Pullman was a huge improvement over what he had remembered. It featured elegant upholstery, and the seats were wide and soft. The improved lighting and the floor where the seats were even had carpet.

The train only made one stop to take on passengers between Bonham and Sherman. Buck changed to the MK&T railroad in Sherman, and his accommodations were about the same as on the previous train. Although the passenger train made five stops along the route, it took less than two hours for the city to come into view.

Buck stepped off the train and onto the platform and stood to take in the massive train station. Then he started on his way, but he didn't recognize anything when he was out on the street. It had been fifteen years since he'd been in town, and there had been only a little over three hundred residents at the time. Now there must have been thousands. As far as he could see, businesses lined both sides of the street. Two mules pulling a streetcar on tracks stopped next to him and the driver asked, "Mister, do you want a ride? It don't cost nothing."

"Yes I do. Thank you, sir."

Buck sat directly behind the mule driver and asked, "Do you go by the mercantile down the street? I believe it's on Pacific Street."

"I go by that old building often, but it ain't no mercantile there anymore. When the war ended and the reconstruction started, some big money men came here and bought that property off Old Man Winters. He and his wife are both dead now."

"I had no idea about that. How many people live here now?" asked Buck.

"The city officials say we have over ten thousand people here, counting the freedmen's towns that are connected to the city."

Buck looked confused and asked, "What in the world are you talking about? I'm not familiar with the term freedmen."

"Back in '60 or '61, the residents of Dallas voted for succession. After the war was over, freed slaves from all over the South started coming here and setting up their own towns. They are now called freedmen's towns."

"I see," said Buck. "Where do all these people work?"

"A lot of cotton is ginned here and shipped on the railroad. We also have a huge trade of buffalo hides. Factories are always being built, and houses are always being constructed. If a man wants a job, he can find it here."

"If the mercantile is gone and the previous owner is dead, then I might as well go back to the train station and catch the next one to Sherman," said Buck.

"I'll be turning up ahead and going back the way we came on the next street over. I'll let you off a block from the station."

"Thanks, I'll sit back and enjoy the view."

"Do you remember Moody Street from when you were here?" asked the driver.

"Yes, I do. I believe me and my friends looked for jobs down Moody. Why do you ask?"

"Just off Moody is what we call Boggy Bayou. It's the red-light district and one of the roughest places in the city. It seems like someone comes up dead down there every day."

Buck and the driver talked until they were a block from the train station. Buck got off the streetcar and headed into the station to catch the train back to Bonham.

Chapter 29

BUCK CHANGED RAILROADS IN SHERMAN AND SAT ON the train to Bonham, reflecting about this trip. It was a relief that what he'd done years ago in Dallas had been reconciled. Even though the store was gone and the owners dead, he still felt good inside that he had made the commitment to go there and try to make amends.

A thought came to mind as he swayed with the railcar traveling down the steel tracks. Maybe he should go back to Cooper, Texas, where his beloved Mary Jane and daughter Belinda were buried. He hadn't been back to their graves since the day they were laid to rest.

He leaned back into the soft fabric-covered seat and closed his eyes. The images he saw made his old, tired eyes moisten up. After all these years, the pain was still present, and he never wanted to lose the memories that were stored in his heart. He opened his eyes and brushed the tears off his cheeks. Then he decided to visit his wife and daughter's burial place. He would go by the bank in Dodd City and withdraw enough cash to have tombstones put up at their graves.

When he exited the train in Bonham, the old gunfighter had a hard time walking. Sitting most of the day had taken its toll on his joints. He went after his horse and buggy. It was late in the day, and he had promised Lucy he'd stop by before going home. With a stroke of luck, she'd go with him to the café and eat supper with him.

Lucy sat on her porch as Buck stopped the buggy in front of her house. "You're back really quick. Did everything go as planned?" she asked.

"Have you eaten supper yet?" asked Buck.

"No, I haven't."

"Come on, let's eat, and I'll tell you about my trip."

Buck and Lucy sat alone at a table when he said, "I didn't recognize Dallas at all this trip. It has over ten thousand people living there, with businesses all up and down the streets. The mercantile is gone, and the owners are both dead, so I came on back. The main thing is I tried to make amends for the wrong I did back then."

"I agree, it's a good thing that you tried," said Lucy.

"Lucy, I'm heading to Cooper, Texas, in the morning for a few days. I was married in '51, and we had a daughter named Belinda. My wife and little girl both died of the pox and are buried at Cooper. I was devastated by their deaths, and I felt guilty for living. I haven't been back to the cemetery since the funeral. I'm going there to visit their graves and have tombstones erected."

Lucy reached out and took his hand in hers. "You should go and talk to your loved ones. I still go talk to my late husband and put flowers on his grave. Buck, you're a good man. I assume that you've done some bad things since you're known as a gunfighter, but what you're doing now is the right thing to do, and I support you in your efforts."

He smiled and squeezed her hand. "I have nightmares about men with no faces coming at me in the street ready to draw on me. It's the same dream over and over again. I know it's from the events of my past, and maybe if I go back and try to get redemption for what I've done, the dreams will stop."

"Whether you get redemption or not, you're doing what's right by going back and trying," said Lucy.

The waitress brought their food to the table, and their conversation stopped until they had finished the meal and were returning to Lucy's house.

"Buck, I want you to go see your wife and daughter. While there, you take care of anything else in your past that bothers you. I'm very fond of you, and I don't want you being disturbed by images, dreams, and injustices, and I sure don't want anything eating at you inside. That's like a big festering sore that won't go away."

"Thanks, Lucy. I'll leave first thing in the morning and ride across the country to be there in a few days. It's been a blessing talking to you about my problems, and I appreciate you so much."

"Oh heck, Buck, just go ahead and say it. You want to be my boyfriend."

He laughed and took her in his arms for a kiss. "Lucy, I want to be your man friend."

She put her hand to his cheek and rubbed it tenderly while she spoke. "You go take care of your personal business, and I'll be waiting for you." She kissed him and climbed down off the buggy. "Buck Reed, you get going, and I'll see you in a few days."

"Yes, ma'am." He took off, proud as a peacock. Lucy was now officially his girlfriend, and his life was starting to look how he wanted it to.

Chapter 30

BUCK WAS IN NO GREAT HURRY THE FOLLOWING morning. He ate breakfast, cleaned the kitchen, and then went outside to feed and water the chickens and horses. He also left extra food set out for Biscuit.

The bank in Dodd City didn't open until nine, so he had plenty of time to saddle his horse, fill his canteen, and pack a small bag of clothing.

The ride to Dodd City took less than an hour, and he went straight to the bank for money to take on the trip.

O.W. came out of his office while Buck was standing in the lobby waiting in the teller line. "Hello Buck, what can we do for you?"

"I'm going on a short trip and need five hundred for pocket money to take with me."

"Coming right up. Follow me to that vacant window, and I'll get it myself," said O.W.

Buck made small talk with his old friend as the man got him his money and promised to stop by again for a chat sometime once he was back in town.

Buck walked out of the bank and was met in the street

by the two young men who had been with Rex the day he disarmed them in front of the saloon.

"Old man, we got a bone to pick with you," said one of the men.

Buck shook his head in despair. This was not how he wanted to start his day. "You boys should go back to where you came from. I'm not in the mood to put up with your stupidity today." Buck drew his gun and pointed it in the direction of the men before they had a chance to react.

"Take your guns out slow and easy and lay them on the ground," said Buck.

Townsfolk stopped to gawk at the exchange going on in the street. "You boys should know by now that I can kill the two of you anytime I want to in a fight. Why on earth do you keep trying to die by calling me out? Now, back away from them guns."

"Please don't throw them in the water trough again. We had the darndest time cleaning them up the other time," said one of the unarmed men.

"I'll leave them in the town marshal's office. Now, promise me that you won't come gunning for me again. Can the both of you do that?"

"Yes, um, I can," said one of the men.

"I won't call you out again," said the other.

"Good, I'm getting too old to be killing young men like yourselves. Stay where you are, and you can pick up your guns when I've left town." Buck mounted up and headed down the street, proud of himself for not killing the two men. A month ago, he would have shot them and not thought twice about it. But now his attitude was different, and he wanted to become an upright citizen in the area where he lived.

Buck took the two young men's guns to the marshal and got on his way. He pushed his horse that first day and by dark, they had made it to Pecan Gap, Texas, where he'd caused damage to the saloon and went to jail. After dropping off his horse at the livery, he checked into the only hotel in town and ordered a hot bath in an hour and a half and one for the following morning to soothe his aching bones.

Once he put his bag in the room, he wanted to go to the saloon and see if the barkeep he had trouble with still owned it. Only a few men were in the whiskey mill, and Buck recognized the barkeep as the same man who had taken a boot to him that morning when he was passed out on the floor. He approached the counter. The owner had his back to Buck until he said, "Barkeep, I'm Buck Reed. Do you remember me?"

The man spun around at hearing the name. "Howdy, Buck, it's been a long time. I hope there are no hard feelings from the last time we saw each other."

Buck could tell the man was scared by how he wrung the dirty towel in his hands.

"I came by to pay you the twenty-nine dollars I owe you for the damage I did back then." Buck pulled out his money and laid thirty dollars on the countertop.

"You don't need to do that, Buck. That was a long time ago."

"I do need to do it, and now me and you are square."

The man reached out and took the money. "Yep, you settled your debt with me, and I'd like to buy you a drink."

"I don't drink anymore," said Buck and went out the door. He paused on the boardwalk and looked down the street to see if there was somewhere he could buy supper. A sign hanging from the rafter of a porch, with faded writing, read *Marge's Café, Home Cooked Meals*. Buck walked to the chow hall and ate his supper before going to the hotel to clean up and a good night's sleep.

The following morning, Buck woke up in pain. His back and shoulders hurt, and his thighs were so sore he could hardly walk. After slipping on his britches and shirt, he made his way to the room where the bathtubs were located. In some of the nicer hotels, the bathtub was in the room and had running water, but this place was older and had a dedicated room with two tubs.

His hot water was waiting for him, and the hot water soothed his sore and aching joints. He soaked until the water started to cool off. Then he dried off and returned to his room to finish dressing.

Buck ate breakfast at the same café. The coffee was strong, and he used it to wash down the ham and eggs. He finished his breakfast, gathered his horse from the livery, and headed to Cooper, Texas, where his wife and daughter had been laid to rest. He hoped he could remember where the graves were.

Chapter 31

As he rode the ten miles southeast toward Cooper, traveling past acres and acres of cotton fields, his childhood came back to him. He saw people, white and black, tending to the rows of cotton hoeing weeds. It had been hard as a boy, working in the cotton fields from daylight to dusk during the spring, summer, and fall months.

It seemed he was either plowing or hoeing weeds until the harvest came in the fall. That was when the work really started. He dragged a cotton sack with the strap around his shoulder and midsection up and down the rows, pulling cotton bolls off the plants. His fingers and hands got cut up from rubbing against the hard, dry parts of the plant as he twisted off the boll. And by the end of the day, his back and shoulders hurt from bending over and pulling the heavy sack, Buck would go home, eat his supper, and go to bed, only to start over the next day.

He figured that his folks were also buried in the same cemetery as his wife and daughter. He might have to ask at the undertaker's office where they were, since he didn't even know what year they had died.

Buck pulled back on the reins when he heard gunshots up ahead around a curve in the road. He couldn't see where the shots came from because a stand of trees stood between him and the direction from which he'd heard the sound.

He removed the safety from his gun and eased his horse forward. At least five or six guns were firing. Maybe someone was taking target practice. He had done that many days on the trail between jobs.

As he rounded the bend, he observed five men on horseback firing in the air, riding around a corral. Some of the pigs and one calf in the pen were dead. Occasionally someone in the homestead would fire an old muzzle-loaded rifle at the men.

Buck knew what was happening; he had been involved in this kind of raid before as a hired gun. Some large rancher or landowner didn't like the small farmers who set up homesteads on public land. The smaller farms took away free grazing and sometimes water from his cattle. The rancher would send men to run the so-called squatters off, and if that didn't work, they set fire to their homes and barns.

Buck never did enjoy this type of work, and the one thing he refused to do was kill women or children. He had been in on running off probably a dozen homesteaders over the years. Now though, he felt they had legal right to occupy the land, and the rancher who ordered his men to destroy these hardworking folks only wanted the land to feed a few more cows.

Buck thought back to his involvement in running off settlers and decided that today he would side with these poor folks and help them out. He urged his horse toward the men who were shooting at the house and was almost in pistol range when one of the riders took a short stick of wood about two feet long with a rag attached to the end that he had probably brought with him and lit it with a match.

Buck knew that the torch would be used to set fire to the house, and he wasn't going to let that happen. He spurred his horse forward and shot the man out of his saddle as he was about to throw the torch at the building.

One of the other riders turned toward Buck and fired twice before Buck shot him off his horse too. Buck brought Red around and was ready to fire at another man when the cowboy threw up his hands.

"All of you drop your guns, or I'll keep emptying saddles," said Buck.

"Put your guns away, boys. He meant what he said. Hello Buck, it's been a long time."

Buck rode closer to the man who had spoken and said, "Benny, is that you?"

"Yep, it's me all right. Are you working for these squatters?"

"Yeah, I'm hired out to them. Who are you working for these days?" Buck asked, still holding his gun on the men.

"We all work for Lester McCallister, who owns the old Flying C Ranch. He bought it about three years ago and needs more land to raise cattle."

"You tell Lester I'm coming by his ranch house in the morning to talk."

"Buck, that might be a mistake. Lester is a hard man, and I don't think he'll be too kindly toward you," said Benny.

"Lester knows me. We've ridden the trail together a

time or two. Be sure to tell him I'm coming to call for a cup of coffee and parlay."

"Okay, it's your funeral," said Benny.

"Or it could be Lester's funeral. You boys gather your wounded and head on out. I have things to do."

Buck rode to the front of the residence where a man, woman, and four kids stood on the porch. Buck put his index finger to his lips so they would keep quiet and motioned them to go inside.

Buck stood in the doorway watching the cowboys bandage up the two men he'd shot with their dirty handkerchiefs and get them into the saddle. He watched the group ride off and went into the house where one room was the kitchen and sitting room. It looked like there were two or three rooms where they all slept.

"I'm Buck Reed, and I just told them men that I work for you folks. What are your names?"

"I'm Randy Rowe, and this is my wife, Betty. The boy over by the stove is Mark, the red-haired girl is Stacy, and this is Evan and George."

"Nice to meet you all. Those men work for Lester McCallister. I know him, and he is a hard man. I'll talk to him tomorrow about not coming after you folks again. Since I work for you now, you'll have to pay me two bits so I don't make myself out to be a liar."

"Are you serious?" asked Randy.

"Yes, I'm serious. He doesn't need to know how much you're paying me. I won't lie, so give me the quarter," said Buck.

Betty went to a row of shelves that held dishes, cups, glasses, and a few cans. She took down one of the cans, removed a quarter from it, and handed it to Buck. "Mr. Reed, we don't have much, and that quarter is a lot of money to us."

"I understand. Don't fret about giving it to me. When this is over, I'll give it back to you."

She smiled and hugged him. "Thank you so much. I thought they were going to burn us up in here."

"Ma'am, they had their orders, and I don't doubt for a second that those men would have killed your entire family," said Buck. "You folks will be safe for the rest of today and tonight. I have to go into Cooper for an important matter. I'll have a parlay with Lester tomorrow and get this settled."

Buck turned to the door, and as he was about to walk outside, he looked back and said, "You stay close to the house tomorrow, and I'll come by and tell you how my meeting with Lester went."

"Thank you, Mr. Reed. We really appreciate you saving us from those men," said Randy.

Buck rode off, asking himself what he had gotten himself into. Lester would not be happy that he interfered in his business, but that was okay. Although he and Lester had ridden for the same boss several times, they'd never been close, and Buck didn't like the man's attitude toward people in general. Lester was a hothead who killed for the fun of it. If it came to a fight when they met, he'd have to kill Lester, and this issue with the Rowes could be over.

Chapter 32

COOPER HAD GROWN IN SIZE SINCE HE'D LAST VISITED. It was still a farming community, but the business section had expanded the offerings of goods to the people. The town now had two hardware stores, three clothing stores, a shoe cobbler, two banks, two saloons, and three cafés. The undertaker's parlor wasn't where he remembered, and he had to ask a passerby where it had moved to.

Buck was surprised when he stepped inside the undertaker's office. The same man who had buried his wife and daughter many years ago sat behind a desk. The elderly man rose from a four-legged stool and came to Buck. "Can I be of service to you, mister?"

"You most likely don't remember me. I'm Buck Reed, and you entombed my wife and daughter back in 1858. They died of the pox, and you buried them in the town cemetery."

The elderly mortician nodded and said, "I remember that well. You took it mighty hard and went kind of crazy after that. I laid your ma and pa to rest next to your wife and child. They're over on the west side of the cemetery, about ten rows from the gate. I put up wooden crosses to mark their graves."

"I was wondering if there is a stonemason in town that could make them all tombstones?" asked Buck.

"Yes, sir. His shop is on the west edge of town, and he does a fine job. His name is Lance Thomas. Tell him that I sent you."

"Thanks for the information. I'm going to the cemetery first, and then I'll go see Lance."

Buck mounted up and rode to the cemetery, standing at the gate for a few minutes with his heart beating fast. The agony came back to him from so long ago when they were taken from him. He closed his eyes and silently said, *God please help me this day?* With new strength, he squelched his anguish and begin his search. The graves weren't hard to find, with the four crude wooden crosses marking them and the name Reed etched on one cross.

Buck removed his hat and stood staring down at the graves. Tears formed in his eyes and he cried, remembering the love and joy he had shared with his beloved Mary Jane. Little Belinda would be twenty-six if she had lived. The tears flowed and the pain he had suppressed all these years gripped his heart like a vise. He fell onto his knees and leaned forward with his hands on their ground.

The memories flooded his whole being, and he stayed on the ground until his legs and arms hurt. Buck got up and said, "I will love and cherish the memories of the both of you until I can be with you again. I have never loved again since the two of you. I'm leaving now, but I'll return as often as I can."

Buck walked back to his horse and mounted up. He looked back at the graves, blew a kiss, and left for Cooper.

He hadn't realized how long he had spent at the graves until he arrived back in town. It was two-forty in the afternoon, and he had spent over two hours at the cemetery. The breakfast he ate was long gone and Buck was hungry, but he wanted to make the deal for the tombstones before he did anything else.

The stonemason sat outside of a little shop under an awning working on a slap of rock with a hammer and chisel.

"Howdy, are you Lance?" asked Buck.

"Yes sir, what can I do for you?"

"I need four tombstones made and placed in the cemetery. One for my wife, one for my daughter, and the others are for my parents."

"Let's go inside and I'll take down all the information you want on the markers."

Inside the office, Buck told Lance about his wife and daughter but informed him that he would have to get the year his folks died from the undertaker. He paid the man and as he left, he said, "I'll be back in a few months to see what kind of job you did on the tombstones."

"Oh, right. I wouldn't expect anything less. I'll do my best, Mr. Reed."

Buck went to the café and ate a good meal of steak and potatoes before going to the hotel for a hot bath and a soft bed. He left his horse at the livery, and on his way to the hotel he passed by a gun shop. A shiny new pistol in the display window caught his attention and he went inside.

"Howdy, are you looking for a new gun?" asked the man behind the counter, putting a pistol back together that he had taken apart with some of the parts still on the countertop.

"I think I may want another sidearm. I favor the Colt Peacemaker. Do you have one?" said Buck.

"I sure do. It's a wonderful firearm that's discreet and dependable. I have it in two-barrel lengths—the seven-

and-a-half model or the four-and-three-quarter length. Which would you like to see?"

"I'll look at both."

The man turned his back to Buck and opened a cabinet where he removed two guns and laid them on top of the counter. Buck took his time and examined each gun separately. He laid the longer-barreled revolver on the counter and asked, "Do you have a shoulder rig that will fit the short-barrel gun?"

"I sure do. I'll go get it for you."

The store clerk came from behind the counter and walked over to where multiple holsters were hanging from pegs in the wall. He took one down and brought it back, for Buck to try on.

"You look like you've used one of these holsters before," said the shopkeeper.

"Yep," said Buck. He slid the gun in the holster and drew it a few times.

"How does it feel?" asked the clerk.

"It's a little uncomfortable. The pistol doesn't slide out the way I want. Can you cut the barrel off an inch or so to fit the holster better?" asked Buck as he laid the gun on the counter.

"I sure can, but you have to pay for it first. Do you want me to put the sight on the end of the barrel?"

"I don't want a sight. How much is the gun?" asked Buck as he pulled his money from his pocket.

"I can sell you the gun, holster, and one box of ammunition for twenty-three dollars."

Buck counted out the money and laid it on the counter. "Go saw off the barrel, and I'll wait on you," said Buck, adjusting the shoulder holster so that it was lower and the gun handle should be lined up better with his hand to draw the gun.

Buck took bullets from the box and filled all the empty loops on his gun belt. The rest he would carry in his pockets after loading the new gun.

The gunsmith returned with the pistol and handed it to Buck. "Here you go. I cut off a little over an inch and a half and filed the end so it will slide on the leather."

Buck put his new gun in the holster and drew it back out. He kept practicing and adjusted the holster a little more before finally opening the cylinder and loading his new weapon. "Much obliged for sawing off the barrel," said Buck.

"You're welcome, sir. If you don't mind, what is your name?" asked the man in a shaky voice.

"It's Buck Reed."

"I knew you had to be good with a gun because you kept drawing it from that shoulder holster like a pro. Say, didn't you live here years ago?"

"Thanks again," said Buck, and he left the store without answering the man's question. He wasn't in the mood to talk about old times. He was glad to have a second gun in case he had to shoot his way off Lester's ranch the following day.

His hotel room had a bathtub and hot running water. Buck lay in the tub and when the water started to cool off, he added more hot water. The soaking helped loosen up his sore muscles and aching joints, and he hoped for a good night's sleep.

Chapter 33

Tilting a chair so the back was against the door handle was a habit Buck had been using for years in hotels. He also closed the window that overlooked the street. There wasn't a lock on the window, but a piece of wood leaned against the wall under it, could be placed on top of the window so no one could open it. Now that his room was secure, he undressed and hung his gun belt on the bedpost closest to his head. He placed the new Colt under the pillow beside the one he would use.

Buck lay awake thinking about going to the cemetery earlier in the day. It was something he should have been doing for years instead of trying to forget the memories that he had. If Mary Jane and Belinda had lived, his life would have been so much different over the last twenty-something years.

He was happy he'd come home to visit his family's resting places. Just knowing that he would one day see them again comforted him, and he went to sleep.

Buck's eyes shot open around midnight, and he reached under the pillow for the short-barrel Colt. What had awakened him? Was it a sound, voices, or boot leather squeaking? His instincts told him to get out of bed and get ready because something bad was about to happen.

He didn't want whoever it was that caused him to waken to know he was up. He gently removed the quilt and eased his feet to the floor. When he stood up, he could see a shadow move under the door. Someone was outside in the hallway, and footsteps could be heard coming up the outside stairway by his window. The man in the hallway must be waiting until the man outside started the action.

This kind of ambush wasn't new to Buck. He carefully moved to the outside wall, and when in position beside the window, he cocked back the hammer and waited. The person on the outside tried to lift the window, but it only moved a half inch. Whoever it was took a step back and began to fire through the window. The glass broke and bullets hit the bed and wall. The assailant in the hall tried to open the door, but the chair kept it secure. With a vicious kick, the lock shattered and the chair broke as the door came open.

Buck fired two shots in such quick succession, they sounded like one as he shot the man coming through the door in the chest. He turned the gun to the window and shot the attacker on the balcony, who was reloading his pistol. The invader tried to close the cylinder, but a bullet hit the assassin and he tumbled off the balcony to the ground, landing with a loud *thud*.

The man in the doorway was dead, and Buck recognized him as one of the cowboys who was going to set fire to Rowe's homestead. Buck lit the lamp about the time the deputy came up the stairs with his gun drawn.

"Mister, you keep them hands where I can see them,"

said the lawman, and he walked to the corpse on the floor. Right behind him was the man who owned the hotel.

"Deputy," said the hotel owner. "You need to get that dead man out of here before he bleeds all over the floor. I'm going after a mop and bucket." He looked at the shattered door, put his hands on his hips, and said, "I'll be dadburn. The scum kicked in my door." He pointed to the window. "And look there. Now I'm going to have to replace the windowpane as well." He was still mumbling as he rushed off for a mop.

"Deputy, these men were going to kill me, and I defended myself. You can see with your own eyes how that one kicked in the door, and the other one emptied his gun at my bed. The glass is all on the inside of the room."

"Yeah, I can tell that's what happened. Do you know who these men are?"

"No, I don't know this one, and I didn't see the other guy's face. Do you know them?" Buck asked.

"I know they work out at the Flying C Ranch, but that's all."

Another lawman came up the stairs, and Buck saw that his badge indicated he happened to be the city marshal. "I have some men coming to haul the corpse out of here. Mister, I suggest you book another room for the night and come see me in the morning so I can take your statement."

"I can do that," replied Buck.

The hotel man came back in and pointed down the hall. "You can use room five." He started cleaning up the blood that had spilled from the dead man's body with a mop and a bucket of soapy water.

Buck gathered up belongings and carried them to his new room. It took him two trips to get all his things. With the door closed and the chair leaned against the doorknob,

Buck lay down and thought about Lester. His old running buddy had tried to have him killed tonight. Tomorrow, he and Lester would look into each other's eyes. Lester was never as fast as Buck, even on his best day, so he'd sent his cronies to do his dirty work. Just the thought of being bushwhacked had Buck's blood boiling. He would get directions to the Flying C in the morning when he gave his account of tonight's action to the law. He knew sure as day that Lester would be waiting for him to show up. In fact, Buck suspected he'd encounter trouble on the way to the ranch.

Sleep took over, and it was daylight when Buck finally got up.

Chapter 34

THE FOLLOWING MORNING, BUCK TOOK HIS SOAKING bath, packed his belongings and carried his travel bag with him to the diner down the street for breakfast. As soon as he stepped inside the eatery, he saw the town marshal whom he met during the night and a deputy he had never seen before sitting at a table drinking coffee. The marshal waved at Buck and said, "Come on and join us for breakfast."

Buck pulled out a chair, but before he sat down, he extended his hand to the marshal. "We didn't formally exchange names last night. I'm Buck Reed."

The marshal didn't change his expression but nodded at Buck. "I'm Will Freeman, and this is my daytime deputy, Bill Bryant."

The waitress brought coffee to the three men and took their orders. Marshal Freeman said, "Go ahead and tell us what happened last night, and then you can leave when we're done with breakfast."

Buck knew what the lawman was insinuating. He wanted the gunfighter out of his town before there was more violence. Buck explained everything from the time something had woken him up until the two men were dead. He left out the trouble at the Rowe's homestead or about his plans to visit Lester later in the day.

Buck laid enough money on the table to pay for all three meals and shook hands with the two lawmen, then walked to the livery stable for his horse. Red was tied up outside under the shade of an oak tree, and the hostler sat in a chair leaned back against the barn, sound asleep.

Buck mounted up and walked Red so close to the hostler that the horse bumped into him, and the man fell onto the ground.

"What'd you do that for? I wasn't bothering anyone," said the man while dusting off his clothes.

"I need to know how to get out to the Flying C Ranch," said Buck.

"I ought not to tell you since you knocked me to the ground," said the man. He took a deep breath and pointed east. "Go east about two miles and then turn northeast on the road once you cross the dry creek. You'll be on the ranch soon after that."

"Much obliged," said Buck, and he took off.

Lester should know by now that he'd be coming from town and most likely using the road. Knowing Lester, he had a third person in town watching the action last night so they could report back to him. Most likely, two men would be hidden on both sides of the road ready to kill him when he crossed the dry creek. *Whoever they are will have a long hot wait today*. He'd bypass the road and travel across the meadows until he found the ranch house.

He only encountered barbed wire at one location, and was able to find a corner where the fence turned and continued on. Based off the location of the Rowe's land and where he was currently, he figured the fenced land belonged to a neighbor. Lester didn't seem to fence off his land like his neighbor did, probably because he wanted to claim all the open land.

Buck topped a rise and saw a large herd of cattle. To the north of them was a house, multiple barns, a bunkhouse, and three outhouses. He needed to get closer to identify any men he might know, but more importantly he wanted a good grasp of the ranch headquarters' layout.

The cattle parted as he rode through them with the reins in his left hand and his right hand close to his gun. The safeties were off both his guns, and he was calm for a man walking into a trap.

Two men left one of the barns and started his way. He recognized one of them as Benny but didn't know the other. The two men rode up to Buck and stopped ten feet in front of him.

"Howdy Benny," said Buck.

"Morning Buck. I reckon you realize Lester is waiting to kill you?"

"Yeah, I've always suspected that he was a coward and is afraid to face me man-to-man. Benny, I'm going to kill your boss for trying to bushwhack me last night. I suggest you don't return to the ranch until this ends. I like you and would rather you stay away," said Buck.

Benny sat on his horse and looked at his old friend for a few seconds. He looked at the man with him and said, "Rusty, I think you and I should go check the water tank east of here."

"I agree with you Benny. Nice meeting you, Mr. Reed," said Rusty, and took off.

"Nice meeting you, Rusty," said Buck. He looked at Benny. "How many men does Lester have with him?"

"There are only two right now. He sent three men to intercept you by the dry creek on the road. I would say that now is a good time to have a face-off with Lester. You know how he is, so don't let him get close to you, or he'll try to break you in half with those tree trunks he calls arms," said Benny.

"I'll be seeing you, old friend," said Buck, urging his horse forward.

As he entered the ranch house yard, a short, barrel-chested man carrying a rifle came out from behind a woodpile. As he put the rifle stock to his shoulder, Buck skinned leather and shot the man in the head. The man fell backward onto the ground as another man came out the front door, firing his gun in the direction of the gunfighter. Buck felt a burning pain in his left thigh but turned his weapon on the shooter and fired twice, ending the threat from the doorway.

Now gunfire came from one of the upstairs windows. Buck pointed his gun up at the window and fired three shots. He holstered the gun and was pulling the shoulder pistol when Lester came out of the house with his rifle aimed at Buck.

"Well, you old coot, it's finally time to meet your maker. I always knew I would be the one to put your lights out for good, and there ain't nary a thing you can do about it," said Lester, smiling.

Buck moved his hand so fast that all Lester had time to do was watch wide-eyed in disbelief, before two slugs hit him in the chest. His mouth came open; he dropped his gun and put his hands over the bullet holes while looking at Buck.

"How did you do that?" he asked, then went down on one knee. Buck rode forward.

"Lester, you were never a match for me." Buck shot one more time, hitting Lester between the eyes. Blood and brain matter erupted out the back of his head as he fell over dead.

Buck dismounted and went where Lester lay, limping on his injured leg. He searched through the dead man's pockets and found a roll of money. Buck mounted back up and turned his horse back the way he had come. He stopped on the rise once he'd ridden past the cattle to check out the pain in his leg. He had blood oozing out of a furrow along his thigh that had already soaked the leg of his britches. It looked like a flesh wound and would have to be tended to soon. He tied a handkerchief around his leg to stop the bleeding and keep the wound from getting dirty. The sawbones in Pecan Gap could take a look at it and put a clean bandage on it when he got there.

Benny and the man who was with him came riding up to Buck. "Well, I see you're still alive and in one piece," said Benny.

"I caught a slug to my thigh, but I'll live," said Buck as he pulled the gun from his holster and started to reload the spent shells. "I have a proposition for you, Benny. The Flying C is yours if you want it. Lester and the two men with him are dead. You can take it over if you let me have forty cows and a couple of bulls, a mature one and a young one. Also I want you to be good neighbors with the small farms around here, especially the Rowes."

"Are you serious? Of course I'll agree to that," said Benny, grinning from ear to ear.

"Can you also bring them to my place between Bonham and Dodd City?"

"Heck yes. I'll have to hire a few cowhands first, but as soon as I have enough drovers, we'll head your way with the cattle."

"I'm going to Pecan Gap to get my leg looked at. You need

to make sure those men down by the creek know you're now the boss. If they give you any flack about taking over the ranch, I would run them off or kill them, but it's your call now. When you start the cows my way, send a telegram to me in Bonham, Texas. I'll meet you on the trail south of Dodd City."

"I sure will. In the meantime, me and Rusty will be waiting on them fellers when they come back from the creek. One of them is Hermon Smith, who is a good cowboy. The other two rode the owl hoot trail with Lester."

Rusty spoke for the first time. "I vote we shoot first and don't give them any options."

"You fellers work it out," said Buck, and he rode off.

That was a good deal he had made with Benny for the cattle. If he hadn't already found his forever home, he would have taken over the ranch.

Buck stopped by the Rowe's place and stayed on his horse until Randy and Betty Rowe came outside. "Mister Reed your bleeding. Do you want me to have a look at your leg?" asked Betty.

"No ma'am. I came by to return that quarter I got off you yesterday. Here it is with interest," said Card and headed her two bits plus the roll of money he took off Lester.

"What in the world is this for?" asked Randy as he saw the money in his wife's hand.

"Call it a gift from the late Lester McCalister. Neither him or his men won't be coming around here anymore. Benny is taking over the ranch and he wants to be a good neighbor. I suggest you do the same," said Card. He turned his horse around and took off leaving the sodbusters watching him leave.

Chapter 35

THE DOCTOR'S OFFICE WAS STILL IN THE SAME building as Buck remembered from the last time he'd been there. He limped through the door to be met by a woman in a white apron soiled with blood spots. "Come on in, mister. I see you've been injured."

"Yes, ma'am. I was shot, but I don't think it's very bad," said Buck.

"Go into the room to your right, shuck those britches, and get on that examining table right now while I get some hot water from the back."

"Ma'am, I ain't used to stripping off in front of ladies that I never seen before," said Buck.

"Well first off, I ain't no lady, I'm Dr. Elizabeth Murray. You can call me Dr. Liz. Second, I've seen just about everything you can imagine. So, do what I say and shuck those britches, or I'll have to cut them up so I can get to your injury."

Buck laughed and stuck out his hand. "I'm Buck Reed, and I guess I'll do what you say for now so you can patch me up."

While the doctor cleaned the wound and examined its severity, Buck said, "I once knew a man with the last name Murray. You wouldn't be kin to Brad Murray, would you?"

"Yep, he's my daddy. How do you know him?"

"We were in the same unit during the war. Brad was a medic and did some work on me one day."

She stopped what she was doing, walked behind Buck, and lifted up his shirt. "You're Buckshot Reed, ain't you?" she asked.

"Yep, but not many people call me that anymore. Is Brad living around here?"

"No, sir. He's a doctor in California. I plan on moving out there to work with him as soon as possible," said Elizabeth.

She applied disinfectant to the wound and bandaged it tightly so no dust would get to it and infect it. She left the room while Buck put on his britches and boots. When he was dressed, the woman returned and said, "You owe me six dollars for my time and supplies."

Buck handed her a ten-dollar bill. "You tell your daddy that I said hi and that he raised a fine doctor for a daughter."

"Thank you, Buckshot. My daddy told me you were a gunfighter. Is that true?" she asked.

"Yeah, I'm an old gunfighter, but I'm trying to settle down and stop being that man." He stuck out his hand to shake hers. "Thanks again for fixing me up. I hope you get on to California so you can work with your daddy," Buck said. He walked out of the office and mounted up.

He was ready for a good meal and some rest before he headed home, so he dropped his horse off at the livery stable and limped to the café. The place was almost empty, and he ate his food without talking to anyone. When he was finished, he went to the hotel.

No one was behind the counter, so he took a seat in one of the four chairs around a small table in the sitting area. It was only a minute or two before the same clerk from the first night came into the room.

"Hello, Mr. Reed. Do you need a room and hot bath for the night?"

"I'll go ahead and take the room, but I think I'll have to take that bath another time. I have an injury to my leg and probably need to keep it dry for a few days," said Buck.

The man handed him a room key and Buck paid for the night. He went upstairs to the same room he had slept in two nights ago. It was still too early for bed, so he decided to go to the saloon for a couple of beers and see if he saw anyone he'd known twenty-six years ago.

Only six men were in the saloon, two at one table just talking and four at another, playing poker.

Buck went to the bar and when the barkeep came over, he asked, "What'll it be, Buck?"

"Just a beer."

"Coming right up."

Buck was on his second beer when the batwing doors opened and two cowboys walked in. He watched them through the reflection in the mirror. Both men reached down and removed the safety straps off their guns as they looked at the men at the tables.

Buck lowered his right hand and removed the safety from his gun as well, waiting to see the men's next move. They came toward him, and when they were within eight feet, they stopped and stood side-by-side.

"Buck Reed, I'm Donnie McCallister, Lester's nephew. I'm here to settle a score with you."

"I have no beef with neither of you fellers," said Buck without turning around from the bar. "I suggest you men leave before you do something that will get you killed."

"We're here to kill you, so turn around and prepare to skin that gun and die."

Buck rotated to his left to face the two men, and as he did, he drew with his usual speed and fired as the two men were still trying to get their guns in position. Donnie fired one slug into the floor before he was knocked backward onto a table that broke. The second man was slower and never had a chance to shoot before Buck put a bullet in his heart that spun him around and then fell face down. Both men lay dead with blood oozing out of the bullet wounds while Buck reloaded his gun.

The event happened so fast that the saloon patrons didn't have time to react and get out of the way. Buck kicked the guns clear of the men's hands as the barkeep ran to the door and hollered into the street. "Someone get the marshal and the doctor. There's been a shooting."

Buck returned to the bar top, drank the rest of his beer, and sat down at an empty table to wait on the law.

In only a few minutes, there were twenty men inside the saloon, nosing around to see who the dead men were but mostly to see who the gunman was who could kill two men coming at him.

Buck sat at the table and told the city marshal what had happened, and the barkeep backed up the story. The marshal wrote the statements down on a piece of paper and when he finished, he asked, "Are you planning on staying around town, Buck?"

"I'm spending the night in the hotel and leaving for home in the morning, if that's okay with you."

"Yeah, that's fine. You be sure to follow through and leave tomorrow."

"Thanks, Marshal."

Buck made his way through the crowd, walked to the hotel, and went straight to his room. He couldn't wait for morning so he could go home, where it was quiet.

Back Home...

Buck made his way through the crowd, walking into a well-lit waiting room. He walked his way to the registration desk to announce his arrival.

Chapter 36

THE NEXT MORNING, BUCK HAD TO SIT ON THE SIDE of the bed bending and straightening his legs for a few minutes to get the stiffness out of his knees. His left leg experienced a slight muscle spasm during the night and the soreness to his thigh had increased since he saw the doctor. After he dressed and packed his bag, he sat on the bed and exercised his legs again before going downstairs to have breakfast and then get his horse. He wanted to head home to relax, and he also wanted to see Lucy and tell her about going to the cemetery. He didn't think he would tell her about Lester or Lester's nephew. He wanted to share his life with Lucy, but some aspects of his life were better not talked about. The unkindly fate of Lester and his nephew might be something that she didn't need to know about. This unfortunate event in his life had taken two lives, and the story ended in the saloon at Pecan Gap.

Buck was almost to Dodd City when he remembered that Wilbur's ranch was southwest of town, and he was most likely close to it. He had time to stop by to have some water and tell him about Lester. Thinking about Wilbur brought a smile across his wrinkled-up face. The two of them had rode across the mountain and through the creek a few times and forged a great friendship while doing so.

Twelve days after Buck and Wilbur parted ways with Sid and John outside Fort Worth, they met up with two other men in a saloon in Clayton, New Mexico. Their names were Phil Durr and Floyd Waters, who were also headed to work in the silver mines. The four of them traveled fourteen days together all the way to Clear Creek Canyon at Georgetown, Colorado.

THEIR FIRST NIGHT in Georgetown turned deadly, but it also opened up work opportunities for Buck and Wilbur. The landscape they traveled over the next six days from Denver to Georgetown took its toll on the horses and men. They went up and down mountain roads and trails through ravines and around thousands of rocks and boulders before riding into the mining town.

Tired, hungry and needing something to wash down the trail dust, the four tired men went into one of the four saloons. This drinking hole was nothing but a large tent with a bar made out of slabs of wood and twelve tables with chairs. The place was full of mineworkers and working girls flirting with the patrons. A drunk miner bumped into Phil, and they exchanged harsh words until three armed males came in and shoved Phil and the drunk out of their paths.

These fellers weren't miners but were what some called mountain men. They were dressed in leather hides, and each carried a repeating rifle and a pistol, plus a bandolier slung sash-style over their shoulders.

Floyd didn't like the three grizzly-looking guys

pushing his friend around, and he took a step in their direction to fight. One of the mountain men drew his gun and shot Floyd in the chest.

Buck saw it all. He reached down and removed the strap on his gun hammer, brought his hand up to his mouth, blew on his thumb and fingers and said, "You fellers came in here looking for a fight, so why don't you skin leather and try shooting me."

Wilbur, who stood beside Buck, had his hand on the pistol grips ready for a fight.

One of the men spit a gob of tobacco juice on the floor and went for his gun. Buck's hand flashed his weapon from its holster and fired before the mountain men realized they had made a deadly mistake. By the time Wilbur started shooting, two of the men were on the dirt floor, and the third one was going down. Buck had emptied his gun and was in the process of reloading when the bartender came at them with a billy club.

Buck closed the cylinder, pointed the weapon at the saloon man and said, "Barkeep, are you sure you want to come to a gunfight with a piece of wood?"

The barkeep retreated and went back behind the bar top. "I'll stay out of it, but I would appreciate it if you fellers would leave."

"You keep your mouth shut," replied Wilbur with his gun pointed at the barkeep.

Phil kneeled next to Floyd and, after checking for a heartbeat, announced to Buck and Wilbur, "That piece of horse crap done killed Floyd."

Buck looked at Wilbur and Phil. "Go through those dead men's pockets and get any valuables they have. I'll watch your backs."

"Now listen here, mister, you can't be taking their

things. That's pure robbery, in my books," said the bartender.

"No one cares what you think, especially me," said Buck. "They killed our friend for no reason, and we're taking their money so we can pay the undertaker to bury him. If you have a problem with that, I'm sure someone will loan you a gun, and we can settle this disagreement."

"I ain't going up against a fast gun like yourself. That would be suicide," said the barkeep, and he walked off.

The next day, word was out about Buck and Wilbur being gunfighters, and it was easy for them and Phil to obtain work as guards who protected the ore wagons on their way to the closest railroad, which was two days away.

When they'd arrived at the mine in the higher elevations in May, snow was still on the ground, and it was freezing cold at night. They worked all summer, but when September arrived, Phil headed out to a warmer climate.

Buck and Wilbur stayed on for another week until fourteen inches of snow had fallen on the mountains. Some of the miners told them that the snow would melt in a few days, but after another three weeks it would probably stay on the ground until late spring. They waited four days for the snow to begin to melt, and that's when Buck and Wilbur left. Unfortunately, they hadn't been paid in three weeks because the payroll wagon had yet to return to the mining operation by the time they left.

They rode toward the mining town of Georgetown, bundled up on their horses with the temperature in the mid-forties.

Wilbur stopped his horse for a second and said, "I think we should waylay that payroll wagon that owes us our wages and take the mine's payroll, and then we ride hard out of Colorado."

"I don't know about that, Wilbur," said Buck. "I'm sure that wagon is heavily guarded, and if we kill anyone, the law will be after us."

"We won't have to kill anyone if we plan this correctly. I'm not so sure the payroll is guarded that well. There have been times that the payroll came in on an ore wagon returning to the mine without any guards," said Wilbur. "I suppose the company men thought if there were no guards, then no one would have a reason to stop the wagon."

Buck only spoke again once they were on the side of the mountain and saw a convoy of ore wagons coming their way from down below. "Let's get off the road out of sight and let them pass. I'm curious about the guards."

Hidden in the timber alongside the road, Buck and Wilbur watched as five wagons and six guards on horseback passed by them. When they were out of sight, Wilbur started back out to the road, but Buck stopped him.

"I counted six guards but only five wagons."

Wilbur grinned. "I was right; they're trying to make everyone think the money is on one of the wagons that just passed us. I bet a sixth wagon will be along shortly loaded with money and should be easy pickings right here."

Buck eased his horse closer to the road and watched down below. He pointed to something coming off the side of the next mountain. "Come on, Wilbur. We have plenty of time to drag some dead trees into the road."

The trees were easy to get into position, and Wilbur said, "You hide over by that boulder, and I'll get the driver's attention. As soon as he applies the brake, you hop in the back of the wagon and knock him out with your pistol butt. Then we'll grab the money and leave Colorado."

Wilbur covered his face with a handkerchief and tied his horse in the trees. When the wagon stopped in front of the trees blocking the road, he emerged from hiding with his gun drawn. The driver set the wagon brake and Buck came from his hiding place, jumped into the bed, crept up behind the man, and hit him on the back of his head. Buck stood behind the seat and took the reins from the unconscious driver's hands so he had control of the team.

Wilbur ran to the wagon and climbed into the spring seat. He reached under the seat and brought out a locked leather satchel about one-foot tall and one-foot wide.

"Here it is. Let's get out of here and ride," said Wilbur.

The two men bypassed Georgetown and were three miles east of Idaho Springs before they stopped to make camp for the night. After they had a fire blazing and water on for coffee, the two new outlaws laid out their bedrolls and Wilbur found a rock to use on the satchel's lock. After a few hard licks, the lock opened, and he lifted the lid. Stacks of greenbacks tied together with twine lay neatly arranged inside the box.

Buck said, "Let's set it on my bed and count our bounty."

They split the money into two piles and counted. Wilbur said, "I've got $8,345.00."

Buck finished his stack and said, "I have $8,655.00." He smiled at Wilbur. "We have $17,000.00."

"Give me enough from your stack to equal half, and then we can burn the bag," said Wilbur.

Buck counted out $155.00 and handed it to Wilbur and started dancing around the fire singing, "I'm rich, I'm rich." Wilbur joined him and the two circled the fire a few more times until Buck said, "We have to leave Colorado as fast as we can. It may take the mine authorities a day before they can get to Georgetown and notify the law."

"I agree," said Wilbur. "Let's fix some supper and turn in so we can get an early start tomorrow. I think we can be in Denver in two more days if we push our horses."

It took them three days to ride into Denver, where they bought provisions and ate a good meal. The patrons who were eating in the café were talking about the payroll robbery, but Buck and Wilbur didn't get into the conversation. They ate their food and listened.

Their journey took them due east out of Denver for fifteen miles before they turned southeast across the rolling plains. The weather was milder as they rode across the open range, full of buffalo grass for their horses to eat. The third day of riding across the plains, they encountered a large herd of buffalo grazing on the native grass. It was an awesome sight to see so many of them together as they migrated across the rolling hills, filling their bellies.

Wilbur pulled his rifle and walked his horse closer to the herd. Buck followed and stopped when Wilbur put the stock to his shoulder and fired once at a calf. The young buffalo fell to the ground, and the rest of the herd ran off, raising up a cloud of dirt and dust off the ground. Buck felt the ground shake, and the sound of hooves was deafening as the mighty beasts swung to the west and ran away.

When the dust cleared, Wilbur took his knife and skinned the young animal. With the skill of a butcher, he carved out the hindquarters and one of the front shoulders. "We have meat for a few days now. Let's find a good campsite close to water and smoke all the meat," said Wilbur.

"Where do you reckon there's any water out here?" asked Buck.

"We follow where the buffalo came from. I'm sure they've been grazing close to a stream or tank."

Five hours later, they made camp on the banks of the Big Sandy. By midnight, their bellies were full, and the rest of the meat was smoked. It would last them a few days until they came to a town.

Chapter 37

Buck and Wilbur parted ways in Fort Worth, Texas, two weeks after killing the buffalo.

Buck went east, and a few days later rode into Dodd City and hung around there for three days getting familiar with the area before going to the bank and depositing his money. He told the banker, O.W., who he had met the first day in town, that he would come back to town occasionally to deposit more funds and the bank had better take care of his hard-earned money.

A traveling salesman who happened to be in the saloon in Dodd City told Buck of a landowner who was looking for top gunhands north of Greenville, Texas. The man doing the hiring had a large cotton operation with land on both sides of Brushy Branch. Settlers were moving in on his holding and taking his farmland, and the landowner wanted them gone.

Buck arrived at the cotton farm two days after he left Dodd City and was surprised by all the equipment, barns, and workhorses. The man's house was huge compared to most homes he'd passed getting there and resembled one of the big plantations he saw during the war.

As he rode up to the main building, two women sat on the porch with aprons tied around their waist, and both wore bonnets to keep the sun off their heads.

"Hello, ladies, I'm here to talk to the man of the house about a job," said Buck.

"My husband, Neal Gilbert, is talking to some more men behind the house. You can go on back."

"Thank you, ma'am," said Buck, and he tipped his hat and led his horse around the house. He heard a booming coming from the yard. Buck turned the corner and stopped. There was Wilbur with two more men standing in front of a tall, skinny man with a mustache and a tied-down gun on his left side, yelling at them something fierce.

The man—Buck assumed this must be Neal—twisted his upper body slightly toward Buck and reached for his gun. Buck had his palmed before the man could take aim.

"Don't shoot! I'm Neal Gilbert, and I was testing you, and I must say that you passed."

"Hello, Neal, I'm Buck Reed, and skinning that gun on a man could get you shot. I hear you're looking for hands, and I'm available."

"Come over and meet the men you'll work with."

Buck tied his horse to a post, walked up to Wilbur, and stuck out his hand. "Good to see you again." He turned to one of the other men. "I'm Buck Reed. Who might you be?"

"They call me Slim." Slim shook hands with the newcomer.

Buck stuck his hand out to the other feller, who said, "I don't shake hands. I go by Odessa."

Buck grinned at the man. "Nice to make your acquaintances, I think."

Neal said, "I'll pay fifty dollars to each of you to run some squatters off my land."

Buck spoke up. "Neal, I'm not one to kill women and kids. In fact, I'm not one to make people move away from their homes for what I view as chicken feed for pay. If you're paying fifty dollars, I suggest you find someone else to do your dirty work." Buck walked to his horse, untied it, and mounted up.

Wilbur said, "I'm with Buck. My gun is worth way more than fifty dollars."

"I'm with these fellers, Mr. Gilbert. That ain't enough pay for what you want done," said Slim.

Odessa never said anything; he spit the piece of straw he was chewing on to the ground and walked to his horse.

"Now, hold on a second, don't get your drawers in a wad," said Neal. "You tell me what a good price would be for you to stick around and persuade those freeloaders to leave."

"I don't work for less than five hundred dollars," said Buck.

"Why, I can't pay that. That's a small fortune around here," said Neal.

Wilbur said, "Now, Neal, you know that's a drop in the bucket of what you make off the cotton around these parts. If that land them squatters on ain't worth more than five hundred dollars, why do you want them gone?"

Neal stood in silence for a few seconds before he said, "Okay, I'll pay it, but you better get them out of here soon, or I'll want my money back. Is that clear?"

"It's clear as mud. I don't trust you, so I want my pay up front," said Buck.

"Up front! Why, I never heard of such nonsense. I'll pay when the job is done and not before," said Neal.

"No, sir. Like I said, I don't trust you, and it would be

a shame for me to hunt you down for the money. I'll take my money up front, or I'll ride."

Wilbur said, "I'm with him. I want my money up front also."

Slim nodded, agreeing with the other two. Odessa smiled.

"Y'all stay right here, I'll be right back," said Neal, going inside the house.

"You played that mighty well, Buck," said Wilbur.

"I didn't play anything. I'm serious with the man. He's so tight I don't trust him as far as I can throw him. I plan on doing my job if he pays me," said Buck.

Neal came back outside carrying greenbacks in his hand. "Okay, here's your money." He counted out five hundred dollars for each man and said, "There are three squatters on my land over by Tidwell Creek. They are each on about a half section of land, and I want them gone."

"I don't know where this Tidwell Creek is. Can you give us directions to their houses?" asked Slim.

"Yeah, I can. I'll draw you a map," said Neal. When he finished making a crude map, he gave it to them and asked, "When will you go see them deadbeats?"

"I think today is as good as any," said Wilbur. "What do you say, Buck?"

"We can have a talk with them. If they don't want to leave, we'll have a come-to-Jesus meeting."

"Let's ride," said Wilbur.

They stopped at the first house, where a man and woman greeted them out front. "Good afternoon, gentlemen," said the man. The woman stood shielded behind him.

"Evening. We work for the man who owns this land,

Neal Gilbert, and he wants you off his property by tomorrow night," said Wilbur.

The man pointed his finger at Wilbur. "This is our homestead, and we ain't leaving. Now, you men get off my land."

Wilbur pulled his gun. "You don't seem to understand. You're going to leave, or we'll bury you over by that cottonwood tree." Wilbur pointed to a crop of trees to the south of the house. He smiled at the man, backed up his horse to leave, and the others followed.

They had similar conversations with the other two squatters before they headed to Greenville for supper and rooms at the hotel.

Chapter 38

THAT NIGHT, SLIM WENT OFF BY HIMSELF TO CHECK out the gaming parlors in town, while Buck and Wilbur went to the saloon down the street from the hotel. They had drank a few shots of whiskey chased by a couple of beers when three men walked in, and one of the men told the piano player to stop playing.

A man at one of the tables stood up and said, "You keep pounding that music box, mister." He had barely gotten the last word out of his mouth when one of the three newcomers hit him on the chin and knocked him to the floor. Wilbur started to rotate on his bootheel to watch the action, but Buck said, "Turn back around. They may be hunting us."

One of the men said in a gruff voice, "You two strangers at the bar, ease away from the counter and face us. You're about to meet your maker."

Buck glanced over his left shoulder at the three men, and as he did, he removed the safety strap from his gun. He moved his face back where he could see the men in the mirror behind the counter, picked up his beer with his left hand, and brought it to his mouth for one last drink. Sat the empty mug down and brought his right hand up and blew on his thumb and index finger.

Wilbur faced the three men and said, "Now, look here. We don't know you men, and as far as I can remember, we ain't done nothing to you."

"Shut up and draw," said one of the men. "You been harassing our kin, and we don't put up with that."

"Yeah, that's right; now get ready to die," said another of the three.

Buck spun on the ball of his feet and fired at the gunslinger who had been doing most of the talking. He was going down when the second man was hit in the chest. The third man had his gun out but was too slow in firing. Buck had shot all three men, and Wilbur still had his gun in its holster.

Buck opened the cylinder and was reloading when the marshal came rushing in with his gun in his hand. "These three came gunning for us, and we killed them," said Buck. "You can ask anyone here, and they'll tell you what happened."

"Barkeep, is that what happened?" asked the lawman.

"Yep, they came in looking for trouble and called these two out. That feller killed all three of them." He pointed at Buck.

"You're free to leave, and I expect you to be clear of town by tomorrow morning," said the marshal.

Buck and Wilbur started for the hotel. Out on the street, Wilbur grabbed him by the arm. "I knew you were fast, but that was something else. You skinned that gun and was shooting before I could even get mine out of its holster."

"I have my moments," said Buck.

The old man came out of the remembrance of his and

Wilbur's past. He shook his head and said, "You need to stop wallowing in the past and pay attention to your actions."

Since he wasn't familiar with where his old friend lived, he decided to ask the man up ahead who was cutting hay with a machine pulled by two Missouri Mules.

"Sorry to bother you, but do you know where the McCallister Ranch is?" asked Buck.

The man pointed to the south and spit before he said, "I sharecrop for Wilbur, and his house is about a half mile down the road. You might walk lightly around him today. He's mighty riled up and not in a good mood."

"Thanks for the information," said Buck, and he took off south.

Wilbur had a beautiful house about three hundred yards off the road. A split-rail fence surrounded the house and a couple of outbuildings. The other structures, like the barn, workers' quarters, and tool shed, were outside the fence.

The house was painted white with green trim, and flowers grew along the front porch. Two cur dogs came running at Buck's horse, barking and gnashing their teeth. His horse paid them no mind and kept walking to the hitching post beside the steps.

Wilbur came to the screen door. "You mangy mutts, go lay down somewhere before I shoot you myself. Hello, Buck, what brings you out here?"

"I'm on my way home and since I was so close, I thought I'd stop by and see how you're doing."

"Get on down and sit a spell. I have a heavy load on my mind today, which may involve you."

"Involve me? What're you talking about?" asked Buck.

"My boy Rex thinks he's God's gift for drawing a gun. I know he's bucked you a couple of times, and you didn't kill him, but I'm not so sure you can turn your back on him the next time. He's ridden off with that scum of a man Sid Dill and his gang. I tried to talk him out of it, but he pulled his iron on me. Can you believe that? Pulling his gun on his own flesh and blood."

"Yeah, I can believe it," said Buck. "Don't be surprised at what Sid might have that boy do. You and I both know Sid will put him to a test, and the outcome will be violent. He'll want to make sure Rex has a stomach for killing before he can be a part of his gang."

"Yeah, and that's what I'm scared of," said Wilbur. "You see, his entire life, I've talked about how fast Buck Reed is, and that boy couldn't wait until he could get a gun and be as fast as you. I'm afraid Sid will make him go up against you, or he may make him kill you by any means."

Buck wiped his hand across his face. "You might be right about that. Sid and I never saw eye to eye on anything, and I always figured I would have to kill him. I'll be on the lookout for trouble, and if there is any way I can get out of it with Rex, I will."

Wilbur looked distraught. "Buck, you do what you have to do. If you had wanted to kill Rex, he would already be dead. I heard about Rex calling you out in town, and you worked your way out of it, but I'm afraid the boy will call out the wrong man, and then it'll be too late."

Buck went over to Wilbur and gave him a hug. "I best be going. I have a dog now, and I'm sure he will want to eat by the time I get home."

As he rode, he couldn't stop thinking about Rex pulling a gun on his pa. That was unacceptable, but Wilbur was probably too scared the boy would shoot him to do anything about it. If Sid sent Rex looking for him, he'd take care of Sid once and forever.

Biscuit came running down the road toward his master before Buck had even turned into the yard. The dog barked and wagged his tail, glad to have company again. Once Buck dismounted, the dog came and sat on its hind end and looked up at Buck. He raised one of his front legs and rubbed Buck's leg with his paw.

"I'm glad to see you too, boy," Buck said, petting the dog on his head and along his back. "Let me put my horse up, and I'll get you something to eat."

With the horse in the corral, fed and watered, Buck gathered all the eggs—four days' worth—and went to the house. He cooked a dozen eggs, two pounds of bacon, and gave a helping to his hungry dog. The trip had taken its toll on the old gunfighter, and he went to bed early.

Chapter 39

WELL AFTER DAYLIGHT, BUCK THREW THE COVERS back and swung his legs out of the bed. He knew better than to stand up too soon, so he sat on the side of the bed and rubbed his knees before finally getting up. Standing wasn't too bad, but his first step made him grab hold of the nightstand to keep from falling.

Taking it slow and shuffling his feet more than actually walking, he finally made it to the kitchen, still in his long johns. By now he was beginning to loosen up and could walk. He threw a handful of wood shavings in the stove, struck a lucifer, and lit the shavings. By the time the fire had caught enough to add wood, he had filled three buckets with water to heat on the stovetop.

The fourth burner plate heated water for the morning coffee. The long trip had hurt Buck more than he had realized the night before. If he sat down now at the table, his swollen knee joints might not allow him to get back up. The best thing to do to loosen up was to keep moving, and with that in mind, he shuffled back to the bedroom to gather the clothes he would wear to Bonham that day.

By the time he returned to the kitchen, all the water was boiling, so he put the three buckets in the tub and refilled them with the hand pump. While the next buckets were heating, he removed the coffeepot, dumped in ground coffee, and poured in a little cold water to settle the grounds.

Buck refilled his half-empty cup and dumped three buckets of hot water in the tub. The temperature of the water felt right, so he stripped off and eased into the bathtub. He experienced relief from the heat and soaked in the hot water, finishing off his coffee. When the water cooled, he got out and dried off. It was much easier to walk now, and he got dressed without much pain.

Biscuit had been sitting at the back screen looking into the kitchen while Buck bathed. He'd known the dog was there but didn't want to say anything because the large mutt could easily tear through the screen door.

"Biscuit, I'll have you something to eat in a jiffy. I'm thinking some ham, biscuits, and gravy."

Both Buck and Biscuit thought the food hit the spot. The dog scarfed his portion down and found a shade to lie in. Buck fed and watered all his livestock before harnessing up the buggy so he could go into Bonham to see Lucy. He would go by the telegraph office to see if he had any messages from Benny, even though he knew it was too soon.

Biscuit ran around the buggy whining and barking as Buck was about to slap his horse's rump. "Come on up here, boy. You can ride to town with me today if you behave yourself."

The dog leaped up and sat on the seat beside Buck. Anyone seeing the two go down the road would've thought they always rode together.

It was almost noon when Buck stopped the buggy in

front of Lucy's house. "Get down and go lay on the porch, boy," Buck said to his dog.

As Biscuit trotted up to the house, Lucy came outside. "What in the world have you brought with you, Buck? That's got to be the—" Buck held up his hand to quiet his girlfriend.

"Don't say it. It hurts his feelings. He's a very sensitive dog."

She laughed. The dog walked up to her and sniffed her legs and then her hands. He sat on his hind end and looked at Lucy.

"What in the world is he up to now?" she asked.

"He's waiting for you to pet him. I told you that he's a sensitive old coot like me. Do you want to go get some dinner?" asked Buck.

"No, I have too much work today. I have already cooked cornbread and soup, and there is plenty for us all. What's his name?"

"It's Biscuit."

"I wonder why anyone would name such a handsome dog Biscuit," said Lucy, laughing and going back into the house.

Buck filled Lucy in on his travels but left out the part about having to kill some men. It had done his heart good to see his family's graves and purchase tombstones. He told her some men would be delivering cattle to his place and that the man would notify him here in Bonham beforehand.

Buck and Biscuit left after eating and parked on the edge of the street in front of the grocery store. Straight across the street was the entrance at the back of the county courthouse that went to the sheriff's office. A man came out through the doorway, and Buck did a double-take when he noticed the peculiar way he moved his right leg.

The man looked like one of those preachers who wore a white collar on his shirt. As the man walked off in the opposite direction Buck had come from, Buck also noticed the man wore a tied-down holster on both hips. If this man was a preacher, he wasn't an ordinary man of the cloth.

His walk was so different from a man's normal gait. He shifted his weight to his right side and instead of bending his left knee, he kept it stiff. He would take a step, swing a leg forward without bending his knee, and take the step.

That has to be Sergeant Marion Delta. There ain't no one that can copy his walk.

He climbed back into the buggy and started after the limping man. When he was beside him, Buck called out, "Marion, is that you?"

The man turned to the buggy, left hand on his gun, ready to draw. He looked like a man in deep thought as he squinted his eyes. "Sergeant Reed. Well, I'll be doggone. Man, it's been a long time since we fought together."

"I saw you leave the sheriff's office and thought it was you. I recognized your walk. How in the world have you been, Marion?"

"Come on, let's get a cup of coffee and catch up on old times," said Marion.

"Sure thing. Biscuit, stay with the buggy and don't let anyone mess with it," Buck said to the dog.

The two old soldiers were sipping their coffee when Buck asked, "Why are you wearing that collar around your neck?"

"I'm an ordained man of the cloth. I gave my soul to the good Lord shortly after the war. I've pastored five churches over the years, but my true calling is ridding the folks of Texas from rapists, murderers, and thieves," said Marion. He took a sip of coffee. "What about you? What have you been doing lately? I used to hear of you but haven't in a few years."

"I'm trying to settle down and have put a stop to all that nonsense I did in my past. I bought a place between here and Dodd City, and I plan on living out the rest of my days there. I've done many bad things, and I'm now trying to make amends for them."

"Buck, if you died today, where would your soul go? Would you go to Hades or Heaven? That's something I deal with every day. A man needs to have some confidence in where he is with God Almighty."

"I've never been much of a spiritual man since I lost my wife and daughter years ago. Until then, we all attended weekly services, and I was even baptized in the river. I sort of blamed God for taking them and leaving me here. I should have been the one he took," said Buck.

"Well, grief can eat at a man, and it happens more than you know. I ain't going to say anything else about it. That's between you and God now. I just want to drink my coffee and talk about old times," said Marion.

"I did some bounty work once in my life and was good at it. My problem was that I brought more men in dead than alive, so I finally quit and rejoined the Army."

"I vaguely recall you talking about that."

Buck took a drink and motioned the waitress to refill their cups. She obliged and as she left the table, Buck asked, "Who are you after?"

The preacher poured coffee from the cup onto the saucer, lifted it with both hands, and slurped up the hot liquid. "Not a word of this to anyone."

"Not a word," said Buck.

"I'm after Sid Dill, John Flemming, Clyde Earnest, and Edgar Bennett. There could be a couple more, but those are the main ones."

"I can't speak for the rest of them, but John and another feller were here about a week ago. I talked to John right down the street from where we're sitting," said Buck. "Sid was always a mean one. And just so you know, Rex Reynolds, Wilbur's son, is with them now. He's a hothead that wants to make a name for himself as a fast gun."

"That ain't good. I've always respected Wilbur and thought a lot of him back in the war. If his boy is with Sid, then I won't give him any slack. I'll gun him down if I have to," said Marion. He shook his head and kicked dirt with the toe of his boot.

"I wouldn't expect anything less. You have your work to do, and Rex chose to ride with Sid," said Buck, draining his cup. "I have to get going and finish my business in town. If you want to bed down at my place tonight, I'll be heading home in a little while, or you can go on your way," said Buck.

Marion thought for a few seconds. "I would like that, if you don't mind."

"Okay, I'll meet you down at the livery stable in about an hour from now," said Buck, standing up to leave.

"You do have a spare bed at your house, right? I ain't one to sleep on the floor unless I have to," said Marion.

"Yeah, I have a spare bed and it's never been slept in."

"Good, I'll be waiting for you in an hour."

Chapter 40

BUCK TOLD THE TELEGRAPH OPERATOR ABOUT THE telegram he was expecting and asked him to deliver the message to Lucy's house. Then he drove his buggy to the grocery store.

Biscuit waited in the shade under the buggy while his owner went inside to buy more groceries. The clerk helped bring out one large box of provisions and Buck carried a second one. He wanted to cook steaks for supper.

Marion was sitting on the porch of the land office when Buck came down the dusty street. Buck waved and kept going as his friend mounted up and came after him.

They made small talk all the way to Buck's place. Both men unloaded the food and put it in the house before tending to the horses. Buck gathered eggs and fed the chickens so he wouldn't have to do it later. There were enough eggs with what he already had to fry with the steaks and potatoes for supper.

Marion pitched in and helped with supper and the two old friends filled up on a delicious meal. Biscuit also had a meal fit for a king.

"Let's refill our cups and go sit in the living room and jaw some before bedtime," said Buck. "I ain't had no company out here since I moved in."

"Sounds good to me," said Marion.

When the two men were comfortable and the dog lay beside Buck's chair, he asked, "Tell me how you became a preacher."

"After the war ended, I came back home to a sad situation. My pa had died, and my brother and his family had moved in with my ma to help with the farm. My brother ain't no farmer and the place didn't produce a quarter of its potential." Marion took a drank of coffee and scooted his chair far enough away from the small table between the chairs so he could cross his legs.

"I came home and took over the farm, and one night I was reading the Bible and something came over me. I can't explain it, but the Word had an effect on me, and I felt this calling to surrender myself for the Lord's work." He reached inside his jacket and pulled out a small Bible and laid it on the table.

"I worked the fields during the day and studied the Word at night," said Marion, tapping his index finger on the Bible. "We raised a bumper crop that year, and I knew it was the grace of God that provided it. I began to preach at our local church, and it wasn't long after that my ma passed away and I sold the farm."

He picked up his cup and took another swallow. "Within a week after selling the farm, I was hired to preach at a church in Jefferson City, Texas. I was on fire, spreading the word and baptizing folks. I had been there six months when I met a beautiful young woman. Jessi and I courted for three months before we were married." He got up out of his chair and went to the window, staring out into darkness.

"Over the next ten years, we moved every two or three years to serve where the Lord led us. During those years she gave birth to my son, James. I was still loving the work that God had led me to, and the churches I went to increased in numbers and spiritual discernment."

Buck got up, went to the stove, brought back the coffeepot, and refilled his and Marion's cup.

Marion got up and walked to the window. "Eight years ago, I was called to a church down by Tyler, Texas. We had been there two months, and the church was growing. I had been to a meeting with some of the men in town and when I arrived home, no one was there. I walked out the back door of the parsonage, and there was my wife and son on the ground, covered in blood. I ran to my wife. After that, it's a bit hazy, but I remember feeling a searing pain on the side of my head."

Marion came back to the chair, sat down, removed his hat, and brushed strands of hair out of the way to expose a scar on the right side of his head. "When I came to, I had to wipe blood from my eyes so I could see. I tried to stand but couldn't, so I crawled on my belly to my wife. She was dead. I then went to my son. He had been shot in the back of his head." Marion was clearly distraught; tears were streaming down his cheeks and his voice quivered talking about what had happened to his family. He took a big gulp of coffee and regained his composure before finishing the story.

"I was mad, brokenhearted, and didn't understand why anyone would hurt my wife and son. As I was holding my son's bloody head in my lap, I called out to God for understanding and vengeance. I laid my boy down and crawled back to my wife, and that's when I heard this voice."

"What voice?" asked Buck.

"It was a voice from Heaven. It said, 'Vengeance is Mine, saith the Lord. My good and faithful servant, go and find the men that did this and do it in the name of the Lord.'"

"God spoke to you?" asked Buck with a questioning look on his face.

"I don't know if it was God or one of his angels, but someone spoke to me, and I took the message to heart. It was like something magical came over me."

Buck sat in silence waiting on his old friend to continue.

"At first, I thought savages had killed my family. I suspect the men that did the horrible thing expected me to think that. But Indians don't usually wear boots, and I also saw blood and skin under my wife's fingernails. She put up a fight, and I knew one of the criminals would have scratch marks on his face. I don't know how long it took me to examine all the evidence the men had left, but I figured out that it was three men. One of them had scratch marks, one rode a horse with two worn shoes on the hind hooves, and the third had small feet. I found his tracks inside the church, where he stole the silver candle stands."

"They killed your wife and son for a silver candle stand?" asked Buck.

"They stole three stands and two gold cups that we used for communion."

"Thieves will take anything and never think twice about it. It never surprises me what they will do for a little money," said Buck.

"Yup," said Marion, and he sighed. "After I buried my loved ones and healed for a few days, I rode after those men. I was able to find the one she marked up with her fingernails two weeks later in a cathouse in Tyler, Texas. From him, I acquired the names and whereabouts of the other two men. Then I gave him the same treatment he gave my wife and cut his throat."

"Did you stay around and talk to the law or see if there was a reward on the guy before you rode off?" asked Buck.

"I stayed and gave my statement to the law. He showed me reward posters for all three of them. I left the sheriff's office and went to a house outside of Tyler and found the other two living with a harlot. I shot them and turned their bodies over the law, and got paid fifty dollars for the whole gang. After that, I started hunting down outlaws."

"It seems that we have a lot in common," said Buck. "My wife and daughter died, and that was what caused me to hit rock bottom and join the Army."

"Yes, I suppose we do have some things in common," said Marion. "Well, it's getting late, and I have a long way to ride tomorrow, so I'm going to turn in."

"Good night. I'll have breakfast for you in the morning," said Buck.

"Thanks, old friend."

Chapter 41

BUCK AND MARION ATE BREAKFAST THE FOLLOWING morning, and after their third cup of coffee Marion said, "I appreciate you inviting me out here yesterday. I probably told you more about my family than you wanted to know, but it was the truth."

"I wanted to know about you. I'll keep it to myself. If you want to take some biscuits and bacon with you, I can wrap them up," Buck said.

Marion pointed to the back screen door. "I would say you might ought to give it to your dog. I think he's about ready to come through that door after it."

Buck laughed. "I reckon you're right about that." He took the leftovers to the dog, and Biscuit consumed them in seconds.

Marion rode off and Buck stood on the porch watching his friend until he was out of sight. He sat down on the porch thinking about what his old friend had told him about his family. Buck didn't say anything, but Marion's story brought back memories about what happened to his family. Buck still felt the sadness of not having them with him. Although there was a sense of comfort in his heart from visiting their graves, a visit didn't overshadow the hurt he still had from losing time.

Out of nowhere, he thought about Ginny Meadows, whom he hadn't seen in almost twenty years. Why had she come to mind? Could he have loved her if he had given their relationship more time? Should he have told her how he hated plowing at her farm? How he had left her was not something he was proud of. She had given him a home and welcomed him as her lover, only to be abandoned. He knew it was wrong all those years ago, and it was time to make amends for his actions. But he would ride into Bonham and talk to Lucy before he did anything.

An hour later, he walked into the wash shed behind Lucy's house and surprised her while she was separating white clothes from dark ones. They made small talk as she continued to work, and then he said, "I have something I need to tell you."

"What have you done?" she asked, standing straight with her hands on her hips.

He explained his relationship with Ginny and why he'd left her, and how he'd never returned to explain or apologize to her for leaving unannounced.

"So, is that bothering you to the point that you think you need to apologize and ask her to forgive you? Or do you want to go back to her and start over?"

"No, I do not want to start over with her. I want to be honest with you and build our relationship without my baggage getting in the way. When I left her, I just saddled my horse and rode off. She probably didn't even know I was gone for a while, and I can only imagine how much that hurt her, and I need to ask her to forgive me."

Lucy stepped forward, gave Buck a hug, and kissed him. "Then go and get it over with. If you think you did her wrong, you probably did. Come see me when you get back; I'll be waiting for you." She kissed him again and returned to her work.

Buck walked to the buggy and took off home to pack a bag. He would leave that very day and spend the night in a hotel in Paris. The following day, he'd ride to Ginny's farm.

Buck didn't think much about what he would say to Ginny until he was in his room at the Lamar Hotel. He began to reminisce about his relationship with Ginny. He'd never really loved her as he should have when he moved in with her on her farm. It had been more of a companionship relationship, and it took care of his needs at the time. He was sick and tired of bounty hunting, and she needed someone to help with the farm work. He should have talked to her when he decided to leave instead of just riding off. That had been wrong, and he wasn't sure she would even talk to him now. But he had to try to apologize for the bad thing he had done to her. He hoped that she still lived on the farm, and more importantly, he hoped she was still alive.

The farm looked the same when he stopped at the closed gate along the path that led to the house. He leaned over the saddle and lifted the latch, and the gate swung open. He walked Red through, closed the gate, and rode on to the house. The white paint he remembered was mostly gone from the sun and wind, and only a little faded color could be seen on the weathered boards.

The barn needed upkeep, as did the fences around the corral and garden. He could tell someone had been growing vegetables in the garden recently, and the fields surrounding the house and barn had a healthy-looking crop of cotton.

He dismounted and wrapped the reins around the

lone hitch post. The door opened and Ginny emerged, holding a double-barrel shotgun.

"Who are you, and why are you on my property?"

"Hello, Ginny, it's Buck Reed, so don't shoot." He removed his hat and said, "I come here to apologize to you for leaving the way that I did. I hope you find it in your heart to forgive me."

"I ought to shoot you right where you stand, you no-good scoundrel. You ran off and abandoned me when I needed you the most."

"I'm sorry, but walking behind a plow wasn't what I wanted to do with my life. I know it was wrong to ride off the way I did, and I'm truly sorry," said Buck as he walked toward the porch steps.

"I don't know where you come from, and I don't care. I'll never forgive you for what you did, so you might as well get on that horse and skedaddle out of here. I don't want to hear your whining about forgiveness."

Buck nodded and put his hat back on. He asked, "Why won't you forgive me? You never really loved me. Our relationship was more like friends. I helped with the work."

She lowered the gun barrel and asked, "You don't know, do you?"

"Know what?" asked Buck.

"I was pregnant with your child when you up and left me, that's why. I had to keep this place going and do everything myself. I felt ashamed going into town with everyone talking about me behind my back, knowing my baby didn't have a father nowhere around." She set the gun against the house and came down the steps to stand in front of Buck.

"I had no idea you were pregnant. I'm so sorry that I wasn't here for you and the baby," said Buck. He was about to say something when Ginny's right fist came at him and landed on his left jaw. Before she could throw another haymaker, he stepped backward.

"I deserved that, but don't do it again." Buck was not one to take a lick for the fun of it. He usually retaliated. "Do I have a son or daughter?" he asked.

Ginny flexed her fingers and answered his question. "I have a daughter, and her name is Carol. She lives in Paris and has a four-year-old son. I never told her anything about who her pa was."

"Ginny, I really want to meet her and my grandson. Will you take me to her?"

"First off, you have no rights to her or my grandson. You never even knew about her. I think it's time you leave and don't come back."

"You didn't say anything about being pregnant while I was here. Yes, I left you, but I didn't know you were with a child. I've done a lot of bad things in my life, but having an offspring is not one of them. Please, I beg of you to let me meet my daughter."

She stood with her head down and her hands covering her face. "Okay, I'll take you to her," she said. "You always were a sweet-talker. Go harness up my wagon, and I'll introduce you to her, but don't expect her to invite you for supper. And don't think for a second you can move back in with me. Me and you are over."

"I understand, and you don't have to worry about me wanting to move in. I have my own place and a woman that I care for in Bonham, Texas."

She didn't reply and went back into the house. Buck walked to the barn and got her wagon ready to travel.

As he rode beside the wagon, the joy of finding out he had a daughter flooded his emotions. He suffered through the loss of one daughter long ago and nothing would take her place, but he wanted to meet the offspring that he and Ginny had produced. His heart continued to thump with the exuberance of getting to meet not only his daughter but also his grandson.

Ginny began to talk on their way to his daughter's house; he found out that she had been leasing her land for the past twelve years to a local farmer. Her health would not allow her to work the soil anymore, and it wasn't financially feasible for her to hire a full-time farmhand.

Chapter 42

When Buck and Ginny stopped in front of Carol's house, Ginny said, "Let me do the talking since I don't know what she'll do when I tell her that her pa is a famous gunfighter."

"I'm trying to put the gunfighting behind me and live a normal life."

"For your daughter's and grandson's sake, I hope you're telling the truth. Let's go see if she's here." Ginny led the way and Buck followed behind her. As she opened the screen door, a young woman wearing a dress made out of flour sacks came to the door.

"Come on in, Mama. Who you got with you?" Carol asked.

Buck took a good look at her face to see if she favored him, and he was glad to see she had blue eyes like his and high cheekbones like her mother.

"Carol, I'd like for you to meet Buck Reed."

Carol put out her hand and said, "My pleasure to meet you, Mr. Reed."

He held her hand longer than he probably should

have and said, "No, ma'am, the pleasure is all mine. It's so nice to meet you."

"So Mama, why do you have a fast gunhand with you, and why'd you bring him here?" Carol asked.

Ginny looked at Buck and then back to her daughter. "Well, you see, Buck is your daddy."

"What! No way you're my daddy," said Carol, going to a chair and sitting down with her hands covering her face as she started to cry.

Buck walked to her and said, "I'm sorry I haven't been around all these years. I didn't know until today that Ginny was pregnant when I left her farm. I hated working the land, and I left. I never came back until today to ask her forgiveness, and that was when I found out about you. I know this is hard to comprehend right now, but I hope we can get to know each other. I'm so glad to meet you and I know I can't make up for the past, but I'm hoping that you'll forgive me for not being there for you growing up."

Carol removed her hands from her face and wiped the tears from her eyes. "You may be the man who got my mother pregnant, but you sure ain't my daddy. A daddy is there for his wife and children, and you ain't never been here."

"I agree with you. But I want to be here for you and your son from now on. I've made a lot of mistakes, but you sure ain't one of them. I hope you will give me a chance to be the pa you never had," said Buck.

"This is a lot to understand, and I need time to think," said Carol.

"Can I meet my grandson?" asked Buck.

Carol thought for a few seconds before she said, "He's asleep right now, but if you come by later, you can meet him."

"Thank you. I'm going to see that Ginny makes it home, and then I'll be back," said Buck.

"Fine! I'll be here," said Carol, staying seated while Buck and Ginny left.

"That went much better than I thought it would," said Ginny when they were out of the house.

"I thought it went well," said Buck. "Does Carol have a husband?"

"No, she and David Newton were planning on getting hitched, but then she got pregnant. He ran off with some floozy that worked in the courthouse in Paris. Carol has had a hard time making a living for her and Timmy. She toiled from daylight to dark on the farm before she moved to town and took a job at the mercantile store. It's hard work, but she ain't afraid to get her hands dirty."

"How about you? You said you lease out your land, but does that earn you enough to pay your bills and have enough to live a good life?" asked Buck.

"It covers the bills, but I don't have any extra, and I can't help Carol. My ticker gives me fits, and the doctor told me I had to stop doing so much."

They rode back to Carol's place and Buck took the wagon to the barn, unhooked the team, and fed them hay before he returned to the house. Ginny sat in her rocking chair on the porch.

He untied his horse and said, "I'll be seeing you, Ginny. I want to thank you for taking me to meet Carol."

"Buck, hold on. I need to tell you that I ain't happy with you, but I forgive you for what you did. I wish I had done the same thing years ago and ran off from this God-forsaken place. Working the farm has taken its toll on my health, but there ain't nothing I can do about it now. You be careful going home."

"Thanks, Ginny. That means a lot to me. I must say, you raised a beautiful, hardworking daughter."

Buck took off back to town to meet his grandson.

The child was in the front yard playing when Buck stopped his horse outside the fence. He watched little Timmy run and play. Carol came to the door and stood watching Buck.

She finally said, "Get off that horse and come on in the house."

Buck did as she said. Inside, she paced back and forth in the living room while he watched, standing with his hat in his hand. She turned and came to him. He was expecting another fist to the face, but instead, she put her arms around his neck and hugged him tightly. He didn't know what to say, but he put his arms around his daughter and wept. They stood holding onto each other, crying for a few minutes.

"I'm so glad I came here today. I've missed so much of your life and want to be here for you," said Buck

"Hush, I don't want to hear what you want to do. I want to see what you do. Words are cheap, but actions pack a punch. I wish Mama had told me a long time ago who my pa was."

"I was as much unaware of you as you were of me, and I admit I did Ginny wrong by leaving the way I did. Today I begged her for forgiveness, and she accepted my apology. That doesn't make it right, but it does open up a dialogue since we share a beautiful daughter," said Buck.

She removed her arms from around her pa's neck and called for her son to come in. When he was in the house, she said, "Timmy, this man is your grandpa."

"Hi, Timmy. Would you come here and give me a hug?" Buck asked as he lowered himself onto one knee. The boy came forward, and Buck gave him a hug. After the embrace from the boy, the old grandfather stood up more easily than he had in years.

Buck stayed another two hours talking to Carol and Timmy before he told them he had to go but would be back soon.

Buck and Carol stood on the porch as he got ready to leave. He pulled out some rolled-up money from his britches pocket and handed it to his daughter. "You take this. Pay bills and buy you and Timmy something nice."

"I can't take your money," said Carol.

"Why not? Everything I own is yours, now that I know you're my daughter. Now take this money, and there's more when you need it." He mounted up and headed back to Bonham.

Chapter 43

Buck was so elated at having a daughter and grandson that he rode all the way home without stopping. It was well after midnight when he arrived, unsaddled Red, and left him in a stall in the barn until morning.

It was still dark when Buck woke up to Biscuit barking and raising a ruckus in the backyard. He grabbed his gun and listened for a few seconds. Then he got himself out of bed and shuffled to the nightstand, on which sat a pitcher of water and a bowl. Two handfuls of water to his face woke him up enough to head to the back door to investigate what was going on outside.

The dog had his mouth clamped down on the chest of a raccoon and violently shook it every few seconds to check if it was still alive. Buck stood barefoot on the back porch with water still dripping off his face and scanned the rest of the yard. He noticed two dead chickens in the pen. It seemed the raccoon had got into the pen and was at work getting his dinner when Biscuit had caught him.

Buck went back into the kitchen and heated coffee water while he put on his clothes and boots. He had to see where the raccoon had broken into the pen and how his dog had entered.

It was getting light outside after he'd had one cup of coffee, and it was time to check the damage to the pen. A hole the size of a bucket had been made in the chicken wire, and he could see paw prints and strands of hair indicating Biscuit and the varmint had both used it. A trip to the barn for a piece of wire was all it took to make repairs. Back at the barn, he harnessed the horse to the buggy before going to the house for more coffee.

After one more cup, he went outside and put on gloves to pick up the dead raccoon and the two dead chickens. He would dispose of them somewhere along the road to Bonham. He figured the buzzards and coyotes needed to eat too, but he wanted them far away from his place.

Red was still tired from the long ride home and was turned out in the pasture to graze. Buck took the buggy and headed to Bonham to see his lady friend. He kept thinking about Carol and Timmy all the way into town.

He was still on a high when he stopped in front of Lucy's house. She wasn't in the wash shed or the house, so he sat on the front porch for about twenty minutes, waiting for her return. Impatient and wanting to talk to her, he loaded back up into the buggy and headed to Main Street. She'd likely be at the ladies' clothing store or the mercantile, where she purchased her washing supplies.

While letting his horse walk down the dusty street, he heard someone call his name. He stopped the buggy in the street and craned his head around to his left. The telegraph clerk was coming his way, waving a slip of paper in the air. Buck hadn't thought about his cattle being delivered since he'd met Carol and little Timmy.

"Mr. Reed, I received this message a few minutes ago.

I was going to the clothing store to give the message to Lucy when I saw you coming down the street."

"Thanks a lot, I appreciate you bringing it to me. Did I hear you say that Lucy is at the store?" Buck asked.

"Yes, sir. She's helping out there for a few weeks. Gladys, the owner, fell and broke her leg yesterday. She's laid up, and she hired Lucy to help until she's better."

"Thanks again for bringing me the message," said Buck, putting it in his pocket.

"I better be getting back to my office. I'll see you around, Mr. Reed."

"You can call me Buck. What's your name?"

"It's Luke West. You have a nice day. Say hi to Lucy for me."

"I'll do that, and thanks again."

Buck took off to the ladies' clothing shop. He felt a little out of place when he walked in since he was the only man in the store, and all the merchandise was for women. A young lady in her early twenties was straightening up clothing on a rack. He asked her, "Excuse me, miss, can you direct me to where Lucy is?"

"Why yes, sir. Just keep going to the back of the shop, and you'll find her in the sewing room."

"Thank you."

Lucy came out of the sewing room. "I thought I heard your voice. Come on back, I'm working in here today."

She put her arms around his neck for a kiss as soon as he was in the room. "I'm glad you're back. How did it go?" she asked.

"It didn't start out well, but it ended excellent. I have a daughter and a grandson. I had no idea Ginny was pregnant when I left, and I deeply regret not being in my daughter's life while she was growing up. That's what I need to talk to you about."

Lucy sat down and looked concerned.

"Sweetie, it's all good," said Buck. "I want to run something by you. You're the one I love, and I want us to be happy together. I also want my daughter and grandson to have a better life than they do now. There are two other houses on my land. One was used by the previous owner as the foreman's residence, and the other for slaves. What if I have them remodeled and let my daughter live in one and Ginny in the other one?"

"I don't like the idea of this Ginny woman living in one of your houses," said Lucy. "That seems kind of convenient for some hanky-panky to me."

"There will never be anything between me and Ginny. I took care of that long ago when I left, and I have no romantic feelings for anyone but you. It was only a thought about her moving. She's in bad health, and it would be good for her to be close to her daughter. That's all I'm thinking."

"What about me and you? What are your intentions for us?" she asked.

"I was hoping we could get married, and you come to the ranch with me."

"That's a possibility, but I want to continue as we are for a while longer and see how we grow on each other. I care for you deeply and hope you respect my thoughts and feelings."

"If that's what you want, I'll respect your judgment, but don't be surprised when I hound you to get hitched."

She stood up, hugged her man, and said, "I think it would be great if your daughter and grandson moved onto your land. They need you, and you need them, especially now that you're trying to make amends for your mistakes in life. I'm also okay with that woman living in one of the houses as long as you keep your distance and she knows I'm your lady friend."

"I've already told her that I have someone who I love. I haven't said anything to Carol or Ginny about moving here. Before I asked them, I wanted to talk to you first and get your opinion."

"When do you plan on asking them?" asked Lucy.

"I'm thinking about taking the train to Paris and to talk to Carol. I'll leave it up to her if she wants to talk to her mom about moving. Ginny would have to leave her home of forty years, and she may not want to. That's up to her and Carol on what Ginny does. I'm only offering the house."

"That sounds like a good plan. You better get going. The eastbound train will be here soon," said Lucy, and she kissed him. "I'll be waiting for you to return tonight."

"Yeah, I better take my buggy to the livery and get to the train station."

Chapter 44

BUCK STEPPED OFF THE PASSENGER CAR AND ONTO the train station platform when he arrived at Paris at eleven that morning. He stopped a porter who was moving suitcases on push carts. "Can you recommend someone who can drive me someplace in a carriage?"

"Yes sir. Follow me outside, and I'll get you a ride."

The porter helped Buck into one of two carriages available for hire. "One other question: what time does the westbound train stop here?" Buck asked him.

"That would be a quarter after three, sir."

"Much obliged," said Buck, handing the man a silver dollar.

When Buck arrived at his daughter's house, Carol wasn't home and the old dad didn't know where to look, so he had the carriage driver take him to Ginny's farm.

As they headed out of town, they met Ginny in her wagon, coming from the opposite direction. "Good morning, Ginny. Do you know where Carol is? I need to talk to her," Buck asked.

"She's most likely working at the seed place. It's south of the square, about a half mile."

The driver said, "I know where it is and can take you there."

"Okay, let's get going. I'll see you later, Ginny."

"You all get in front of me. I'll sit here for a few minutes and let your dust settle, and I'll be along directly."

"Thanks Ginny," said Buck. The driver turned his carriage around and headed back to town.

He found Carol in the back of the seed warehouse, sewing sacks full of seeds with a long needle and thread. Timmy ran around, playing with a stick like it was a gun. "Hello, Carol. Do you get off for dinner, or do you work through it?" Buck asked.

"I came in early today so I can take time to eat. Are you buying?"

"Yes, I'm buying. I have a carriage waiting to take us."

"I'll meet you at the wagon. I need to get Timmy cleaned up and tell my boss where I'm going."

After eating their food, Carol, Timmy, and Buck continued to sit at the table while the boy ate dessert. Buck said, "I came here today to talk to you about something important. The land I own has two other houses besides the one I live in. I don't know how to say this, so I'll be frank. I would love for you and Timmy to come live on my ranch and take over running it. I have cattle on the way there as we speak, so you can make a good living off the herd. You can even move your ma in with you or into the other house if you want, provided she's willing to sell her farm. I have plenty of money in the bank for us all to have what we need, and with the calf crop each year, you would have enough income to purchase more cattle. When Timmy gets older, he can take over for you."

She stared at him without saying anything for a few

seconds. "I'm surprised you would do something like this. I can't answer now, but I sincerely appreciate you offering us houses. I need to talk to Mama and see what she wants to do. I don't feel right leaving her alone since she has sacrificed for me all these years."

"I agree. I want you to know that Ginny and I don't have any romantic feelings for each other. I have a lady friend in Bonham that I want to marry someday. If you and Ginny decide to take me up on my offer, I'll need a few days to have the houses worked on, and then I can send some men in wagons to haul your belongings to the ranch."

"Are you going back today?" she asked.

"Yes, I'm catching the three-fifteen train home. You can send me a telegram with your decision."

"Okay. I better get back to work so I don't get fired. Thanks, Buck, for coming and talking to me."

As they left the café and were on the boardwalk, someone said behind them, "Carol Meadows, I want to talk to you, honey."

Buck started to turn around, but Carol took his hand in hers and stopped him. "Don't. It's Ben Ivers, and he's probably drunk."

"Carol, you better stop and talk to me, or I'm liable to kick that old man you're with into the dirt."

Buck wasn't one to take a threat lightly and faced the man. "Come on and try to kick me into the street."

"Hold it, you two," said Carol, stepping between the two men. "Ben, I'd like you to meet my pa. His name is Buck Reed."

Carol moved out of the way, and Ben took a step backward and almost fell off the boardwalk. "I'm a little drunk and think I'll go somewhere else. I don't want no quarrel with you, Mr. Reed."

Buck pointed his left index finger at Ben. "Don't ever let me hear you disrespect my daughter again, or it might get my dander up."

"Oh, yes sir. I didn't mean to disrespect you. My apologies, Miss Carol." He stumbled off the boardwalk into the street and started off as quickly as he could walk.

"That was quite interesting," said Carol. "Your reputation must reach farther than I thought. I never seen Ben so nervous before."

"No one is going to disrespect my daughter or my grandson," said Buck.

When they returned to the seed store, Buck said his goodbyes and had the carriage driver take him back to the train station.

While waiting for the train to arrive, he pulled the telegram out of his shirt pocket. He had forgotten that he even had it. Benny had left yesterday with the herd and should be at Buck's spread the day after tomorrow. That was good news, but there was a lot to do at the ranch to get ready for the cattle. The fences needed to be checked to be sure they would keep the cattle in, and he would have to get someone to cut hay, or buy some for the winter, which was coming soon.

Buck was deep in thought when he heard the engineer blowing the train's horn as it approached the station. He walked to the boarding platform and waited for the cars to come to a stop.

The hour-long trip back to Bonham gave him time to think about all the details he needed to take care of, but the number one thing on his mind was seeing Lucy. He wanted to talk to her and discuss a lot of ideas about the ranch. It seemed like life was going a hundred miles an hour, and he needed to put a good plan in place if Carol moved to his ranch. Lucy would know how to help him.

Chapter 45

BUCK COULD ONLY TALK TO LUCY FOR A FEW MINUTES since she was busy at the dress shop, so he went home to feed Biscuit, tended to the chickens, and cooked supper. It had been a long, tiring day and he was spent both emotionally and physically. Reading always took his mind to a different place, and after one chapter of Moby Dick, he went to bed.

The next morning, the revived old dad felt better than he had in months. He attributed it to a sound night of sleep without nightmares. While Buck and Biscuit ate breakfast, he decided to ride around his land to make sure the fences were up.

He wanted to look at the meadows and see if there was a pasture where he could cut hay for the winter. He also wondered if there was a water tank on his land, or if Bois d'Arc Creek was the only water source for his property.

It took him most of the day to ride the entire boundary of his land, and in doing so, he found a spot where someone had an active campsite along the creek bank.

They had made camp in a runoff gully that flowed water to the creek when it rained. He figured out quickly that it was the escaped Indians that the Army patrol was looking for. He wouldn't do anything about it as long as they left him alone and didn't try to steal from him.

Buck rode back into the barn and dreaded dismounting. He'd been in the saddle so long that he knew he'd be sore. When he eased out of the saddle, his left leg gave out, but he was able to grab hold of a post to keep from falling. It scared him so much that he broke out in a cold sweat. Buck took his time getting his legs to work before removing the saddle and caring for his horse.

By the time he finished at the barn and fed the chickens, it was time for supper. Biscuit followed him everywhere and kept looking at his owner with sad eyes, like he wanted something.

Buck cooked bacon, eggs, and potatoes and made extra so his dog would also have plenty. Biscuit wolfed down his food in seconds.

"Dang, boy, you must have been starving today," said Buck as he took his time to savor the taste of his food.

After he cleaned the kitchen and poured himself a glass of water, he went out on the porch. With the dog by his side and close enough to pet, Buck started talking to him.

"Biscuit, we have cattle coming to the ranch tomorrow or the next day. Unless I tell you to get after them, you'll have to leave them alone. We also may have a woman and little boy come to live down there in that other house. The boy will need looking after, so I want you to protect him when he's outside."

The dog rose from the floor, and the hair on his back stood up. Biscuit showed his teeth and growled. Buck knew they were in danger, so he moved as fast as he could to get in the house for his rifle. He had on his pistol, but this time, a little more firepower might be necessary if it was the Indians whose camp he was at today.

He stood in the doorway as six armed Indians on horses came to a stop in his yard. Buck stepped onto the porch, set the rifle against a post, and asked, "What can I do for you, fellers?"

"I'm William Redhorse. People call me Standing Horse. We need meat, beans, and coffee. I have money for the things we require."

"I'm Buck Reed. I own this land, and I know you have a camp on the creek on the back of my property. I don't have enough of the items you request, but I can get what you need when I go to Bonham."

"We have a two-day supply. Thank you, Buck Reed. We will be back in two days." With that, the braves turned their horses and rode off around the side of the house.

Buck sat back down and decided he'd get the men the provisions they wanted. He would give them one cow to eat as well, if his cattle came in time.

All the traveling and riding had caused tiredness to take over his worn-out body, and he went to bed. Slightly after midnight, Buck saw his wife and little Belinda in his dreams. He reached out to them but couldn't touch them, and it angered him so much that he woke and sat up in bed and looked at his pocket watch on the nightstand.

He pondered about the dream and then reflected on Carol. Life was strange at times. He'd lost Belinda and his wife, but gained Carol and Timmy. Such a miracle could only have happened by the grace of God. Then he thought about what Marion had asked him when he had spent the night at his house.

Where would he go if he died today? He had killed, stolen, lied, and broken almost every one of the Ten

Commandments during his life. Still, he remembered that he had decided on Jesus and had been baptized when he and Mary Jane were together and went to church every Sunday.

This was the first time he had even considered Christianity in years. How could God forgive him for all the bad things he had done? Now he had a daughter and grandson and hoped God would bring them here to live close to him.

Buck went back to sleep after assessing all the blessings he had received in his life.

When he woke up the following morning, the sun was already up, and after getting dressed, he cooked his and Biscuit's breakfast standing on still-tired, aching legs. After the chores around the ranch were finished, he shaved, took a bath, and dressed for a trip into Dodd City to buy the provisions the Indians had requested and to replenish his carrying-around cash.

Buck harnessed his horse to the buggy and was loading up his dog when he heard a volley of gunshots coming from the back of his property. He grimaced, knowing that men were most likely dying down by the creek. He heard Henry repeating rifles. The Army patrol had found the Indian camp.

Not wanting to get involved, he and Biscuit took off toward Dodd City. He had turned east on the main road when he changed his mind about his destination. Buck made a U-turn in the road and headed toward Bonham instead. He wanted to talk to Lucy and needed to find someone to cut hay for the cattle. He'd also see if he had a telegram from Carol.

The telegraph office was his first stop, but there was no message, so he went to the west edge of town to the livestock pens, where locals brought their horses, cows, chickens, and sheep to market once a week to buy or sell. He hoped someone would know a farmer he could hire to cut his hay.

Under the porch cover of an old shed, three older men sat whittling on pieces of cedar, making figurines.

"Howdy, men, I'm Buck. Do you happen to know anyone who cuts and gathers hay?"

One of the old men put his small carving in the bill pocket of his overalls and said, "Peter Bench has one of those newfangled baling contraptions, and he makes his living by cutting hay. I saw him in a meadow this morning on my way into town."

Buck didn't say anything, but one of the other men did. "Francis, tell him where you saw Peter working. He's waiting for the location."

"Oh, yeah, I reckon you need to know what pasture," said Francis. "You will see him a mile west on the north side of the road. You can't miss him."

"Thanks. Have a good day," said Buck, and he headed off.

The old feller had been right. Buck spotted a team of workhorses pulling a sickle-bar cutting machine and another team pulling a hay rake, right where the man had indicated. Buck waited until the man on the cutter was close to the road and waved him down.

"I'm looking for Peter. Would that be you?" asked Buck.

"Yep, that's me. What can I do for you, mister?"

"I'm Buck Reed, and I have a small ranch east of Bonham, about two miles east and three north. I'm having cattle delivered either today or tomorrow, and I need hay cut for the winter."

"I can sure do that. I'm booked for the next few weeks, but I can get to it after that. Let me look in my book." The man pulled a writing pad out of his pocket and started counting on his fingers. "I can be there in about fifteen days. The grass should still be green by then."

"Good. Do you also put it in the barn, or do you know someone who does?"

"I can do it all for you, Buck. I have a good crew that hauls it to the barn and stacks it for you. How many acres do you want to be baled up?" asked Peter.

"I don't rightly know. I have forty head of cattle coming, but I'm thinking about buying another forty head, so let's plan on enough to feed a hundred head of cattle."

Forty and forty ain't no hundred, that's only eighty," said Peter.

Buck wanted to laugh but didn't. "Some of that eighty will have calves to feed."

Peter nodded. "Yep, I reckon so. It'll take me three days to cut that much. If it takes longer, that's fine with me. I ain't got nothing but time."

"Thanks, Peter. I'll see you in a little over two weeks," Buck said, and he walked back to his buggy.

He had just passed the telegraph office when he heard his name called out. The operator had a piece of paper in his hand, waving it at Buck. Buck moved the buggy to his right and stopped so he could take the message without getting out of the seat.

"Thanks a lot, I appreciate you stopping me."

"You're welcome. I'll be seeing you, sir." The man turned and went back inside while Buck read the message. It was from Carol, and said, *We will all move.*

He left the buggy where it was and was getting down from it when the telegraph operator spoke from the doorway. "Buck, do you want to send a reply?"

"Yeah. Say, 'I will contact you when the house repairs are finished.'"

"Yes sir. You go ahead and tend to your business. I'll catch up with you on the charge the next time you come in."

"Thanks, I'll be seeing you." The old dad smiled and slapped the horse's reins, on his way to find Morell. Buck hoped he was working at the furniture store today and wouldn't have to hunt the man down at someone's home doing work.

Chapter 46

Buck was in luck. Morell was loading a table into the wagon bed when Buck pulled up outside the furniture store. He stood for a second before getting out of the buggy.

"Hello Morell," said Buck as he approached the man.

"Hey Buck, how you doing?"

"I'm fine. Are you available to work on my other two houses?"

"I can be. I only work here in my spare time," said Morell, wiping his brow with a handkerchief. "What do you want done, and how soon do you want me to start?"

"I want the insides remodeled, as well as any repairs that need to be done on the outsides, plus paint. The old foreman's house will have a lady and her small child living there, so she'll use at least two bedrooms. The old slave house will have a single lady in it, and she is getting older like me," said Buck.

"Me and my boys will go out there today and make a list of everything I think that needs work," said Morell. "I recall they are in pretty bad shape, and if you want water in them, it will probably cost upward of a couple of hundred dollars to make all the repairs."

"That's fine. I also want bathtubs in both houses with water pumps. If you need to hire more men to help you, that's okay. I need them ready as soon as you can, especially the interior, so everyone can get moved in," said Buck.

"I may hire a few fellers I know, and maybe we can work on both houses simultaneously. I can also have some of my boys' friends dig the ditches for the water lines. That will save me a lot of time since the ground is so hard right now. We sure are in need of rain," said Morell. "When I have the repairs listed, I'll start gathering the material. I think we may get started tomorrow, if that's okay with you."

"You get started, and I'll ensure the lumberyard and hardware store sell you what you need. I'll most likely be gone while you're at my house, so go ahead with your plan."

"I'll take care of it, and I sure appreciate the work, Buck."

"Thanks, Morell. I'll see you in a day or two."

Buck went to the lumberyard and arranged for the carpenter to get what he needed. Next was the hardware store where he confirmed his account was still active. While there, he picked out the bathtubs for both houses.

On his way to the ladies' clothing store, he saw Rex Reynolds enter the saloon wearing a red shirt and a black handkerchief tied around his neck. Seeing him in Bonham was a little strange, since his pa had told him Rex was working for Sid and he hadn't seen Sid today. Maybe Sid or John was also here and out of sight. Buck kept a keen eye out for either of the two men as he walked along the boardwalk. He looked inside all the businesses on his way to the ladies' shop.

Buck told Lucy everything that had happened since they'd last talked, including the news about Carol moving to his ranch.

"Buck, I really am happy for you. I can see how pleased you are by the beautiful smile you have on your face. I'm sorry, but I can't talk right now. I have a customer waiting on the alteration that I'm working on."

"I understand. I wanted you to know the updates. Give me a hug, and I'll leave."

They hugged and he left the shop and found Biscuit still sitting in the back of the buggy. "Biscuit, come on down and get a drink of water, then we'll get something to eat at the café."

They had to walk past the saloon, and while doing so, he looked in over the tops of the batwing doors but didn't see Rex. He assumed the boy had only stopped in for a quick beer and was already gone.

Buck walked into the café and ordered two plates of food. He told the waitress the second order was for his dog outside, and she could put the food on something besides a plate if she wanted to.

Buck sat close to the window so he could watch the street. He was curious why Rex was in town by himself. Where were Sid and the rest of his men? Maybe Rex wasn't riding with them after all and was there looking for work.

The meal was delicious, and Biscuit was already in the back of the buggy when Buck came outside and got in his rig. He thought about the items the Indians had requested, but decided it might be a waste of money if the Army patrol caught up with them on the creek. If the military didn't kill them, then he'd buy the food tomorrow.

On the way home, right before he came to the road that turned north off the main road, he saw the Army patrol coming toward him. They were leading five Indians on ponies, with their hands tied behind their backs.

"Afternoon, Lieutenant Webb. I see you found who you were looking for," said Buck.

"We always get who we go after, sir. We had to kill three of the savages and bury them down by the creek. Then we burned what was left of their camp."

"I don't remember giving you permission to bury three bodies on my property," said Buck.

"I had no choice. Those bodies would've stunk by the time we got them back, so we buried them," said the lieutenant, smiling.

"Who's your commanding officer at Fort Sill?" asked Buck. "I'm sure I can be compensated for them Indians buried on my property, especially if my former commander, who is now General Oliver, contacts him."

"That ain't necessary. I'll tell my commander and send you the money for their burial spot."

"Thank you, Lieutenant. Next time, you need to ask for permission."

Buck slapped the reins to the horse's rump and took off with a smile. After all these years, he still liked messing with Army officers.

He hoped his cattle had arrived, but there was no sign of them when he got home. After caring for the horse, he opened the wire gate so the wranglers could turn the cattle into the pasture when they showed up.

Chapter 47

THE FOLLOWING MORNING, BUCK WAS BESIDE himself, anticipating the arrival of the cattle. At eleven, he said to the dog, "Go get a drink and prepare for a run. We're going to go down the road a piece and find the herd."

They were a mile west of Dodd City when he spotted dust to the south. It had to be his cattle. He and Biscuit headed in that direction until they intercepted the drovers a half mile south of the road.

Buck walked Red up to the man riding point and said, "I'm Buck Reed, and these are my cows. I'm sure glad to see you fellers."

"Hello, Buck, I'm Andrew Wells. I work for Benny. We got slowed down having to cross through farmland country."

"That's fine. We're almost to the main road and can use roads the rest of the way."

"Okay. Does that dog know how to work cattle?"

"I don't know, but we'll find out when they get on my

property. I'm not much for eating dust, so I'll lead the way to my ranch," said Buck.

Although Buck had worked on numerous spreads, he had never been a cowboy. He was a hired gun employed to protect the owner or run off squatters. Once, he was hired by Big John Connor, who was at odds with another rancher over water rights. That situation could have escalated into a range war, but the two hard-headed ranchers had been able to come to an agreement.

When the small herd was near his house, Buck rode back to Andrew and said, "The next place is mine. I have the gate open, and all we have to do is turn them in."

"It's not that easy," said Andrew. "We'll have to block the road to make them turn into the gate. I'll grab a couple of men, and we'll go ahead and be ready for the cows."

Buck, Andrew, and two men lined up their horses across the road. As the cattle got close, Buck called out to Biscuit, "Okay, boy, here is where you earn your keep. Let's put those cows in the pasture."

The dog just stood and looked up at his owner until Buck swept his arm toward the open gate, gesturing for the dog to get to work. Biscuit ran after the lead cattle and got close enough to nip at the leader's heels. The first cow turned toward the gate and the rest followed. Biscuit ran back and forth along the offside, nipping on the cows' heels and pushing them through the gate. He barked and ran at the cows to get their attention, falling back every now and again.

When the cattle were safely in the pasture, Andrew said, "That dog of yours has worked cattle before—he knew just what to do. He'll be a valuable hand to help you."

"I agree. How many heads did you bring me?" asked Buck.

"There is a total of forty-four cows and one bull. Most of the cows are bred and should be dropping calves this winter. I suggest you hire a cowman to help you out. I don't figure you know diddly-squat about raising cattle."

Buck laughed. "Does it show that much? You're correct, I've never worked with cattle. I think I'll take your advice and hire someone to work around the ranch. If I make any money off the land, I might buy more cows and another bull."

"Do you own a full section of land?" asked Andrew.

"Yeah, and there's a creek flowing through the land and one stock tank, so we've got plenty of water. I thought I could buy another forty head and be fine on grass. I have a man coming in a couple of weeks to cut enough hay for a hundred head," said Buck.

"I don't see any problem with another forty head as long as you have hay for the winter."

Buck felt good about having his plan approved by a seasoned cowhand. Maybe he could make a go of ranching, even if he was a little late getting into the game.

"Well," said Andrew, "it's been nice meeting you, Buck. I'd like to stay and get acquainted, but my hands and I have to head on back."

"You be sure and tell Benny that I appreciate the cattle."

"Yes sir," said Andrew. "Come on, fellers, it's time to head out home."

Buck watched the drovers ride off before he went to the barn to care for his horse. Getting the cattle on the property relieved a little of the stress he had encountered the last few days wondering when they would arrive. Andrew was right. He needed to find someone to work for him as a ranch hand who could perform the doctoring and care of the cows, especially during the winter months since he didn't want to face the cold feeding hay and breaking ice so the cattle could get water.

It was still too early to prepare his and Biscuit's supper, and although the cattle delivery had eased his stress, he couldn't stop thinking about everything that still needed to be done. That was enough for him to go into the house for a pencil and paper.

Buck sat on the porch with the dog lying next to his chair and was deep in thought when Biscuit sat up and put a paw on his thigh. The dog wanted a little attention, which was his way of showing affection. Buck started to rub his hairy friend behind his ears.

"You surprised me today, boy. You knew what to do so the cattle would turn into the gate. I'm now wondering what's next in our adventure together." Biscuit lay back down, and the old man began to write down his list of things to do.

Later that night, a dream took over his sleep. He was walking back and forth across a dusty road, searching for something on the ground. When he looked up, three men sat astride lathered-up horses, who took deep breaths through flared nostrils. He couldn't make out who the cowboys were, and their presence caused him deep concern.

"Who are you, and what do you want?" Buck called out.

"Don't you remember the times we met in the street, in some distant town, and you killed each one of us?" asked a voice, but he didn't know which man had said it because none of them had moved their lips.

"Get away from me. You're not real!" shouted the lone Buck Reed.

Something fell at his feet. Three guns lay on the ground in front of him. He looked back up to the silhouette of the three faceless men. Their guns were pointed at his chest.

Buck woke up startled by his dream. His body was covered in sweat, and his hands were still shaking as he shook his head to clear out the images.

He splashed a hand full of water on his face to help put the dream out of his mind. Hopefully, one day, he would stop having the nightmares. This had been the first one in days, and he wasn't looking forward to more of them.

Wide awake now at three a.m., he heated water so he could soak in the tub and had a hot cup of coffee before breakfast. The dream was nothing more than that; it was a dream that he had experienced many times before, and it would soon be gone from his thoughts as the day got started.

Chapter 48

Dodd City looked the same as it did four weeks ago when he decided to live out the rest of his days close by. The lone man dressed in a black duster rode down the street. Out of habit, he took notice of each person on the boardwalk as he passed them by. Buck stopped in front of the bank, dismounted, removed the duster, and laid it over his saddle before going up the two steps and entering the brick building. Only one customer was at the teller's window, but today Buck's business wasn't with the teller.

He strolled to the open door of the manager's office and said, "Good morning, O.W."

"Why hello, Buck. What can I do for you?"

"I need two thousand dollars, if you don't mind."

"I don't mind at all. Are you buying more land?" asked the banker.

"No, I'm buying more cattle and remodeling the other two houses on my land. You won't believe this, but I discovered a few days ago that I have a daughter and a grandson. Her name is Carol, and his is Timmy. She and the boy are moving into the old foreman's house, and Carol's ma will live in the smaller residence."

"Is that a fact? I'm glad you have family who will be close to you. Does this mean you and the girl's ma are getting back together?"

"No, we had our fling years ago. I have no romantic feelings for her, and we're not even good friends," replied Buck. "I have a lady friend in Bonham who has gotten my attention, and I'm hoping we can continue to expand our relationship."

"That's good. I was afraid you would get bored and lonely out there alone. Now you'll have plenty of time to get to know your daughter, and especially your grandson. All boys need a father figure in their lives to keep them on the straight and narrow, so they don't get into trouble," said O.W.

"So I'm told, and that's the way my pa felt. His straight and narrow was a leather strap to my butt. But that's in the past, and I need a ranch hand to work for me. I had forty-five head of cattle delivered to me yesterday, and I plan on buying a few more. If you know of someone who's good with livestock, I would sure like to talk to him," said Buck.

"I know of a feller who needs work and lives fairly close to you. His name is Albert Henry, and he has a wife and seven kids. They have a quarter section north of you about a mile or so, and he needs a job. He grew up on a large ranch in west Texas, so I'm sure he knows how to tend to livestock. His ma and pa sold it out and moved over by Sherman when he was around twenty. He raises cattle but needs more land and a bigger herd to support the large family. I'm sure he could help you around the ranch as a part-time hand."

"Thanks. If I ever get my money, I'll go talk to him," Buck said, smiling.

The banker stood up. "I'll go get your money."

O.W. put the money into stacks of bills and tied them with twine. "Here's your cash. Say, I also know a feller close to you who has young cattle for sale. He lives a mile north and east, and his name is Bernard Sena. He's a little opinionated, but he does have good cattle."

"I've met Bernard, and he's a bully used to getting his way. He brought the sheriff with him the first day I was on my land and tried to run me off."

O.W. laughed. "That sounds like Bernard, all right. I see his plan didn't work, and I'm glad about that. You go see him and say that I sent you. He won't give you any problems since he owes me a lot of money."

"I'll think about it. It was good seeing you again, my friend," said Buck. He tipped his hat to O.W. and walked back outside. As he scanned the street, a man coming out of a store caught his attention in his peripheral vision. He quickly looked again, but the person he'd seen was turning the corner onto a side street. Buck could have sworn the feller resembled John Flemming. Oh well, John wasn't his problem. He had more important things to do, like talking to Albert and seeing if he wanted some work. He might even go see Bernard about buying cattle. That might be a way to become friends with the man.

The first time he'd ridden into Dodd City years ago came back to him as he rode out of town. He had walked his horse up the street, taking stock of the city. It was quiet, with only a few people milling around. The buildings were weatherbeaten and wind blasted. A few horses stood at the hitching rails in front of the hardware store, the grocery store, and of course, the saloon. A stray dog or two ran out into the street, and a rooster crowed every now and again. A few of the townsfolk that were moseying along the boardwalk glanced his way but kept moving toward their destination.

He stopped at the café, sat at a long wooden table, and ate his food while minding his own business. The blowsy woman who waited on him demonstrated no interest in conversation with the middle-aged man wearing a tie-down gun. She had most likely seen his type many times before.

He finished his meal, paid his tab, and took his horse to the livery stable. The stable hand asked, "Come far?"

"Quite a piece. How's the nightlife in town?" asked Buck.

"Not much goes on around here except a little drinking at the saloon." The man looked down at the gun swung low with the tied-down holster on Buck's hip. "You come here looking for work?"

"Not really, just passing through," replied Buck.

Buck was finished with where the conversation was going, and it wasn't none of this man's business what he did. He turned and walked to the two-story frame hotel he had passed on his way into town. The room was simple, with a bed, one straight-backed wooden chair, and a wash-stand with a basin, a pitcher of water, and one glass. A mirror hung on the wall above the basin.

Once his small travel case and saddlebags filled with his books were stowed under the bed, he wanted to check out the town on foot. As he walked down the boardwalk, a heavy-set man wearing a three-piece suit and a low-crowned cowboy hat stopped him.

"Hello, stranger, I'm Oren Windom, but my friends all call me O.W. I own the bank in town, and if I can ever be of service, then stop on in."

Buck reached out and shook the friendly man's hand.

"I'm Buck Reed, and I might stop in tomorrow to talk to you about an important matter."

"That would be fantastic, Buck. You can come by any time after eight in the morning. The coffee and talking are always free."

"I'll see you tomorrow, O.W."

He liked the ebullient banker and planned to go see him the next day. Buck continued down the street to the saloon, where four men sat playing poker at a table. Two men stood at the bar having beers, and off against the far wall a man with a half-empty bottle of whiskey and one glass had his eyes focused on the newcomer. Buck made his way to the bar and ordered a beer. Buck noticed the man had a notch out of the top of his right ear. It was odd. He could have been born that way, or someone had cut it off in a ruckus.

While sipping his beer, the feller with the notched ear rose and walked to the bar. "You any good with that gun, or is it just for looks?"

Buck turned slowly to face the man. Buck's left elbow rested on the bar, and his right hand was at his side by his gun. Buck gazed into the man's brown eyes, and before either man said another word, someone at the card table called out, "Ambrose! Sit back down and mind your business."

Buck kept his eyes on Ambrose and couldn't tell who had hollered at the man. He hadn't gone into the place looking for trouble but was ready if it came his way.

Ambrose smiled at Buck. "Sorry, mister, I didn't mean you no harm. I was just curious."

"That's fine. I'm just passing through and wanted a beer before going to bed. No harm done."

The man went back to his table and had a drink. One

of the men playing poker asked Buck, "If you're looking for work, I can use another gun."

Buck turned to see who spoke. "I'm sorry, I'm not looking for work. I'm passing through."

The man laughed. "So are we. Ambrose is with me, and we're on our way back to Abilene, where I own the Cactus Ranch."

"Much obliged for the offer," said Buck, who drained his mug and was about to leave when the banker he met earlier came through the door. Buck stayed at the bar and watched O.W. greet each man in the room before he came to the bar and said, "Let me buy you another beer, Buck."

The two men spent another hour at the counter carrying on a conversation about Buck's plan to settle down somewhere and retire. O.W. didn't pressure him for information, but did ask if he would come talk to him tomorrow. They spent the rest of their conversation discussing Fannin County and its people.

The following morning, he was in O.W.'s office a little after eight. He told the banker what he did for a living, how much money he had, and that he needed a good man to manage his finances. He and O.W. made some arrangements, and Buck deposited his share of the money that he and Wilbur had stolen off the silver mine's payroll.

One cent had never gone missing in all the years Buck had trusted the banker with his money. O.W. was as honest as the day was long and was a good friend.

Chapter 49

A MAN IN HIS EARLY THIRTIES WHOM BUCK ASSUMED was Albert, and two younger boys were dragging limbs from a fallen tree on the north side of their house. By the look of the branches, brittle and bare of leaves, he figured the tree had died, and they'd chopped it down before it fell and caused damage.

The man stopped whacking off the smaller limbs and watched as the well-dressed older gentleman stopped his horse not five feet from him.

"Howdy, I'm Buck Reed, and I own the section a mile west and a mile south with the freshly painted house and barn."

The man stepped forward and stuck his hand out, and Buck leaned over in the saddle to shake. "I'm Albert Henry, and these are my boys, Herbert and Walter. What can I do for you, neighbor?"

"I've been talking to O.W. at the bank, and he told me you might want to take on some extra work. I have forty-five head of cattle and plan on buying a few more, and I need someone to take care of them. I don't know come here from siccum about cows, and I'm not in the best of shape anymore, so I need someone to care for them and do whatever doctoring they might need."

Albert listened and nodded like he agreed with Buck. "I could sure use the extra money, all right. I reckon I could do it, especially since your place is not more than a few miles from here."

"How much do you suspect I should pay you to do all the work with the cows?" asked Buck.

"How many more are you planning to buy?"

"No more than sixty head right now. I have Peter Branch scheduled to cut and bale enough hay for the winter. I also made a deal with him to have his men haul and stack the hay in the barn. I've already ridden out the entire fence line, and it's in good shape," said Buck.

"How about a dollar a day? Can you pay me on the first of every month?"

Buck leaned over in the saddle again and stuck out his hand to seal the arrangement. "Thanks, Albert. I'm riding to Bernard Sena's ranch to see about buying more cattle. I'll let you know how that turns out on my way home, if that's all right? Me and Bernard haven't always seen things in the same light."

"Yes, sir, that'll be fine. I suspect we'll still be here chopping on this tree. I'm cutting it up for stove wood."

Buck was happy that Albert had agreed to work for him. Now he would see if he could talk business with Bernard.

The dogs were the first to warn Bernard's ranch head-quarters that they had company. Bernard stood on the porch with a double-barrel shotgun, and another man stood in the bunkhouse doorway holding a rifle.

"Hello, Bernard. I'm here on business, not to fight. Are you interested in doing business with me?" asked Buck.

The rancher set the scattergun against the side of the house. "Climb off that horse and sit a spell while you tell me what our business is," said Bernard.

Buck eased off the horse and stood for a few seconds to get the blood flowing in his knees before he dropped the reins, walked up the steps, and sat in one of the four chairs on the porch. "O.W. sent me out here to see if you had some young cattle I could buy."

Bernard crossed his arms and said, "I have a lot of cattle, and if the banker sent you out here, he must have loaned you some money."

"No, that's not the reason I'm here. The bank has been keeping my money for about ten years or so. O.W. sent me out here because you owe him money. But that's not my concern. I have forty-five head, and I'd like to buy a few more. My daughter is moving here, and I'm going to turn the ranch operations over to her, and I want her to be able to make a living."

"How many heads do you want?" asked Bernard.

"Fifty cows and one bull should be enough for now."

"I'll take thirty dollars a head," said Bernard.

"That's mighty steep for around here. Maybe I should go to the sale barn in Bonham and do my business," said Buck. He didn't know what a reasonable price was, but he figured Bernard would jack the price up and he hadn't been wrong.

"What do you figure is a fair price for crossbreeds, especially young cattle that's already bred?" asked Bernard.

"I'm thinking I should be able to buy fifty heads for a thousand dollars. That seems like a fair price since you don't have to hire extra help to drive them to market," said Buck.

Bernard appeared to think about the deal Buck was

willing to make. "I'll take the thousand and have my men deliver them tomorrow, if that's satisfactory."

Buck pulled the money out of his pocket and counted it. He handed ten one-hundred-dollar bills to Bernard and stuck out his hand to seal the deal. "It's been nice doing business with you, neighbor. I'll be going. I appreciate your hospitality."

"You come back again, Reed."

Buck took off and stopped by Andrew's place to tell him that the cattle from the Sena Ranch would be delivered tomorrow.

"When I see them come by, I'll mosey over and look at the herd. I want to give them a look over and see if we need to do any doctoring on them. I'm sure a lot of the cows will be dropping calves soon, and it would be good to kind of keep a record of when I think that will happen," said Andrew.

"Good, I'll see you tomorrow."

Chapter 50

MORELL AND HIS TWO BOYS BROUGHT TWO WAGONS loaded with lumber, water pipe, and bathtubs to the house where his daughter would live. They were unloading one of the wagons when Buck rode up.

"Hello, men, I see you're about ready to get started." Buck didn't get off his horse since he didn't want to have to get back on to go the short distance to the barn.

"We're goin' to unload these two, go back to town for two more loads, and start rebuilding this house tomorrow. I have another crew coming the day after tomorrow to start on the little house," said Morell.

Buck took off his hat to wipe the sweat off his forehead. "That's good. I'd like to move my daughter here as soon as possible. If you need me for anything, I'll be at my house," said Buck, and he rode off. He was excited that the houses were getting worked on so soon and that the rest of the cattle would be delivered tomorrow.

Buck sat with Biscuit on the porch after they had filled their bellies that evening, and he remembered the guy in Dodd City that he thought might be John, but wasn't sure.

Then he thought about seeing Rex in Bonham two days ago. He hoped Sid and his gang didn't have something planned in town. Sid and Rex were two problems he would likely have to face sometime. Killing Sid wouldn't make him lose any sleep, but he didn't want to go against Rex. His pa was a friend, and it would destroy their relationship. Maybe that hadn't been Rex in the red shirt. Maybe it had been someone else who only resembled the young man.

Buck rested well that night, and didn't have any night-mares for a change. The following morning, he was having breakfast when Morell and his boys arrived and started working on Carol's house. After cleaning the kitchen and gathering all his dirty clothing, he went outside to tend to his animals. The chickens were glad to leave their pen and began pecking at the ground in the backyard, gathering insects and tiny pebbles. It still amazed the old man that chickens filled their craws with gravel so the eggshells would be hard.

Morell's two boys carried old boards out of Carol's house and made a pile so they could be burned later. Buck couldn't see any of the Texas cattle grazing in the pasture. He figured they were on the back side of the property by the creek. He walked to the gate and opened it, antici-pating that Bernard would soon bring the cattle he'd purchased.

Buck didn't want to leave the gate unattended, so he put a chair under the shade of a post oak tree, where he had a good view of the pasture and the opening.

He was glad he and Bernard had conducted business like good neighbors. Their first meeting hadn't gone that well. The rancher had overstepped his bounds, coming onto his property and telling Buck to leave. Who knew he and Bernard might become friends over time.

The sound of bawling cattle coming down the road brought him out of his thoughts. The dust rising off the dirt road hid most of the riders, and all he could see was the lead bull and a few cows.

Buck stood up to go to the road when Biscuit ran from behind the house and made a beeline to the gate opening. He was in position when Bernard and one other cowboy came to block the road for the cattle to turn into the pasture. Biscuit took over and focused on the lead bull, making the colossal animal turn to its left and into the open gate. The rest of the cattle followed as Biscuit ran back and forth, nipping at their heels. Buck watched the dog work and knew that someone had trained the mutt well.

Once the cattle were all in, one of the cowhands closed the gate while Buck walked to the fence to talk to Bernard.

"Morning, Buck," said Bernard.

"Hello, neighbor. Thanks for bringing the cattle over. The well is at the back of the house if y'all want a cool drink," said Buck.

"We're fine. I wanted to get your cattle delivered before it got too hot. I've grown tired of the hot days and I'm ready for fall temperatures," said Bernard, wiping his face off with his handkerchief.

"I don't like the heat any myself, and I appreciate you bringing them over. I should have enough cattle now to keep my daughter and Albert busy," said Buck.

"I have more for sale if you want a few young heifers," said Bernard. "We best be heading home. The hands still have work to do. I'll be seeing you, Buck."

"Thanks again, Bernard."

Buck turned toward the pasture to see what Biscuit

was doing. The dog was creeping around watching the cattle. Buck called out, "Come here, boy."

Biscuit ran to Buck and sat on his hind end while he got rubbed behind his ears and petted. Buck had always known the dog was special, and now he was not only special but a real asset to the ranch.

Buck spent the rest of the day milling around the place, working in the barn, filling the wood box in the kitchen, and seeing that the chickens had feed and water.

The next morning, he gathered up all his laundry to take into town for Lucy to wash. While there, he would also send a telegram to Carol and buy more groceries.

Buck had seen Jubal and Lester unhitch the horses from their wagon when they arrived that morning. As he left his house to go get the buggy, Buck watched them go to the corral and bring the large animals to the wagon as he walked down to the house to talk to Morell.

They had made much progress in the kitchen area by ripping out all the old cabinetry and some decayed flooring.

"You fellers have been mighty busy in here," said Buck.

Morell put down a hammer and untied his carpenter apron. "Yes sir, we have. The boys should be finished tearing out the rotten wood in the rest of the house tomorrow. I plan on working on this kitchen rebuilding the cabinets."

"Can you give me an estimate of when you'll be finished now that you've started?" Buck asked.

The carpenter rubbed his hand over his mouth and cheeks while thinking about his answer. "I think we can be finished with both houses in three weeks. That being said, your daughter can probably move in after two weeks.

We can work outside the house after the houses are occupied."

"Thanks. That gives us a good starting point on moving her up here," said Buck, shaking Morell's hand. "I'll see you sometime tomorrow."

Buck was returning to his house when Albert rode up. Biscuit growled, but Buck settled him down.

"Hello, Albert. The cattle are most likely on the back side of the pasture by the creek, if you want to look them over," said Buck.

"I'll ride over there. Do you own this entire section of land?"

"Yes. I've owned it for around ten years, but I've only recently moved in."

"I see. Well, I'll go find the cattle and tell you what I think when I return."

"You go right ahead. I'll close the gate behind you," said Buck.

Buck decided to wait another day before going to Bonham. He wanted to be home when Albert returned so he stayed busy doing chores and was in the kitchen when Biscuit barked once, and then he heard Albert's horse walk behind the house.

"Buck, are you in there?" Albert asked.

Buck came to the back, wiping corn meal off his hands. "Yeah. I'm mixing up some cornbread. Biscuit, this is our friend, so leave him alone, you hear?"

"I looked the cattle over. I don't think they'll start dropping calves for another few months, so we should be okay until then. You have a healthy herd, and they'll be fine on grass until December."

"That's good news," said Buck. "I'll leave it up to you to decide when you think you need to come and look after them. I don't cowboy, and I'm not going to start now. The next time you come over to check on the cattle, I want my dog to go with you. He's a good cow dog and can come in mighty handy."

"Thanks, Buck, a good cow dog is worth his weight in silver. I'll be over most days. If it's all right with you, I may cut a gate in the back of the pasture to ride across the country to get here."

"That's fine by me. You do what you think is best."

"I'll see you tomorrow," said Albert, and he rode off.

Buck went back to fixing supper.

Chapter 51

Two good nights of sleep without nightmares had started to make the old man feel better. Early the next morning, Morell's wagon came into the yard and Biscuit raised a ruckus. Buck got out of bed and stretched before walking into the living room so he could see down to Carol's house.

Sure enough, the carpenters had come to work, and there was another wagon in front of Ginny's house today. Things were coming together; if he had no setbacks, his daughter could move to the ranch in a couple of weeks.

Buck hitched the horse to the buggy and loaded the laundry he was taking to Lucy in the back. He figured the ladies' dress shop needed her for a few more days, but knew she had to keep up with all her customers' clothes too.

Bonham was alive with people milling along the boardwalks on both sides of the street. As he turned the buggy west onto 6th Street, a block north of the square, he slapped the reins against the horse to make it go faster. Two men on horseback got his attention riding away from his location. One man wore a red shirt, and the other resembled John Flemming from the back.

The men were three blocks ahead of Buck, and he hadn't gained on them by the time they veered off on the street that would lead them out of town heading north. When he turned the buggy in that direction, the two riders were nowhere in sight.

Buck returned back the way he had come and went to Lucy's house to drop off his laundry. He couldn't stop wondering if the men had indeed been Rex and John. If it had been them, he figured they were scoping someplace out for a robbery, and most likely it would be the bank.

Buck rode on to the ladies' dress shop to talk to his lady friend. The shop only had two customers in it as Buck made his way to the sewing room. Lucy stood up and put her arms around his neck.

"I'm sorry, dear," she said. "I've been so busy between here and keeping up with my work at home that I haven't been available for you to visit. I'll be finished at the shop this week. Gladys is on crutches now and thinks she can sit back here and do the alterations."

"I'm fine with you working here. I've also had a lot on my plate with buying cattle, getting the houses remodeled, and trying to think of everything that needs to be done before Carol can move. All of that is coming together, and it's getting better every day. I put my laundry in your wash shed, but I'm in no hurry. You catch up on everyone's before you start on mine."

She kissed him. "You go do whatever it is you need to do and come see me the next time you're in town."

"Bye, darlin'." Buck tipped his hat to her and walked through the store. At the door, he touched his hat brim and smiled at the ladies.

Biscuit lay in the back of the buggy looking off to the

west as Buck sat in the buggy seat. "What're you looking at, boy?" asked Buck. He glanced over in the same direction but couldn't tell what had gotten the dog's attention. He decided he should give the county sheriff a visit and tell him his thoughts.

Buck walked into the Fannin County Sheriff's office. The sheriff sat leaned back in his chair with his booted feet on the desktop, sound asleep and snoring up a storm. Buck whistled, and the man awoke and reached for his gun.

Buck said, "Don't get excited. It's only a humble old citizen coming to tell you something."

The sheriff sat upright and wiped his eyes to get the sleep out. "You, sir, are by no means a humble citizen. Now, what's so important that you had to abruptly wake me up? I was up most of the night over a man beating up his wife."

"I was told that Rex Reynolds was riding with Sid Dill and John Flemming. I told the city marshal that John happened to be in town a few days ago. He said he would tell you what I said."

"Yeah, he told me, but I ain't seen hide nor hair of either one of those men," said the sheriff.

"I was in town three days ago, and I'm almost positive I spotted Rex going into the saloon. I walked by there a few minutes later, but he wasn't in the place. Today I saw a man in a red shirt with another man who I believe was John. I'm not certain it was them, but it sure looked like them from where I was."

"This Rex feller, does he wear a black handkerchief with that red shirt, and is a little cocky?" asked the sheriff, getting up and taking down two cups off a shelf on the wall for coffee.

"Yep, that's him. Have you seen him in town?" asked Buck.

He handed Buck a hot, steaming cup of black coffee. "I saw him in town several times and talked to him once. The conversation was sort of one-sided, as I did most of the asking. His answers were short, and he didn't seem to have any real explanation for why he's in town."

"That makes me think he has orders not to talk to the law or cause any problems. I still think Sid is planning something here in Bonham."

"That may be the case, but if we don't know what it is or when it'll happen, I can't do a lot to prevent it," said the sheriff, taking a sip of his coffee.

Buck blew on his before he took a swallow. He made a face and asked, "What did you put in this coffee, tar?"

"I like it strong," said the sheriff, smiling, and then took a sip.

Buck continued, "I can feel it in my bones that something will happen. When it does, I'll be at your disposal if you want my help. This is my home now, and I want to be part of the community."

"Buck, I appreciate you coming in and talking to me. I'll call on you if I need help," said the sheriff and took another swig of coffee.

Buck had all he could stomach of the coffee and set his cup on the desk. "I best be going. I still have a few more things to do."

"I'll be watching for Rex and that gang he rides with. You come back anytime, Buck," said the sheriff, sipping his coffee.

Buck walked out and as soon as he could, he spit a couple of times, trying to get the bitter taste of the foul-tasting java out of his mouth. That had been the worst coffee he had ever drunk.

The butcher shop was on the east side of the square. He wanted to see if he could purchase a few bones for Biscuit to gnaw on. The butcher was a big man, well over six feet tall and weighing over two hundred fifty pounds. He wore an apron over his clothes that had blood stains in various locations.

"Howdy, you want some meat?" he asked.

"Yeah, I'll have a couple of steaks, and I'll have some bones for my dog if you have any," said Buck.

"I can do both of those for you. I'll be right back." The butcher went through a door behind the counter and returned carrying the steaks wrapped in white butcher paper and the bones in a bent-up pail. "Are you the gunslinger that's sweet on Lucy Smith?"

"I'm Buck Reed, and yes, I'm sweet on Lucy, but I am not a gunslinger, as you put it. I'm retired from all that, and I'm now a rancher. How much for the meat and bones?"

Buck paid his bill and left without saying anything else. The man had rubbed him wrong by calling him a gunslinger, and he didn't appreciate it.

With all his business done, Buck stopped in the dress shop one more time to tell Lucy goodbye. Then he headed home before his steaks went bad. He would cook the meat tonight and give Biscuit one of the steaks plus the bones to chew on.

Chapter 52

MORELL AND HIS CREW HAD LEFT EARLY TO PICK UP more supplies in town. They would have them loaded today so they could get back to work first thing in the morning. Buck cooked dinner and had given the dog a bone and Biscuit took it to the front porch, lay down, and got busy gnawing on it.

Buck followed the dog outside and sat in his chair like he did some afternoons. He hadn't been sitting long when the dog suddenly stood up with the hair bristled on his back.

"What's wrong, boy?" asked Buck, looking in the same direction as the dog.

Biscuit took a step to the edge of the porch, and Buck reached out and put his hand on the dog's back. He saw the dust first, and then the horse and rider coming down the road. He rose from his chair, concerned why someone would be running their horse coming toward where he lived. Jubal Farr, Morell's oldest son, pulled his horse up in front of Buck.

"Jubal, what's the matter?"

"There's been some trouble in town, and Miss Lucy has been shot. She's at Doc Steele's office."

"Is she hurt bad?" asked Buck, his voice changing to a frightened tone.

"I don't know. I was told to come and get you."

"Okay, cool down your horse and give him some water while I get my things."

Buck went into the house and hurriedly packed his travel bag, strapped his shoulder holster across his chest, and buckled the other gun and holster around his hip. He opened the drawer on the nightstand and grabbed a box of shells before he walked to the barn, where Jubal finished tightening the girth strap on his horse. "Thanks for saddling my horse, Jubal. This saves me valuable time," said Buck, and he mounted up.

Even though he was upset and worried, he knew better than to ride Red hard all the way to Bonham. His old aching joints wouldn't take the pounding, and running the horse that far would wear out his mount. The short trip had an agonizing effect on Buck's mind. He started to remember the lost feeling he'd had when Mary Jane and Belinda died. It was so overwhelming that he stopped the horse, removed his hat, and prayed.

"God, I don't rightly know what to say, but I need help for Lucy. She's been shot, and I beg of you to spare her life. Amen."

He was anxious to ride into Bonham and see her. Not knowing the extent of her wound, he had come prepared to stay with her as long as she would let him.

Men from town equipped with rifles had taken up positions around the two banks. Two businesses, the hardware store and the dress shop, had broken windows. A few armed men were stationed on the hotel balcony and across the street behind the false front of the grocery store. He counted ten women gathered outside Dr. Steele's office, and two of them had on a holstered gun. He dismounted and let Red's reins hang as he made his way through the ladies.

Buck burst into the doctor's office and found Lucy in the second room he looked in. She lay on a narrow bed with her eyes closed, and the doctor had a white sheet covering her up to her throat. "Lucy, it's me, Buck. Are you awake?"

"I-I can't see you, Buck. Where are you?" Her voice was slurred, and her eyes were closed as she tried to raise her left hand.

The doctor came into the room carrying a tray with bandages on it. "She's in no pain at the moment. I gave her laudanum, and she is pretty much out of it. The bullet hit her at a slight angle, tore a two-inch crease between two ribs, and came on out. Those ribs are most likely broken and will be mighty sore for a month or more. I'm going to keep her here tonight for observation. You're welcome to stay if you want," said the doctor, pointing to a chair against the far wall.

"I'll stay a spell, but if I sit in that straight-back chair very long, you'll have to give me something for pain," said Buck, moving the chair beside the cot. "Do you know why she was shot?"

"I'm not sure, but she's not the only one who took a bullet," said Dr. Steele. "One of Peter Bench's men was killed as he drove a wagonload of hay through town. Everyone is saying the shooting was intentional, and the shooter got smack dab away."

"That's strange that a man would shoot up the town for no reason," said Buck. "But crazy things happen."

He took Lucy's hand and held it until his hand began to get numb, and he had to let go. His back and legs were beginning to hurt since he had been there at least an hour. The doctor came back in to check on Lucy, and Buck said, "I need to get some exercise to stop my knees and back from aching. If she wakes up while I'm gone, you be sure to tell her I'll be back."

"She won't wake up for quite some time. You go do whatever you need to. I'll keep a watchful eye on her."

"Thanks, Doctor," said Buck, putting the chair back against the wall and walking outside. He wanted to know who the shooter was and what the sheriff planned on doing about it.

There were more people in town than he had seen since coming to Bonham, and it seemed that all the men were armed and ready for battle. The men he had seen when he arrived were still on guard at the bank. Around a dozen men were on horses outside of the sheriff's office. Buck figured they had volunteered to join a posse and go after the shooter. Weaving through the crowd, he finally stood in the open doorway of the county sheriff's office.

The sheriff was talking to the city marshal for Dodd City when Buck interrupted the conversation. "Sheriff, do you know who shot Lucy?"

The lawman looked at the old gunfighter and lowered his eyes. "Yeah—the man wearing the red shirt and black handkerchief. He emptied his gun in the street and then hightailed it north. I figure he's heading to the Red River and into Indian Territory."

"Could be," said Buck, rubbing his chin and thinking. "There had to be a reason why he did it. I can't imagine for the life of me why Rex Reynolds would shoot Lucy and that man on the wagon."

"He could have been drunk, but the barkeep said he never came into the saloon today. Another feller said he saw Rex ride into town a few minutes before the shooting started," said the sheriff. "We're goin' to try to pick up his trail and catch up with him before he can get across the river."

"You have plenty of men, so I'll stay back and watch after Lucy. Marshal, why are you here?" asked Buck.

"I was here on business at the courthouse when the shooting started. I reckon I'll go with the posse after Rex. That boy has gotten a little too big for his britches, and it's time to bring him down a notch or two."

About that time, the conversation was interrupted by a commotion outside.

"Get out of the confounded way. I have an important message for the sheriff!"

Luke West, the telegraph operator, stood outside the office waving a piece of paper at the sheriff.

"Let the man through," shouted out the sheriff.

"This just came over the wire."

The sheriff took the message and turned white as a sheet as he read it.

"What does it say?" asked Buck,

"Outlaws robbed the bank in Dodd City and killed the banker. They got away with all the money and took two young children as hostages."

Buck was shocked to say the least to hear that his friend had died and that all his money had been stolen by Sid Dill and his worthless gang. He immediately sat down on the porch step trying to think. It took him a few seconds to let it sink in and gather his thoughts before he asked, "Are you sure it was O.W. that got killed, or was it one of the bank employees?"

"The telegram said it was Oren Windom, the banker," said the sheriff and showed the message to Buck.

Buck looked at the telegram and said, "O.W. is a good friend of mind, and I'm having a hard time processing his death. Why would they shoot him? He didn't even carry a gun," said Buck and removed his hat to wipe the sweat with his shirt sleeve that had formed from the bad news.

"I reckon that you were right about that bunch. I just don't know why Rex would shoot up the town," said the sheriff.

"Rex shooting people here in town was a decoy, so the main group could rob the bank. They knew no law would be in Dodd City because the city marshal is here. O.W. was not only a good friend of mine, but all of my money was in his bank. I suggest you get going with that posse, or you'll never catch them."

Buck walked back through the crowd heading back to the doctor's office. He could hear the sheriff giving orders and looked back as the men rode north out of town.

Chapter 53

BUCK KNEW THAT THE POSSE HAD NO CHANCE OF catching up to Sid and his men. The outlaws had over an hour's head start, and the posse couldn't follow them into Indian Territory. The robbers would cross the Red River and stay in some town to drink and live well until the money ran out, or they would fight among themselves and split up.

Buck was consumed with anxiety and rage over his money being stolen as he sat back down in the doctor's office. It was sad that O.W. had been killed, but the loss of money was devastating to his and his daughter's future.

Lucy was awake but still groggy when he took her hand and tried to talk to her.

The doctor came in and said, "Buck, I'm going to keep her sedated for a few days so she can start the healing process."

"I'm glad she's going to be okay," said Buck.

The doctor smiled and nodded.

"The bank in Dodd City was robbed today, and they killed the banker who was my friend," he said. "They also stole all my money. I'm sure they're headed to Indian Territory, where it's safe for them because the local law has no jurisdiction there. The US Marshals won't be after them for a while since they get their orders from Fort Smith, and by then the gang will be someplace else."

"Mr. Reed, if you want to go after the men who took your money and killed your friend, then by all means, go. I'll see after Lucy and make sure she gets the best care I can give her."

"I feel guilty about leaving her here this way," said Buck.

"Buck, you have to get your money baaacckkk," said Lucy in a slurred voice. She squeezed his hand.

"Oh dear, it's so good to hear your voice," said Buck. "For a little while there, I thought I would lose you."

"You ain't goin' to lose me, you old coot. Now get after those men and come back soon," said Lucy. She closed her eyes and drifted off to sleep.

Buck placed her hand on the bed. "Doctor Steele, you take good care of her, and I'll be back as soon as I can. If something happens to me, please tell her I love her."

Emotions took over about him leaving Lucy while leading his horse down the street to the mercantile. He had a lump in his throat like he was about to cry. It was so bad that he almost went back to the doctor's office, but it was also paramount he go after the men who killed his friend and get all the money back.

The street was still crowded with townsfolk when the old gunhand walked into the store. There he was met by Sammy, the lady who had helped him before.

"Good afternoon, Buck."

"Hello, Sammy. I need a small coffeepot, a skillet, and enough provisions for a couple of days."

"I'm guessing that you want to take these items on the road?" she asked.

"Yes, I'm going to be gone for a few days and must be prepared."

"Hmmm, let's see. Coffeepot, skillet, spoon, and fork. Oh, we need to get you a cup also. How about a bedroll? Will you need that too?" she asked as she wrote down the items.

"Yes, I need all that plus coffee, bacon, and whatever else you have that I can carry. I need to travel as light as possible."

"You go over to the canned goods shelves while I gather these things, and I'll also get you something to carry it all in."

Buck selected one can of beans, a can of peaches, and two potatoes. When he placed them on the counter, Sammy gave him a cloth bag for his provisions and the utensils. He was looking over the bag when she brought him a bedroll already rolled up inside a ground tarp.

"I have everything you'll need for a few days. Is there anything else?" she asked as she picked up a pencil and notepad to calculate his debt.

"I don't think so."

"That will be two dollars."

Buck paid the young lady and as he walked toward the door, she said, "You be careful out there, Mr. Reed." He smiled back at her and went outside, where he tied a sack on each side of the saddle horn and the bedroll behind the cantle. He mounted up and looked back at the doctor's office before heading east out of town.

Leaving Lucy laid up was one of the hardest things he had ever done. If things went wrong, he might never see her again, but he wasn't going to tell her that. This was going to be a long hunt, and if he caught up with Sid Dill, the meeting would most likely be a deadly one.

Thinking about Sid, he knew that he would have to kill the man if he got the chance. But how many men did he have with him, and what about John and Rex?

Buck and John had always been friendly with each other, but John made an alliance with Sid, and if John was present when Buck confronted Sid, he would have to kill both of them. As for Rex, that was something he would have to play by ear. He hated to kill his friend's son, but Wilbur needed to understand that Rex shot Lucy and killed another man in Bonham to distract the law.

All these thoughts went through his mind, and then he happened to think about the bounty hunter Marion. Where was he? He had said when he left that he would go to Dodd City and find Sid. Did he go somewhere else, or did he and Sid tangle, and was Marion dead?

What about Wilbur? Did he sit at home and do nothing, or go after the robbers? His money was stolen also. There were so many questions and so few answers.

If Marion happened to be in Dodd City, they could join together to track down the gang. Most likely, Sid and his men had hightailed it to the Red River north of Paris. If the gang did cross the river, Buck surmised that Sid would take his men to a settlement where the east train line and the north line intersected. There, the bank robbers would have access to the St. Louis-San Francisco Railway and could go north into Kansas and Missouri or south back into Texas.

But he couldn't put the cart before the horse. He needed to gather information in Dodd City, and it was coming into view.

Chapter 54

MEN WITH RIFLES AND HANDGUNS HAD TAKEN offensive positions along the street, ready for the outlaws to return. Buck shook his head at the townsmen's stupidity; the outlaws were not coming back. They had all the money, so why on earth would they return? There were even two men in the bell tower of the Methodist Church watching the road going east and west.

It had been two hours since the robbery, and a group of men and women were still congregated around the front of the bank. An older man in a three-piece suit with his tie undone waved his arms and tried to talk over the upset people gathered in the street. Buck heard the man try to assure the deposit holders that the law would catch the robbers and get their money back. The people didn't seem to buy what the man told them.

Buck rode in among the mob and stopped his horse. "I'm Buck Reed, and most of the money in the bank belonged to me. Now, shut up and let me ask some questions."

Men and a few women shouted that they were also depositors in the bank and wanted to know how they would get their funds back. A shot was fired, and everyone stopped talking, and a few people even went down to the ground and covered their heads with their hands. Buck drew his gun to return fire until he realized it was Wilbur who had fired the shot and making his way through the people.

"Everyone shut your traps and let Buck talk. The sooner he gets information, the sooner he'll be on the outlaws' trail to recover your money. Go ahead, Buck, ask away."

"Thanks Wilbur. How many men robbed the bank?"

The man in the suit said, "I'm Mayor Willy Robuck and I think it was probably a half dozen, by all the shooting."

Buck stared at the man. "I don't want to know 'probably' how many. I want the facts. Did anyone see them ride into town or ride out of town?"

A boy of about fifteen wearing pants two sizes too short said, "Mister, I saw them come out of the bank. One of them held onto a girl of about twelve, and another one had a girl that was a little older. I saw three men come out of the bank and ride north with those two girls behind the last two men."

"Can you describe the three men?" asked Buck.

"The man who had the younger girl had a big stomach and was not very tall, and I figure he weighed two hundred thirty pounds. He wore a black shirt with gray striped britches. The man who had the second girl was taller and thinner, and he wore a black hat. The last man seemed different than the other two. He wore a shirt without any sleeves. I reckon he cut them off to stay cool or something. He had a shaved head and one of his ears was missing."

"So you only saw three men?" asked Buck.

The boy nodded. Buck looked at the crowd. "Did any of you see anything more?"

A woman stepped forward and removed her bonnet. "I was down the street a couple of blocks and saw those men ride into town. There were four of them. Bill described the three that came out the front door, but I think one went out the back door with the money. Bill, did you see the men carrying a money sack?" she asked.

"No ma'am, I didn't see no sack," said Bill.

"Can you describe the fourth man for me, ma'am?" asked Buck.

"He was riding a fine black stallion, and the man dressed nicely in a checkered shirt, and wore two guns with pearl handles. The man with no shirt sleeves rode a paint horse and the other two had sorrels."

"Thanks, ma'am, and you too, Bill. Oh, one more thing. Did anyone see which way they went when they left?"

"I saw them heading north about two miles west of town," said a man. "They rode pretty fast, but I didn't know they were outlaws."

"Could you tell if they still had the children with them?"

"Yep, a few of them were riding double."

"Does anyone know the two girls they took?" asked Buck.

Everyone shook their heads no. "Do you suppose it was a front to make us think they took hostages?" asked Wilbur.

"I'm thinking that's it. Sid probably made a deal with

some family to use the girls, and Sid would give their daddy some money to use them. Did you see four men riding north?" Buck asked the man who had said they turned north two miles east of town.

"Yes, sir, I saw four men and those two girls."

"Has anyone seen a man come through town wearing a preacher's collar in the last couple of days? His name is Marion Dixon."

"Yeah, he was here two days ago. I believe he was going to Paris from here. He said he was looking for a man named Sid. Do you suspect that this Sid feller is the one who stole our money?" asked the man in the suit.

"Yes, it was Sid Dill and his gang."

Another man in the crowd said, "If you're going after them, I would like to come along."

Buck shook his head from side to side. "I'm sorry, but I work alone. You men stay with your families, and I'll do my best to get our money back."

Wilbur said, "Buck has experience with this sort of thing and with what he has to do. We'll only slow him down and get in his way. I've seen him in a fight and he's really good, so leave him be."

"Thanks, Wilbur. Could I talk to you in private?"

"Sure, let's go over there by the hardware store."

Buck led Red across the street and stopped when no one but Wilbur could hear him.

"Wilbur, have you talked to Rex?"

"No, but he wasn't part of the gang that did this, and that's a good sign," said Wilbur.

"Not really," said Buck, and he wrenched his face and took a deep breath. "Rex shot up Bonham, and one of the bullets hit my lady friend Lucy. She's going to mend over time, but he also killed a man in a wagon hauling hay.

Wilbur, Rex is wanted for murder in Bonham. Sid knew that the city marshal would be at the courthouse in Bonham. Sid wanted to cause a ruckus over there so the law wouldn't come running to the bank when his men robbed it. Sid recruited Rex to commit the act in Bonham to throw the gang off the trail. A posse is after Rex as we speak."

He could tell by the anguished look on Wilbur's face that the news was hard on him. "Buck, I'm truly sorry to hear about your lady friend and that feller who died. I failed as a father with that boy. I should have done things differently by him, and maybe he would have turned out better," said Wilbur. "I need a favor. Please don't kill my boy. I hope it's in your heart to spare his life."

"I can't guarantee anything, because part of whether he lives or dies will be up to Rex. He's chewing at the bits to pull iron on me to get a reputation. I hope he doesn't try that on Sid either. Sid ain't all that fast, but he's the kind of man that will shoot Rex in the back and grin while doing it."

"Yeah, I tried to talk to him about that, but he flew off the handle and left. I wanted to tell you that Marion was here. He said he would be back if he didn't find Sid in Paris. I'm concerned since he hasn't shown back up."

"I can't worry about him now. I have to get going before the trail grows cold. What's the quickest way to the river crossing at Arthur City?"

"On the east side of town, head north for six miles and then go northeast until you intersect with the road to Arthur City just west of Powderly. You may know it as Lenoir. They changed the name when the railroad came through. You do know that the railroad has a stop at Arthur City, don't you?"

"No, I wasn't aware of it, but I don't think that matters

to Sid unless the town has plenty of whiskey and no law. He'll go into the nations, where he feels safe for now."

"I won't hold you up any longer. Be careful, old friend, and don't trust Sid or anyone with him."

Buck tapped his heels to his horse and headed out.

Chapter 55

THE DIRECTIONS HE'D RECEIVED WERE EASY TO follow, and Buck didn't waste time looking for the tracks of four running ponies. The facts of what had happened at the bank and the information about the gang's supposed hostages were all he needed to know. Those girls probably lived in Indian Territory. Buck happened to think they had poor parents and with a little bit of questioning folks, he would soon learn who they were and where they lived.

The outlaws had spent a considerable amount of time planning the robbery, and they would go someplace they had already used as a hideout. It had to be close enough for them to travel back and forth to Dodd City to organize the robbery.

The question that kept coming back to him was, where would they leave the girls? He was sure Sid had made a deal with their folks to use them as decoys. Buck should have asked more about the two girls back in town. Had they come to Dodd City with their parents? Did they show up at the bank at a random time? Did they ride into Dodd City with the outlaws?

The one-man posse rode along the main road that passed through Powderly. The road seemed wider than he remembered since the last time he had passed through, back after the war was over. He didn't stop, instead continuing toward the river.

Arthur City, if you could call it a city, was no more than a train stop, café, general store, and a few scattered houses. The café was across from the train station, and most likely, the bulk of their business came from the train while it took on water. Buck stopped and ordered a plate of food and asked the lady if he could also buy a few biscuits for the road.

The food was good, and as the waitress was clearing the table, he asked, "Did you happen to have four men stop by around noon for dinner? One was wearing a shirt with no sleeves."

"Yep, four hard-looking men and the two Dewitt girls, who are from across the river. Why do you ask?"

"I need to talk to the girls' folks. Can you tell me where they live?"

"They live on the sharecropper farm a little north and east of the river crossing. It's a shotgun house with a red barn."

"Thanks," said Buck, and he left.

His horse had no trouble crossing the river, due to the water only being thirty feet wide, and at the deepest section the water only came to a little past his ankles. Red had some difficulty making it out of the riverbed due to the thick sand. North of the Red River, he saw the red barn and removed the safety off both his guns before he rode up to the front of the house. "Hello in the house. Anyone home?"

Two barefooted girls came out and stood with their

hands shielding the sun from their eyes. "What do you want, mister?" asked the tallest one.

"I'm a weary traveler and need to water my horse and rest a spell. Would you ask your folks if I can draw water from your well and sit under the shade of that big oak over by the barn?"

A dirt farmer wearing bib overalls with no shirt underneath and a pair of worn-out brogan boots with no laces stepped from the doorway, holding a shotgun. "You girls get back inside and tend to supper." He motioned to Buck with the barrel of the shotgun. "Get off our land and don't come back."

"Okay, I just wanted some water for my canteen and horse. You don't have to be so inhospitable," said Buck as he pulled the reins to his left like he was leaving. His right hand pulled the shoulder holster gun out and fired one shot.

The man dropped the shotgun and grabbed his upper arm where the bullet had made contact and traveled clean through.

"Now, let's have a nice conversation," said Buck, still holding the gun on the man. "Both of you girls, come on out here with your hands empty."

The man slid down onto the dirt and leaned against the house with his face wrenched in pain. When the girls came out, Buck said, "One of you go get a rag to wrap around his arm, and one of you grab that gun by its barrel and drag it to me."

Buck sat on his horse holding his gun and waited while the girl brought him the shotgun. The other girl returned with a length of cloth and tied it around the man's arm. "Now mister, we play a game called truth or suffer. I'll ask a question, and you don't have to suffer if you tell the truth. If you lie to me, I will hurt you. Is that clear?"

All three nodded that they understood the game.

"I know the two girls were with Sid when he robbed the bank. Where's the money that he paid you to use them?"

The man said, "We ain't got it yet. Sid said he'll be by later in the week to pay us."

Buck raised his gun and fired, grazing the man's other arm. "See, you lied to me, and now you have to suffer more."

The man looked like he was in a lot of pain now. The youngest girl said, "It's in the house. I can go get it. Just don't shoot my brother anymore."

"Then go get it and make it snappy," said Buck.

"Mister, you're making a big mistake coming here," said the injured man. "When Sid finds out, he'll come gunning for you."

"That's my plan. I happen to know Sid, John, and Rex. They wrote out their death sentences when they stole my money. Now, tell me who was with Sid and John at the bank."

"Woodrow Gallon and Harley Sissons."

"Where will I find Woodrow and Harley?" asked Buck.

"Woodrow lives in the settlement north of the Indian School called Goodland. The railroad building and the train station are at the new town, and Woodrow owns a saloon there called Bogie's. Harley is staying with Sid and John in a house that Sid owns somewhere."

The youngest girl came outside with a tin can and gave it to Buck. She remained standing by his horse with her head down. He removed a roll of greenbacks and passed the empty tin back to her.

"Mister, don't take all our money. Sid only gave me fifty to use the girls and if you take it all, we won't have any left for food," said the man.

Buck counted out fifty dollars and said, "Girl, look up at me." He handed the money to the young lady who was now looking up at him. Buck looked at the injured man and said, "I have one more question, and this one determines whether you live or die. Where was Sid going to hole up?"

The man said, "Don't tell Sid I was the one who told you, or he'll kill me and my sisters after he kills you. They have a house on the north side of Durant Station on Chuckwa Creek."

"See, that was a fun game. Don't be a fool and try to warn Sid that Buck Reed is coming for him, or I'll have to come back and play another game with you folks. One last thing before I leave. What's your name?"

"It's Ezekial Compton. Most folks call me Zek."

Buck wheeled his horse around and rode off, taking the shotgun with him. When he came to the main road, he broke open the barrels and removed the two shells, dropped the weapon and continued on. The man at the house was lucky that his sisters were there, since they were the first to answer his questions, or the brother might be dead.

Chapter 56

It was dusk when Buck rode past the wooden sign that read *Goodland*. This was the Indian school that Ezekial mentioned, so the town must be close. He kept going north another few miles and rode into the settlement where Woodrow owned a saloon.

The place had an up-and-coming commercial appearance from the looks of buildings under construction. Businesses seemed to be booming by the amount of folks on the wooden boardwalks along the streets on both sides of the tracks. Farther away from the railroad right-of-way, he could see that houses lined the streets to the west and east.

Buck located the saloon on Main Street. It was a tent saloon with a false front, and the four hitching rails in front of the drinking hole couldn't accommodate any more horses. Buck dismounted in front of a leather goods store and left Red while he checked out the saloon. Most likely rot gut whiskey and chalk beer happened to be the drinks of choice and the place was no different than all the other bars the old man had seen throughout his life.

Two buildings south of the saloon, on the corner of

Main and Duke streets, sat a grocery store with a three-story hotel above it. A painted sign attached on the second floor advertised the Webb Hotel with an arrow pointing to a stairway leading upward. Buck had passed by a livery only two blocks south of his location and took Red there for feed, water, and rest. Walking back to the hotel gave his legs time to get some circulation going from sitting in the saddle so long. The climb up the flight of stairs to the second-floor lobby was not his favorite thing to do, but it was necessary if he planned on sleeping in a bed tonight.

Once in his room and lying on top of the bed, he thought about how to handle Woodrow. If Sid and the others were at Durant Station, that meant he had a fifty-mile ride ahead of him. Time was of the essence, and it happened to be a quarter after six. He'd sleep for four hours and then go get Red and be ready to leave immediately after he found Woodrow. He would ride all night and arrive at Durant Station sometime tomorrow.

The hotel clerk had been more than helpful and had a meal delivered to the old man's room so he wouldn't have to climb the stairs again.

With his hunger pangs diminished, it was time for sleep before he went to look for Woodrow and get some of his money back.

Buck came out of his room at ten-thirty and descended the stairs without seeing anyone in the small hotel lobby. The night air felt heavy with humidity as he walked to the livery.

He had the boy that slept at the stable saddle Red, and then Buck led his mount down the rutted, dirt street looking for a place to leave him while he found Woodrow. One of the hitch posts in front of the saloon had no animals tied to it, and Buck left Red there with the reins draped over the top of the cross beam.

With both guns ready for action, Buck entered the dimly lit, smoke-filled tent that stunk of cigar smoke and body odor. He stood watching for a few seconds until a scantily dressed floozie came to him and asked, "Hey sugar, want to have a drink with me?"

"No, I'm not looking for company tonight."

The woman looked sad and walked off. He had seen places like this go up in a day or two where there was money to be made. Men came here to drink, talk, play cards, and spend time with the bargirls.

A short, heavy-set man moved around the room straightening up the chairs and picking up used glasses and mugs off the tables. He had leaned over a table to grab a mug when Buck said. "Hello, Woodrow, how have you been?"

The man jerked his head up and said, "Who are you and what do you want with me?"

Buck drew his gun and said, "I'm here to collect the money you helped steal in Dodd City."

"Mister, I don't know what you're talking about. I'm an upstanding businessman. I don't rob banks."

Buck smiled. "I never said you stole the money from the bank, but now that you've fessed up to it, I want my money back."

Woodrow stood there with a mug in his right hand and a rag in his left hand. He seemed to be deep in thought on how he was going to get out of this situation by the way he kept shifting his eyes side to side, looking for some help in the room.

"In case you're wanting to try something, I'm Buck Reed and I don't have a problem with killing you right here, right now. I know you were with Sid and John at the bank. It just so happens that the money you stole belonged to me. I know Sid has already paid you your share, so fork it over, or I'm going to take target practice on your knees and elbows."

Woodrow's shirt had wet spots forming on it and droplets of sweat formed on his forehead. He started wadding up the soiled rag in his hand that was used to wipe off the top of the tables. Buck knew what was coming next. Woodrow threw the rag at Buck and reached for something behind his back when a slug hit him in the muscle above his right knee.

Woodrow fell to the hard packed-dirt floor and screamed out in pain, grabbing his leg.

"I told you what would happen. Stay still, and let's see what you have hidden behind your back." Buck took his foot and shoved the man over enough where he could remove the seven-inch knife from a scabbard attached to the back of Woodrow's belt.

Buck pitched the blade away and put the barrel of his gun against Woodrow's other knee. "Now, where is the money you stole for me? Or do you want me to shoot you in the other leg also?"

"It's under the counter in a strong box. Not all of what's there came from the bank. Some of that money is my hard-earned savings," said Woodrow, clearly in pain.

Buck walked behind the counter and saw the box underneath a crate full of whiskey bottles. With his booted foot, he shoved the crate to the floor. With his eyes watching the bar owner on the floor, he pushed the box with his foot until it was clear of the counter and opened the lid.

Buck pointed his gun at a man watching the action. "Come over here and put this box on the table and take out all the bills."

The man complied and handed the money to Buck,

who placed it into his left front pocket. "Thanks, mister. Now go sit back down."

Buck stood beside the injured man's head and spoke loud enough that everyone in the tent could hear him. "This is what will happen to anyone who steals, or tries to harm me." He reached down and hit Woodrow on the back of his head with his gun butt before walking out to his waiting horse.

Five hours later, Buck sat in the saddle on the banks of the Muddy Boggie River, waiting for the break of day. There was no way the old man would chance crossing in the dark. At daylight, he planned to urge Red down the bank and cross where other travelers had. With any luck, he'd be at Durant Station by dark and find a place to eat and sleep.

Chapter 57

DARKNESS COULDN'T BE MORE THAN AN HOUR AWAY as Buck and his tired horse walked through the small town where the MK&T Railroad had laid tracks and built a station. A wheelless railcar parked on the railroad siding had the words *Durant Station* painted on the side. Next to the railcar sat Durant Station's General Store, and next to it in a large wooden building was where the rail workers and local cowboys had a drink or two, the Railway Saloon.

A little farther up the dirt street was a café, blacksmith, and a clothing store. The lack of a hotel happened to be one business that he didn't see in the town. The old tracker needed food and rest, but he also wanted to find Chuckwa Creek before dark, so he continued north and saw a sign with directions to Caddo.

Buck turned his horse off the road when he glimpsed a paint horse coming his way about a half mile from the north. It was almost dark now as he concealed himself behind some brush. He watched the heavy-set man ride by and remembered that one of the robbers rode a paint. Curious to see where the man went, Buck followed far enough behind that he could only just make the figure out in the dimming light.

The feller stopped in the back of the saloon and had finished staking out his horse on a patch of grass when Buck rode up and drew his gun.

"Howdy, I'm from Dodd City, Texas. You and I have some business to discuss."

"I don't have anything to talk to you about, and I don't appreciate you pointing a gun at me."

Buck cocked the hammer back. "We can discuss our affairs with you standing and remaining in one piece, or we can do it with you lying on the ground in severe pain. Your choice."

"I ain't got nothing to say to you, mister. Now, leave me be so I can go have a shot or two of rotgut."

Buck smiled at the man and knew he was up to something. "What's your name? So they can write it on your grave," said Buck.

"It's Harley Sissons, and it could be your grave, not mine." He moved his right hand slightly, and Buck saw something fall into it. He fired one shot. Harley went down to his knees and raised a two-shot derringer at Buck, but it was too late. A bullet between his eyes toppled him over, dead as a doornail.

Buck reloaded his gun in case someone from the saloon wanted to tangle with him too. When no one showed up in a couple of minutes, he blew out a big breath of air and eased out of the saddle as best as he could. He had to stand holding on to the saddle for a few seconds before he made his way over to Harley and searched for money. Sure enough, he found a roll of cash in each of the dead man's front pockets, and in one of his saddlebags was a nasty handkerchief with a roll of greenbacks in it.

Since no one came to see what the shooting had been

about, Buck led Red to the street and headed north, hoping to see light coming from a house down by the creek.

The moon didn't give him enough light to make out any structures along the stream from the road. It was pitch black and useless to go on in the dark. He would go back toward town, find a place to sleep for the night, and continue his search in the morning.

He was ready to stop in the woods and sleep on his bedroll when he saw a sign in front of a weatherbeaten two-story house: *We rent rooms* was all it said. He looked at his watch and the time was 8:03. He figured someone could still be awake and knocked hard on the door. A middle-aged woman with her hair in a bun opened the door holding a kerosene lamp in front of her.

"May I help you with something?"

"Yes, ma'am. I saw your sign and wondered if I could rent a room for the night."

"You sure can. I don't allow whiskey, women, or tobacco in my house. If you agree to those terms, it'll be three dollars for the night, and I'll serve you breakfast for another four bits."

Buck reached into his pocket and pulled out his money. He gave the woman four dollars and said, "I won't be here for breakfast. I have something important to do at daylight, and I'll be out for a while. When I'm finished with my business, I'd like something to take on the road with me."

"I can fix you a little something. Follow me, and I'll show you to your room. It's at the back. There's a door back there you can use since you're leaving early."

She showed him the room and said, "I have a horse pen out back and feed for sale in the shed. You can put your horse in there if you want."

"How much for the feed?"

"That'll be a dollar."

Buck handed her the money, walked back outside, took Red to the pen, and fed him some oats.

Geneva had turned down the bed covers, opened both windows, and placed a pitcher of water on the nightstand by the time he came back in carrying his travel bag.

"If you need anything, I'm on the other side of the house," said Geneva.

"Thanks. I have everything I need," Buck said, removing his shoulder holster. Geneva left and the tired man took off his boot and shirts and went to sleep with both guns within easy reach.

The following morning before sunrise, he stood in front of the mirror with the lamp next to him so he could see to shave. He wondered why he spent the time to shave when he was planning on killing at least two men this morning. Old habits were hard to break, and a clean-shaven face seemed to be something he did at the start of every day. He liked looking good and needed all the help he could get with his wrinkled face and gray hair. Speaking of gray hair, it was getting a little long and would need to be cut soon.

Once he was clean-shaven and his gray hair had been slicked down with water, he dressed, strapped on his guns, and packed the last of his things. A soft knock on the door almost made him draw his gun.

"Come in."

The door opened, and Geneva stood in the dim light, already dressed. "I wanted to make sure you were up. Is there anything you need before you leave?" she asked.

"There is one small thing. Do you know if there is a house on the banks of Chuckwa Creek?"

She made a face like she was deep in thought and then

smiled. "There is a house a little over a quarter of a mile away on the rock bluff that overlooks the creek. It ain't much, but I think some man bought it off a Choctaw Indian and is fixing it up. There's a trail through the trees that will take you there. It's just past where the big rock is beside the road heading to Caddo."

"Much obliged for the bed and the information," said Buck, taking up his bag and walking out to get his horse.

Chapter 58

THE ROAD GOING THROUGH DURANT STATION appeared to be empty at the break of dawn, but Buck kept aware that trouble could be lurking in the shadow. If someone found Woodrow and reported it, Sid and John could be sitting in ambush waiting on him.

A few houses had smoke ascending from stove pipes and chimneys. Some folks were most likely cooking breakfast and maybe preparing all their meals for the day.

He kept a keen eye out for the rock and trail that led to the house where he hoped Sid was holed up. The trail was no more than a narrow path through trees and brush, and he let the horse find its way down the slender route.

Buck was tense, and that state of mind caused him to remember twelve years earlier when he sat in a saloon minding his business in a mining town in southern Colorado. Two hired guns working for the man who owned the silver mine and ran the town came into the saloon to throw the gunfighter out of town. It seemed that their boss thought Buck was there to cause him trouble when, in fact, Buck was resting a few days before he rode on.

Both men wore fancy two-gun holsters and sported clothing that made it evident they were not miners. They wore riding boots, shirts with two pockets, and a handkerchief around their necks. They must have purchased their britches from the same store because they were alike.

The shorter of the two men said, "Mr. Samson wants you to leave town right now. You can ride out, or we'll bury you over on the hill."

Buck gulped the last of his beer and said, "Since you put it that way, I reckon I'll be on my way. If you men don't mind, I'll go get my travel bag out of my room."

"We don't mind. In fact, we'll walk along with you to make sure you don't run into any problems," said the taller man, who rested his left hand on his gun butt.

The two hired gundogs walked behind him to the little boarding house where his things were. The safety straps were still on his guns, and he was basically fair game if the men wanted to kill him. He couldn't let them see his fear as he walked in front of the men.

Another man dressed in range clothing was leading Red toward the rooming house from the opposite direction, and that made Buck even more anxious. Now he had three men to deal with.

Both men followed him to his room and waited at the door while he stowed his few items in his bag. While packing, he removed the safety strap off his gun without either of them seeing him do it.

They followed him outside and stood about ten feet behind his horse so he was always in their view. That was when Buck began to stress out and get angry. He tied his bag to the saddle horn, backed away from the horse a few steps, squared his shoulders with the two men, and said,

"Fellers, it looks like you took on the wrong job today. You made me feel bad by hound-dogging me to leave town, and now I've decided that your boss can plant the two of you on that hill."

The taller man lowered his left hand toward his gun, but Buck reacted faster and cleared leather, firing at the two men. He then turned his gun to the third man, who was so surprised that he stood stunned.

"If you want to live, shuck that gun belt and run to your boss," said Buck.

The man did as he was told, and as soon as he took off, Buck mounted up and rode toward the Samson Mine office. A man who he figured was Samson stood smoking a cigar as he watched him approach. Buck stopped when he was even with the man.

"Two of your hired stooges are dead in the street. I suggest you be more careful about who you decide to run out of town. I was only passing through," said Buck, and he started off.

"Hold on. I'm Phillip Samson. I can use a man with your skills. How does seventy-five dollars a month sound?"

Buck laughed at the man. "I'm not interested in working for you, and even if I were, I cost ten times that amount," said Buck. He rode out of town.

The path in front of him took a sharp turn, and a tree limb hanging over the trail almost hit Buck in the face, which caused him to stop thinking about the past. Leaning over as far as he could, he missed the limb, and when he sat back up, he saw the house he hoped was Sid's.

Leaving Red down the trail three hundred feet, Buck crept through the timber and rocks with both guns ready for action. He saw the front, one side, and most of the corral out back. There were only two horses in the pen, and one looked like the one John had been on the day he was at Bonham. Buck didn't recognize the other mount.

It wasn't the best time to barge into the house since they were likely in two separate rooms. He would have to work mighty quick to take them without them returning fire. So, he would wait until the men inside came outside to relieve themselves, and that was when he would make his presence known.

Chapter 59

THE BACK DOOR SLAMMED OPEN AND OUT CAME JOHN, still in his long johns and carrying his rifle. He made a beeline to the trees and was emptying his bladder when Rex came out of the house, unarmed, with just his pants on.

Rex stood about twenty feet from John and did his morning business too. Buck entered the opening where the house was located and stopped twenty feet behind the two men.

"Tuck it in and turn around real slow," said Buck.

John turned his head and looked back at Buck. "Hello, Buckshot," said John. "What're you doing here?"

"I'm tracking down two murderers who stole my money from the bank in Dodd City. Now, drop that rifle and come around real slow!"

Rex had his hands in the air, but John hesitated, and Buck was ready for him. John twisted to his left and brought up the rifle. Buck drew and fired twice, but it sounded like one shot. John tumbled backward and was dead before he hit the ground.

Buck pointed the gun to Rex. "Walk over there and pick up the rifle. I'll give you the same medicine John got."

"I ain't going to do it, and I ain't no murderer."

"Did you shoot up Bonham yesterday morning?" asked Buck.

"Yeah, but I didn't kill anyone."

"Actually, you did," said Buck. "You killed the man who was hauling a wagonload of hay, and you put a bullet in my lady friend."

"I didn't mean to kill anyone, I swear. It was a freak accident that two people got hit by a bullet," said Rex, and he started to whimper.

"That's what happens when you ride with the likes of Sid Dill. You had dreams of becoming a gunfighter, and now you'll either die by my gun, or you'll hang for your crimes. Now, lie on the ground so I can tie you up."

Buck took a coil of rope off one of the saddles that hung on the horse pen fence and tied the boy's hands and feet. "I'm going inside to get your shirt and boots. Where did you and John hide your share of the bank money?"

"Mine is still in my saddlebags, which I used as pillows. I don't know where John put his. Untie me, and I'll get the money for you and find John's share," pleaded Rex.

Buck ignored him and went inside the house. He found John's money in his britches pockets. He added it to the money Rex had in his saddlebags, then searched the rest of the two rooms before taking Rex his clothes. "Before you get dressed, I want to know where Sid is."

"I don't know. When we got to town, he left us and rode south. He told us to come to the house and wait for him. John said Sid has a girlfriend south of here on the Butterfield Stage line where the road intersects with the road that goes east to a settlement called...I can't remember the name."

"Okay. We can find where he turned east later. You try anything, and I'll kill you like I would a rabid dog."

Buck untied the boy long enough for him to get dressed and saddle his horse. He then tied him back up and helped him into the saddle. He led Rex's horse on foot, along with Red, until they were a short distance from the house.

Buck stopped at the boarding house and collected the sack of food that Geneva had prepared for him—fried chicken and biscuits.

Buck received many looks as people gawked at him leading Rex through Durant Station. They weren't used to seeing anyone arrested other than a few drunks by the Lighthorse Police. Buck wasn't going to take the time to find out if the US Marshal was in the area. He was taking his prisoner back to Texas.

They left town and headed south, and Buck dropped Red back so he was almost beside Rex. "I'm curious about something. Did a bounty man named Marion happen to come around?"

"Yeah. We were camped on Pine Creek south of Powderly when Sid heard a noise of some kind and went into the trees thinking it was the law. In a few minutes, this man came into camp singing a church song and asked if he could have a coffee. I thought he was a preacher since he wore a white collar like preachers wear sometimes."

"Who all was with you that night?" asked Buck.

"It was me and John by the fire. The man asked where Sid was. John went for his gun, but the preacher man already had his gun aimed at him. About that time, Sid came rushing out of hiding and fired his gun at the man. Sid shot him three times in the back, and the feller fell face-first onto the fire, spilling all our coffee. I dragged him off into the woods and left him there."

"That sounds like Sid. He always was a coward and a back-shooter," said Buck. "You make darn sure we don't miss that road that Sid rode east on. You're in a position to receive the brunt of my anger."

"I won't miss it," said Rex. "John said it's the road that goes east to a farming town called Cale Switch. There is likely a sign where we need to turn. John also said that Sid bought the woman a house with a white fence. That's all I know."

Chapter 60

THEY'D COVERED CLOSE TO SIX MILES WHEN REX SAID, "I think the road is up ahead. That looks like a sign on the edge of the road. Are you taking me with you to find Sid?"

"You'll go for a ways, but not when I get close. I don't want you doing something stupid and getting me shot," replied Buck.

They turned onto the road with Buck in the lead, and a quarter of a mile later, the road made a double curve. Lo and behold, Sid Dill was riding toward them on his horse.

Buck removed the strap off his gun and kept moving toward the man he was going to kill. Sid stopped his horse and put his right hand on his gun handle.

"Hello, Sid," said Buck. "I reckon it's time to work out our differences."

"I suppose so—me and you ain't never got along. When I'm through with you, I'm going to kill that yeller-bellied boy of old Wilbur's that you have tied up," said Sid.

"I hear you had John shoot the banker and you also shot Marion in the back," said Buck. "Today I don't have my back to you, so pull iron whenever you build up enough nerve, you cold-blooded coward."

That last remark caused Sid to get so mad that he started to slobber, and that's when he pulled his pistol out of its holster. He was bringing the weapon up to fire when the first bullet from Buck's gun hit him in the chest. The force of the bullet almost unseated him from the saddle, but the man hung on and brought the weapon up again. Two more quick shots lifted him from the saddle and toppled him to the ground. His horse reared up and was kicking his hind legs, frightened from the shooting and Sid tumbling off backward off its hind end. Buck eased his way over to it and settled it down before he removed the bulging saddlebags off the back of the saddle.

The bags were heavy and full of stolen money. The old man dismounted, hobbled to the dead Sid Dill, and took all the money Sid had in his pockets. Even with everything he had recovered so far, the money still didn't seem to be enough.

Buck mounted up and led Rex's horse, making his way toward Cale Switch until he saw a house with a white fence. He tied the horses to the fence, walked to the door, and went inside without knocking.

No one was inside. When he looked out the kitchen window, he saw a woman in the garden hoeing weeds. He started his search in the woman's bedroom, and he discovered a cloth bag under the bed stuffed with money.

Buck took the bag and returned to his horse, tied the bag on, and headed for Dodd City.

The two men rode their horses hard until they arrived in Colbert. They stopped long enough to water the horses and eat chicken and hard biscuits at Mr. Colbert's store before going across the Red River on the ferry. They were still far from Dodd City.

They walked their horses through Denison, Texas, and Buck turned east. He cut across country to save time and miles. When they came to the main road that ran from Paris to Denison, they stayed on it until they were close to Bonham. Buck didn't want anyone in Bonham to see him and Rex, so he rode south around the city.

It was dark when they skirted around Dodd City and rode further south.

"Are you taking me home?" asked Rex.

"Yep, I'm taking you to your pa. It'll be up to him to decide your fate."

Wilbur's dogs raised a ruckus as the two men came down the lane to the ranch house. Wilbur walked out to the front porch when Buck pulled up with Rex tied on his horse.

"Wilbur, I didn't kill him. Now he's your responsibility. It's on your shoulders to do what's right. I'm going into Dodd City with the money and then home."

"Thanks, Buck," said Wilbur. He stepped off the porch and reached up to untie Rex.

Buck said, "Wilbur, if Rex ever crosses me again, I won't hesitate to kill him." He rode off into the night to deliver the stolen money.

It was after midnight and all the businesses in Dodd City were closed except for the saloon, which Buck stopped at. He walked inside, and the place grew quiet when the men who were still there drinking saw he was back.

"I've got the bank's money on my horse."

Chapter 61

A FEW OF THE MEN IN THE SALOON WERE ECSTATIC TO hear they'd gotten their hard-earned money back. Buck drank a beer while someone went after the city marshal and another man went to get O.W.'s widow so she could open the bank safe.

When the money had been securely locked in the bank, Buck gave instructions to the city marshal, the widow Windom, and everyone who had gathered outside the bank. Under no circumstances was the safe to be opened until the county judge could be present and oversee the counting of money. Buck rode home.

Biscuit was waiting on him down the road before he got to his house.

"Did you miss me, boy?" asked Buck as he kept riding.

After taking care of his horse, he fried some bacon and shared it with his dog. The old man was exhausted and fell asleep in his easy chair where he read. Sometime before morning, he woke up and got into bed for a few more hours of rest.

The dog raising a ruckus, caused him to open his eyes

the following morning. Buck heated water for coffee and a hot bath. He felt like his body was coated with a ton of dirt, and a good soaking wouldn't hurt his old bones either.

Buck headed into Bonham in the buggy with Biscuit riding in the back. As he came to the main road, there were Wilbur and Rex on horseback.

"Morning Wilbur. Are you taking Rex to the sheriff in Bonham?"

"Yep, I am. He has to take responsibility for his actions."

Rex's hands were free, which was a concern. "Do you trust him enough to let him ride into town with his hands untied?" Buck asked.

"I ain't goin' to do nothing. I'm turning myself in," said Rex.

"Fine, let's get going. You fellers take the lead," said Buck.

Buck let the two riders get in front of him a couple hundred yards so he didn't have to eat their dust. "Biscuit, you watch out for that young one. I don't trust him at all."

Wilbur and Rex stopped at the sheriff's office. Buck waited in the street as they dismounted, to make sure Rex didn't try anything.

Wilbur took hold of Rex's left arm and started for the office door. Rex looked back at Buck and smiled. Buck pulled his shoulder holster gun as Rex grabbed the pistol from Wilbur's holster.

Rex fired point blank into the side of his pa's head. Blood and brain tissue erupted out of the side of Wilbur's head as he fell to the ground. Rex quickly pointed the gun toward Buck, who was already shooting at the murderer.

Rex took three bullets in the chest before he stumbled and fell on the ground, and his life's blood oozed out of the holes in his chest. Buck went to him and kicked the gun from his hand.

"I thought I could take you," the boy said in a weak voice.

Rex died with his eyes open.

Buck spent the next two hours explaining what he knew about Rex, John, and Sid to the county sheriff and county prosecutor. At the end of his interview with the sheriff, he asked, "Are there any wanted papers on Sid or John?"

"Yep, there is. I dug through my stack of wanted posters and found them. You're due two hundred dollars from the state," said the sheriff.

"Give it to the family of the man that Rex shot. I'm sure they'll need it," said Buck.

The county judge commended Buck for his good work recovering the stolen money and bringing in a killer.

Buck checked on Lucy, who was sitting in a chair when he arrived at the doctor's office. She jumped up and used her good arm to put on the back of his neck where she could kiss him. After the kiss, she said, "I've missed you, Buck, and I'm so glad you're back in one piece." With several more kisses, they sat down and he told her most of the story about getting the money back.

That afternoon when he left Lucy, he accompanied the judge and sheriff to Dodd City to oversee counting the bank's money.

Buck had brought back two hundred thirty dollars more than the thieves had stolen, which the judge gave to him for his troubles.

By the time the judge and sheriff left for Bonham, Buck was ready for a long-overdue rest. He and Biscuit went home.

The next four weeks saw a change in the townsfolk in

Dodd City and Bonham. They accepted the old gunfighter as one of their own and expressed their appreciation for tracking down the murders and getting their money back. He wasn't Buck Reed the gunfighter anymore. He was Buck, rancher and friend.

Lucy was mended and back to washing and ironing for her customers in eight weeks. Buck went to Bonham daily to help her carry wash water and tote the baskets of clothes. He didn't want her lifting anything heavy for a few more weeks. He asked her to move in with him, but she refused. He even asked her to marry him, but again she refused. Her exact words were, "Buck, I love you and want you in my life, but I also love our relationship, and right now, I want to continue to be your lady friend and for you to be my man friend."

Buck laughed and said, "I love you, Lucy, and I'll do what you want, but I will keep asking."

Five weeks after getting the money back to the bank, Carol, little Timmy, and Ginny moved into the two houses Buck gave them. He waited two weeks after Carol was there before he turned the ranch over to his daughter. She had big plans, and when she told him what she wanted to do, he said, "Dream big and do whatever you want. The ranch is yours and Timmy's."

Three months passed and Buck sat on his porch, drinking coffee, while he watched Carol and Albert wade through the dewy grass to get a good look at the cattle grazing beside the house.

Little Timmy played between his house and the barn, throwing a ball and watching Biscuit run after it. The dog had taken up with the boy and spent his days following Buck's grandson around everywhere he went.

Buck took another sip of his coffee and closed his eyes. This was the first time since his wife and daughter had died that he felt alive and content. The nightmares hadn't shown up in weeks, and his aching joints were even better. He pushed the past from his thoughts and said to himself, "You have a home, a good woman who loves you, a daughter and grandson close by, money in the bank, cattle in the pasture, and a bright future in North Texas." Old gunfighters never die, they just smell like it.

A Look at: Life After War
(Sawyer McCade 1)

The war is over. The battle within has just begun.

Sawyer McCade was trained to fight, to survive, to kill. With the Confederacy fallen, he returns home to Kansas—only to find his family farm burned to the ground and his parents murdered. Every brutal instinct the war carved into him screams for vengeance.

But Sawyer made a vow: he will not be ruled by bloodshed. Leaving the past behind, he heads to Texas to forge a new life on the open range. Cattle, not conflict. Hard work, not war. And maybe, just maybe, a chance at peace.

Then a desperate message from his sister changes everything. The people who destroyed his family are still out there, and the law won't stop them. If Sawyer doesn't act, he risks losing what little he has left. But seeking justice means confronting the darkness inside him—the part trained to hunt, fight, and kill without mercy.

Will he stay the man he's trying to become, or become the weapon he was trained to be?

AVAILABLE MAY 2025

About the Author

Monty was born and raised in Southeastern Oklahoma in the small town of Sawyer, which is nested along the banks of the Kiamichi River. He's owned horses and cattle, riding the former and working the latter. Over the years, he formed a deep connection and respect for the Old West and the courageous folks who braved the wild frontier.

Monty is an avid reader and is particularly enthusiastic when it comes to Western authors and novels. His love of reading sparked his desire to write his first short story. He loves writing about real places and landmarks from the 1800s. In college, he wrote a ten-page paper about his grandmother, born in 1886, who married at fourteen and took in five orphaned nieces and nephews shortly thereafter. Monty's love for history and penchant for storytelling earned him an A+, and he hasn't looked back since.

Now retired, he loves to travel, fish, spend time with his four grandkids, and tell stories. He looks for inspiration for future books wherever he goes, and he is a member of the Western Writers of America Inc.

www.montygarnerauthor.com